"Oh, Hazard. I can't bear that this sweet little creature might die like all those others."

Without thinking, Erin pressed a hand over his. Squeezed. "We'll find the answer. I just know we will."

Hazard's eyes narrowed. For a moment he stood perfectly still, absorbing the shock waves that seemed to be exploding through him at the mere touch of her.

From his vantage point, Cody watched the unfolding scene with a slightly bemused expression. Old Wes Wilde used to say that love never happened when it was convenient. If Cody didn't know better, he'd guess that right now, while Wes's son was fighting the bitterest disappointment of his life, he'd just been shot with a double whammy. In the form of Cupid's arrow.

Cody figured he'd just keep his thoughts to himself for a while. Because, unless he was badly mistaken, those two didn't have a clue about what was happening between them. But it would come to them, sooner or later. His guess was soon. Very soon.

Dear Reader,

This is a very special month here at Intimate Moments. We're celebrating the publication of our 1000th novel, and what a book it is! *Angel Meets the Badman* is the latest from award-winning and bestselling Maggie Shayne, and it's part of her ongoing miniseries, THE TEXAS BRAND. It's a page-turner par excellence, so take it home, sit back and prepare to be enthralled.

Ruth Langan's back, and Intimate Moments has got her. This month this historical romance star continues to win contemporary readers' hearts with *The Wildes of Wyoming—Hazard,* the latest in her wonderful contemporary miniseries about the three Wilde brothers. Paula Detmer Riggs returns to MATERNITY ROW, the site of so many births—and so many happy endings—with *Daddy by Choice.* And look for the connected MATERNITY ROW short story, "Family by Fate," in our new Mother's Day collection, *A Bouquet of Babies.* Merline Lovelace brings readers another of the MEN OF THE BAR H in *The Harder They Fall*—and you're definitely going to fall for hero Evan Henderson. *Cinderella and the Spy* is the latest from Sally Tyler Hayes, an author with a real knack for mixing romance and suspense in just the right proportions. And finally, there's *Safe in His Arms,* a wonderful amnesia story from Christine Scott.

Enjoy them all, and we'll see you again next month, when you can once again find some of the best and most exciting romance reading around, right here in Silhouette Intimate Moments.

Yours,

Leslie Wainger

Leslie J. Wainger
Executive Senior Editor

Please address questions and book requests to:
Silhouette Reader Service
U.S.: 3010 Walden Ave., P.O. Box 1325, Buffalo, NY 14269
Canadian: P.O. Box 609, Fort Erie, Ont. L2A 5X3

the WILDES of
WYOMING —
Hazard
RUTH LANGAN

Published by Silhouette Books
America's Publisher of Contemporary Romance

To my own Wild Bunch.
Pat, my middle son, this one's for you. With love.
And of course, for Tom. Founder of the dynasty.
Acknowledgment:
I wish to thank Kent Ames, D.V.M., of the Veterinarian
Teaching Hospital of Michigan State University
in East Lansing, Michigan.

 SILHOUETTE BOOKS

ISBN 0-373-27067-4

THE WILDES OF WYOMING—HAZARD

Copyright © 2000 by Ruth Ryan Langan

RUTH LANGAN

Award-winning and bestselling author Ruth Langan creates characters that *Affaire de Coeur* magazine has called "so incredibly human, the reader will expect them to come over for tea." Four of Ruth's books have been finalists for the Romance Writers of America's (RWA) RITA Award. Over the years, she has given dozens of print, radio and TV interviews, including *Good Morning America* and *CNN News,* and has been quoted in such diverse publications as *The Wall Street Journal, Cosmopolitan* and *The Detroit Free Press.* Married to her childhood sweetheart, she has raised five children and lives in Michigan, the state where she was born and raised.

IT'S OUR 20th ANNIVERSARY!
We'll be celebrating all year,
Continuing with these fabulous titles,
On sale in April 2000.

Romance

#1438 Carried Away
Kasey Michaels/Joan Hohl

#1439 An Eligible Stranger
Tracy Sinclair

#1440 A Royal Marriage
Cara Colter

#1441 His Wild Young Bride
Donna Clayton

#1442 At the Billionaire's Bidding
Myrna Mackenzie

#1443 The Marriage Badge
Sharon De Vita

Desire

#1285 Last Dance
Cait London

#1286 Night Music
BJ James

#1287 Seduction, Cowboy Style
Anne Marie Winston

#1288 The Barons of Texas: Jill
Fayrene Preston

#1289 Her Baby's Father
Katherine Garbera

#1290 Callan's Proposition
Barbara McCauley

Intimate Moments

#997 The Wildes of Wyoming—Hazard
Ruth Langan

#998 Daddy by Choice
Paula Detmer Riggs

#999 The Harder They Fall
Merline Lovelace

#1000 Angel Meets the Badman
Maggie Shayne

#1001 Cinderella and the Spy
Sally Tyler Hayes

#1002 Safe in His Arms
Christine Scott

Special Edition

#1315 Beginning with Baby
Christie Ridgway

#1316 The Sheik's Kidnapped Bride
Susan Mallery

#1317 Make Way for Babies!
Laurie Paige

#1318 Surprise Partners
Gina Wilkins

#1319 Her Wildest Wedding Dreams
Celeste Hamilton

#1320 Soul Mates
Carol Finch

Prologue

Gold-tipped clouds hovered over the peaks of the rugged Tetons. A chill breeze swept down from the mountain range and spread across the grazing land, rippling the grass. There was a sense of calm as dusk settled over the vast Wyoming countryside.

At the moment, the beauty of the scene was lost on twenty-year-old Hazard Wilde, who had been up since dawn. After tending to the herd, he'd driven into the town of Prosperous for supplies, something he did several times a week, even though the little community was located more than fifty miles from the ranch. Then he'd been forced to waste precious time tinkering with the old, battered truck's engine, hoping he could keep it running for another hundred thousand miles, before turning his attention to repairing a leak in the barn roof.

Now, with evening falling, it occurred to him that he hadn't eaten anything except a bowl of cereal that morning.

Chance, two years older than Hazard, and Ace, at seventeen, the baby of the family, had been immersed in their own chores, until they had mysteriously left several hours earlier, without a word about where they were headed. It took all three brothers, working around the clock, just to stay one step ahead of the mounting bills. At the moment, Hazard was feeling that he was carrying the lion's share.

"Hey, Hazard. Big news." Chance and Ace Wilde pushed their way through the milling cattle until they reached their brother's side.

"Your news can't be as good as this." Hazard was kneeling in mud, created by melting snow, examining a newborn calf. "This is our future. Right here. Enough of these and the Double W will survive nicely." He barely looked up. "Well? What do you think?"

His two brothers waded in and stood looking over his shoulder.

"Very healthy." Chance slapped him on the back. "Nice work, doctor."

Hazard beamed like a proud father. "Thanks." He sat back on his heels and watched as the new mother began to lick her infant clean. "It might take me a another ten years, but someday I'll earn that title."

Satisfied, he wiped his hands on his filthy jeans as he got to his feet. For a minute longer he watched the scene between mother and newborn, then turned to his brothers. "Okay. What's your news? Where've you been while I was out here busting my hide?"

"You first." Chance turned to their youngest brother.

Ace was grinning from ear to ear. "I just hired a firm to take some soil-boring samples. You know, to check for coal or uranium."

Hazard looked thunderstruck. His reaction wasn't lost on his brothers. "You did what?"

Ace's smile faded a bit. He was annoyed that his brother wasn't showing the proper enthusiasm. "I said I hired a firm—"

"I heard you." Hazard looked from Ace to Chance, then back again. "What'd you use for money?"

"I won a couple hundred last night at Clancy's. I figured I'd better spend it on something I wanted, before it slipped through my fingers." Ace was looking pretty smug. "So I gave the Hudson Boring Firm a hundred down, and I'll pay the rest on monthly installments. And I gave some to Chance." He turned to his oldest brother. "Okay. Your turn. Tell him your news."

Chance was struggling to hold back the excitement, but it was a losing battle. He stood a little taller as he said proudly, "I just bought an oil rig."

"An oil rig." Hazard's jaw tightened.

Recognizing that look, Chance reached into his pocket and held out an official-looking document. "Before you say anything, read this."

Ignoring the mud and blood on his hands, Hazard unfolded the document, then looked up with barely concealed contempt. "This says oil was discovered on the Hope ranch. What's that got to do with us? They're hundreds of miles from here."

"It's worth a risk, Hazard. If the oil's here, my rig will find it."

Hazard's eyes narrowed. "I'm here trying to set aside enough to pay last year's taxes, and the two of you are off spending a fortune on some damned toys."

"Hey." Ace's smile disappeared. "They're not toys. They could determine our future."

"Or sink us deeper into debt. And for what?" When his younger brother started to turn away, Hazard grabbed him by the shoulder. "Listen to me, Ace. The important thing here is the land and the animals. We can't be blinded by dreams of fast money.''

"Who says?" Ace shoved his brother's hand aside. "You think you love this land more then I do? Is that it? Are you saying that just because you're happy wallowing in the mud with your cows, your work is somehow nobler?"

"I'm not interested in being noble. I just want to hold on to the Double W. I love this place.'' He turned to Chance, who had remained ominously silent. "I would have thought you'd know better. If we keep wasting money on foolish schemes, we're going to lose everything Dad worked so hard to give us. Or have you forgotten his dreams for us?"

Now it was Chance's turn to lose his temper. "I don't need you to remind me what Dad wanted for us. I've sacrificed as much as you for those dreams."

"Really? Then how do you explain going into debt for a stupid oil rig?"

"Stupid? Is that what you think?" Chance's fist shot out, catching Hazard by surprise.

From the time these three had been toddlers, this was how they had always worked off their frustration. The act of hard, bruising, physical punishment was like a cleansing when their blood ran too hot for words.

Hazard reacted instinctively, returning the blow with one of his own.

"Yeah. Stupid.'' He took a punch to the midsection, which had the air whistling out of his open mouth, before he countered with one to Chance's jaw that had teeth rattling. "And so are you if you wasted good money on it.''

While Chance was still reeling, Hazard turned on Ace with a snarl. "Instead of mining for coal and uranium, why don't you mine that brain and see if it's still there.

For all you know, one of your pool-hustling buddies may have already won it, and you just haven't noticed.''

He was stunned by the blow that sent him to his knees. He shook his head to clear it. Somehow, when he hadn't been looking, his little brother had managed to grow a foot taller and acquire some muscles.

When Hazard got to his feet, Ace moved in, his face contorted with rage. ''You think, 'cause I'm the youngest, that I don't know anything. Well I know this much. You aren't the boss here, Hazard. And you can't make me do things just because you say so.''

''I didn't say—'' Hazard's protest was cut off by a hard blow to the nose that had blood streaming down the front of his shirt.

With a grunt of pain he returned punch for punch, until both he and Ace were bloody and winded. When Ace paused for a moment to catch his breath, Hazard used the advantage to shove as hard as he could, sending his younger brother sprawling in the mud.

Now that his blood was boiling, he didn't seem able to turn off the rage. That had always been his curse. Slow to anger, Hazard was like an enraged bull once he'd been pushed over the line.

He turned on Chance, his fists raised in invitation. ''Come on. I'll take you on now.''

''Damn right you will.'' Chance led with a right and followed with a left uppercut that sent Hazard hurtling backward.

He got to his knees in the mud, then came up in a frenzy, landing a blow to Chance's midsection that made him double over. When Chance straightened, Hazard hit him with a grazing blow to his temple that had him staggering to his knees, and had Hazard shaking his wrist to ease the pain.

"Come on. You want some more?" With his fists raised, he stared from one brother to the other.

Seeing no takers, he felt oddly disappointed. Then, as the anger slowly began to drain away, exhaustion took over. He managed a shaky step backward, before he found himself sitting weakly in the mud.

For long minutes all that could be heard was the sound of their labored breathing, as the three brothers waited for the last of their temper to dissolve. It was always like this. The fury. The storm of fists. And then a tentative attempt to resolve whatever had triggered the fight in the first place.

Chance's voice broke the stillness. "What gives you the right to decide what we can and can't do with the land?"

Hazard struggled to calm his breathing. "Because I'm the only one showing any sense. Look around you. This is a ranch."

"A ranch buried in debt," Ace muttered.

"Maybe. But we've got over two hundred head of cattle. With any luck, after this spring calving, we'll have maybe two hundred fifty."

Ace gave a snort of disgust. "If all the calves make it. And then we'll have two hundred fifty cattle that have to be fed. And slaughtered. And hauled to market."

"We'll do it."

"No. You'll do it," Ace said. "It's your baby."

"All right. I'll do it. And you know why? Because we've got a hundred thousand acres of prime range land."

"There. You see?" Chance looked from Hazard to Ace, then back again. "You just said the magic word. Land. Don't you see?" He got slowly to his feet, pressing his hand to the dull ache in his shoulder. By morning it would be throbbing, and he'd be stiff and sore in a dozen different parts of his body. His only satisfaction was knowing his brothers would be equally sore. "This land has more to offer than just food for cattle."

He held out a hand to Ace, who got to his feet slowly and in turn offered a hand to Hazard, until all three brothers were standing.

The cattle had moved off when the fighting had begun, giving the three men a wide berth. Now Chance, Hazard and Ace stood, caked with mud, oblivious to the bite in the air.

"Look at this." Chance put a hand to Hazard's shoulder and pointed.

In the distance, the tips of the Bighorn Mountains were bathed in golden moonlight. "For as far as the eye can see, it's all ours."

"Don't you think I know that?" Hazard pointed for emphasis. "Every time I look around, I think about how much it cost Dad to leave us this legacy. He worked himself into an early grave. I just don't want us to do anything that might cause us to lose it."

"We're not going to lose it." Chance draped an arm around his shoulders, signaling an end to the feud. "But there's room enough here for all of us to chase our own dreams. For me, that dream is finding oil. I've always believed it's here. I know it is. It's just a matter of time until I find it."

Ace nodded, glad to see his brothers willing to move beyond their fists. Though, in truth, he enjoyed the battles as much as the truces. His father used to say he'd come out of the womb ready to fight his older brothers for his place in the family. "I'm just as positive I'll find coal and uranium. It's been here for thousands of years, just waiting for me to come along and claim it."

They both turned to Hazard, who was still frowning and mulling.

He thought over what they'd said, then slowly nodded, knowing he'd overreacted. "Okay. I guess that's fair. As long as you agree not to do harm to the grazing land or the cattle. They're just too precious to me. I guess you could say they're my dream. And always have been." He stuck out his hand. "So. Can you agree to drill for oil and dig your mines without harming what's already here?"

Chance nodded, then slapped his hand.

With their hands still joined they turned to Ace.

After a moment's hesitation, their youngest brother added his hand to the pact.

"I'll go you one better. Let's race," he said with a smirk, "to see whose dream brings in the first million."

Their frowns disappeared, replaced by matching grins so dazzling, they had set the hearts of every female in the nearby town of Prosperous into overdrive at one time or another.

"You're on, Bro." They lifted their hands over their heads and gave a high-five.

As they turned away, Ace rolled his shoulders. "I'll say one thing about ranching, Hazard. It's sure given you a hell of a punch."

Hazard gave him a halfhearted jab, then draped an arm around his shoulders. "Just keep that in mind, Little Brother, if you decide to mess with me in the future."

Chapter 1

"Hey, Hazard." Ace poked his head in his brother's room.

Hazard looked up from the microscope with a frown. With all the demands of ranch chores, it had taken him every bit of ten years to earn the title Doctor of Veterinary Medicine, but it had been worth it. In between college credits, his hard work and determination had turned the Double W into the largest, most productive cattle ranch in the state of Wyoming.

At first he had turned a small portion of his bedroom into a mini-laboratory, so that he could run tests and blood cultures on ailing cattle. Now, after years of caring for the thousands of head of cattle at the Double W, an entire suite had been added next to his bedroom, which housed a fully equipped laboratory.

"Yeah? What do you want, Ace?" As always, when he was immersed in a medical problem, he had to struggle to bring himself back to the real world.

"Maggie wants to know if you're joining us for breakfast."

"Oh. Sure. Tell her I'll be there in a minute."

"Uh-uh. Right now. Or she said to warn you there'll be nothing left."

Hazard shrugged, then got to his feet. As he followed his brother through the sprawling ranch house to the kitchen, he noticed Ace's suit and tie. "Where're you off to?"

"Colorado. McCormick asked me to drop by his mining operation."

"Is he thinking of selling?"

Ace shrugged. "I doubt it. But I'm interested in buying. I've been investigating his operation. It's a winner. I'm thinking I can relieve him of 50 percent." Developing WildeMining had been a long, slow process. But Ace had finally raised his operation to a level of earnings that matched the ranch and the oil company headed by Chance. His had been the last of the operations to earn a million dollars, with the ranch coming in first and WildeOil running a close second. But, though it had taken longer, WildeMining was now a successful business. And looking to expand. "But I figure I'll just play it by ear. See what he wants."

"And maybe take him for a few thousand in eight ball."

Ace's grin was quick. "You got that right. Poor old McCormick never seems to learn his lesson."

"Just remember. When a guy loses to a pool hustler, he rarely wants to invite that same hustler into his business."

"Not unless that hustler is as charming as yours truly."

They were both chuckling as they entered the kitchen.

The minute they stepped inside, their brother, Chance, and his new bride, Maggie, stepped apart.

"No necking allowed before breakfast." Ace took his place at the table.

"See?" Chance tugged on one of Maggie's curls before crossing the room. "That's why we need our own place. Then we can make out wherever we want."

"You thinking about moving?" Hazard helped himself to a glass of freshly squeezed orange juice. As he drank it, he thought again how much better things had become since Maggie had come into their lives. For years they'd lived on nothing but greasy, overdone burgers and carry-outs from the E.Z.Diner in Prosperous. Now they ate like royalty, thanks to his sister-in-law's gourmet cooking.

"I've always loved that spot up on Tower Ridge. Maggie and I are thinking about building our dream house there."

"You'd take away the best cook we've ever had?" Ace looked from his brother to the woman who was just placing a platter of pancakes on the table.

Maggie kissed her brother-in-law's cheek. "Don't worry, Ace. I'll have you and Hazard over to dinner every other night, until you get wives of your own."

"Which means you'll be stuck with us forever." Ace speared a couple of pancakes and began drizzling them with syrup. "I don't know about old Hazard, there, but the woman hasn't been born who's going to snag me into marriage."

At Maggie's arched brow he shot her one of the famous Wilde smiles. "Not that there's anything wrong with marriage. It works just fine for you guys. But I have no intention of falling into that…" He let the word die as Maggie lifted a skillet over his head in mock anger.

Just then a lean, white-haired cowboy walked in and

respectfully hung his hat by the door before greeting them. "Morning, Maggie. Morning boys."

"Cody." Maggie gave him a warm smile as she handed him a glass of juice. "Sit right down. We're having an interesting discussion about marriage. Have you ever been married, Cody?"

"No, ma'am." He settled himself in a chair. "Marriage and cowboys just don't mix."

Maggie took her place at the table and turned to Hazard. "How about you? Are you of the same mind as your brother about the state of matrimony?"

Hazard shrugged. "I guess I could take it or leave it. But I think Cody's right. I doubt there are many women who'd want to put up with the life I lead. Half the time I'm out the door before dawn tending the herds. The other half I'm up on one of the ranges, bunking with the wranglers for weeks at a time."

"Besides all that, you're ugly," Ace said as he downed his third pancake.

"Yeah." Hazard landed a punch to his shoulder that would have staggered most men. "That's just what Beryl Spence was telling me the last time I dropped by Clancy's for a beer."

Cody joined in the laughter. "She sure was falling all over herself to wait on you, wasn't she?"

"Couldn't keep her hands off me," Hazard said with a self-satisfied, purely masculine grin.

"Beryl Spence." Ace closed his eyes and pressed a hand to his heart. "That woman has the greatest—"

Another punch to his shoulder had his eyes opening wide. "Hey."

"Hey, yourself." Hazard flexed his fingers. "Watch your mouth around your sister-in-law."

"It's only Maggie."

That had Chance punching his other arm.

"Okay. I get the message." Rubbing his arms, Ace emptied his plate and got to his feet. "I've got to get started. Alex and the crew have the plane ready and waiting." He turned to Cody. "Sorry to spoil your breakfast. But I need a ride to the airstrip."

The old man sighed as he pushed himself away from the table. "You think you could keep some of these pancakes warm, Maggie?"

"I'll do better than that. I'll make you fresh ones as soon as you get back."

"You got yourself a deal, Maggie, girl." He hurried across the room and snatched up his hat before turning to Hazard. "When will you need me?"

"Take your time. I've got some lab work to do. Then I think we'll head on up to Peterson's herd. And, Cody?"

The old man turned.

"Tell Russ to plan on coming along. We'll need to load up some carcasses and haul them back here for testing."

"He's already up at Peterson's."

"He is?"

Cody nodded. "Stayed up at their bunkhouse last night."

When Ace and Cody were gone, Chance looked at his brother. "What's all this lab work?"

Hazard shrugged. "A couple of the newborns in Peterson's herd started out healthy, but ended up dead just days later."

"Wolves?"

Hazard shook his head. "Nope. At least not those he got to right away. A few were eaten by wolves, but Peterson thinks they were dead first."

"Did their mothers reject them?"

"Not according to Peterson." He pushed away from

the table. "I'm going to run a couple more tests, just to see if I can find any kind of infection."

Chance's eyes narrowed. "Isn't that the experimental herd you were so proud of? The herd that was going to be completely free of chemicals?"

"Yeah. That's the one." He turned. "Thanks, Maggie. That was a great breakfast, as always."

"How about some coffee to take with you?"

He smiled. "Thanks. That'd be nice." He accepted a full cup before striding away.

When he was gone, Chance stared after him. "He's right, you know."

"About what?" Maggie was already clearing away the dishes.

"About no woman wanting to put up with his hours. Since we were kids, Hazard has worked harder than any of us. He can't seem to separate himself from the land and the cattle. I'll bet that's all he even dreams about."

Maggie walked up behind him and pressed a kiss to his neck. "Maybe you haven't noticed, but he's a man. And a devilishly handsome one, at that. I'll bet there are dozens of women who'd be willing to put up with his long hours, as long as they could have just a little bit of whatever time he has left over."

"Hey. Have you been admiring my brother when I wasn't looking?"

She laughed. "I have. He's almost as handsome as his older brother."

He pulled her down on his lap. "Let's say we sneak off to our room before we head on over to Tower Ridge."

She brushed her mouth over his. "I think I could be persuaded."

Just then the door slammed inward, and Ace paused to gape at them. "Sorry. I forgot my keys."

"Then get them and get going," Chance barked.

"Hey. Don't get so huffy. You two ought to leave that for a more private time."

"That's just the trouble. There is no private time in this place. It's like living in a zoo."

"Okay." Ace snatched up the ring of keys from a hook by the door and shot them a grin. "I'm leaving now. You can go back to doing…whatever it is you were doing."

When he was gone Chance kissed Maggie hard and quick. Then he got to his feet. "That does it. We're going out to Tower Ridge right now. And next week I'm getting an architect up here to start drawing up some plans. We need a place of our own."

"There were two more over here." Peterson led the way, with Hazard and Cody and Russ Thurman trailing behind, until they reached a mound of blood-spattered snow.

"Wolves?" Hazard bent down, noting the trail of blood that led to the brush just beyond.

"Yeah." Peterson was one of the many cowboys who lived on the Double W, tending the herds of cattle. Those who were single stayed in the more than half a dozen bunkhouses scattered across the ranch. Because he had a wife and children, Peterson was provided with a ranch house of his own. And because of his years of loyal service to the Wildes, he had recently been named official ranch foreman.

"Dragged the carcass in there and were having themselves a nice dinner, until I ran them off with my rifle. But from the looks of it, I'm thinking the calf was already dead when they got to it."

"What makes you think that?"

"There were three more right over here." He walked a short distance and stopped.

Hazard knelt down and studied the dead calves, looking for some sign of injury. There appeared to be none. He glanced at Cody. Though the old cowboy was no veterinarian, Hazard trusted his judgment. The old man had been around cattle all his life.

"What do you think?"

Cody scratched his head. "Don't know what to make of it. I've seen a lot in my day, but this one beats all. Still, they had to be sick. Probably some new strain of virus in cattle."

From his pocket Hazard withdrew a surgical knife and located a clot of blood in a vein. Then he located the cows, still heavy with milk, and obtained samples of blood into syringes.

"You think their mothers have some sort of infection?" Cody asked.

"I hope so. At least then we'll have our answer. And we'll know how to treat it."

"If these calves are dying of infection, won't it be passed on to the wolf population?" Peterson asked.

"It could. If they don't have an immunity."

"So this could spread beyond the herd."

Hazard shrugged, not wanting to take his mind in that direction. The problem, unless caught soon, could become immense. "Until I know what I'm dealing with, I don't have a clue." He stood and idly wiped his hands on his pants.

Then he turned. "Russ, bring the truck up here and help Cody load these in the back."

Russ Thurman was a big, burly cowboy with rusty hair and ruddy complexion. Though only a couple of years older than Hazard, years of heavy drinking had already thickened his middle. He moved the plug of chewing tobacco from one side of his mouth to the other, then turned away and spat a stream of juice. "Why don't I bury them right here?"

Hazard shook his head. "I'll need the carcasses in case I have to run more tests." He turned to his foreman. "Let's look at the rest of the newborns. See any sign of sickness?"

"No. That's what has me worried. I didn't see any sign of sickness in these either. One night they're fine. The next morning they're dead."

As the two men walked away, Cody turned to Russ, who was still watching and listening, and quietly chewing. "Want me to get the truck?"

Russ shook his head. "Naw. I'll do it." He walked away, jingling the keys in his pocket.

Minutes later, he and Cody loaded the dead calves in the back of the truck, then settled themselves in the cab and kept the engine idling, blasting warm air and a radio station that played nothing but country.

When Hazard returned, he shook hands with Peterson, then climbed in behind the wheel, grateful for the warmth.

"The calendar says spring. But the weatherman hasn't heard the news yet," he muttered as he put the truck in gear and started off.

"Looks like more snow." Russ pointed to the clouds hanging low over the Bighorns.

"Just what we need." Hazard frowned. "Calving begins and we get another snowstorm."

"I wouldn't worry. There's not too much snow in those clouds." Cody idly rubbed his knee. "These old bones always warn me when a big storm's coming."

"I need some good news right now. So I'll hold your bones to that prediction."

The old man laughed.

An hour later they rolled up to the bunkhouse, where Hazard brought the truck to a stop.

"Home sweet home." Russ's tone was sarcastic as he opened the door and climbed down.

He held the door. "You coming, Cody?"

"That depends." The old man looked toward Hazard. "You need me for anything more?"

"Not right now. I'll probably just start running a few tests. See if I can come up with anything."

As the old man climbed down Hazard called, "Whatever tests I'm going to do on these carcasses should be finished tonight. If you two want to come by the house in the morning, you can pick up the truck and see to their disposal."

"Don't you worry, Hazard. We'll take care of it."

As the truck rolled away, Cody looked after it, then dug his hands in his pockets. "I hate seeing him worried like this."

Russ shrugged, spat a stream of juice. "No big deal. Just a couple of dead dogies. Happens every spring."

"Maybe." Cody turned up his collar and headed for the bunkhouse. "I just hope we don't find any more."

A few days later, Hazard peered into the microscope and studied the cells with a critical eye. As far as he could see there was nothing out of the ordinary. Yet the animal, who only yesterday had been taking its first tentative steps and learning the scent of its mother, was now dead. As were dozens like it.

He rubbed the back of his neck, stiff after so many hours bent over microscopes and test tubes. It wasn't unusual to lose a number of calves every spring. Between the harsh environment and the wolf, a natural predator, they were bound to lose a few. But this year the numbers were far too high and were concentrated in the very herd on which he'd pinned so many hopes.

Something was wrong. And it nagged at him that he couldn't come up with a solution.

He glanced at the clock. Nearly three in the morning. There would be time for only a couple of hours to sleep before he would have to face another day.

He stood and made his way to the bedroom, stripping off his shirt as he did. Sitting on the edge of the bed, he kicked off his boots, then stripped and climbed naked under the covers.

But sleep wouldn't come. He kept seeing the dead calves in his mind. So many. All without a single mark on their bodies.

If it was a new strain of virus or bacteria, left untreated, it could wipe out an entire herd in a season.

He sat up, then resolutely slipped into his jeans and made his way to the computer. There was no time to waste. He needed help now.

He would begin with the state board of veterinary medicine. See if they'd heard of any new strains attacking cattle in the area.

He went on-line, found what he was looking for and began the first of more than a dozen requests for information on any and all viral and bacterial infections that might be attacking vulnerable, newborn calves.

It was almost six in the morning when he connected with his old university professor, Dr. Marlon Wingate, who offered a tiny ray of hope.

The message was terse. *Dr. E. Ryan, from Harvard University, is considered best in that field. A brilliant laboratory researcher. Fortunately for you, the doctor is serving a year's fellowship at the University of Wyoming*

*in Laramie and is currently in your area to lecture at the
university in Cheyenne. I could request that Dr. Ryan
travel to your ranch to observe firsthand and gather blood
samples. Is there a place on the premises where the doctor
could conduct tests?*

Hazard's fingers flew across the keyboard. *I have a
small, but well-equipped laboratory here at the ranch. Dr.
Ryan is welcome to share it. The Double W will, of course,
assume all expenses and is willing to pay whatever the
doctor requires in compensation.*

He waited impatiently for the reply. At last it came.

*Dr. Ryan considers the mystery intriguing. Will arrive
sometime late afternoon.*

Hazard wrote, *Thank you, Professor Wingate. I owe
you, big-time.*

The response was slow in coming, as the old man's
fingers fumbled over the keys. *Your gratitude is thanks
enough, my young friend. I hope I haven't raised your
hopes prematurely. But if anyone can find the answer to
your problem, it is Dr. Ryan.*

Hazard made his way to the shower, then dressed and
headed off to the barn. There was no sense in thinking
about sleep now. It was time to start another round of
endless chores. But right now he'd just been given something even better than sleep.

Hope. It burned brilliantly in his mind. All he wanted
was a simple solution to this mystery. And then he could
get back to the business that consumed him. That had
always consumed him. The business of ranching.

Erin Ryan drove along the two-lane highway, oblivious
to the beauty of the countryside. She drove a car the way
she did everything in her life. With complete concentra-

tion. Two hands on the wheel. Seat belt fastened. Rearview mirror carefully adjusted.

She'd been driving for what seemed hours without seeing another person. Except for the small town of Prosperous, which had already faded into the distance, she could have been on a deserted planet. For a young woman who had grown up in Boston, this held a strange fascination. Though she had been in Wyoming for several months, it still seemed like an alien world. One from which she was oddly detached. Except for her work in the laboratory, she seemed to have no connection to life in this rugged environment.

As the sprawling ranch house came into view, she was more than a little surprised. Built of stone and weathered gray wood, there were charcoal-gray shutters at the windows and a charcoal shingled roof. It soared to three stories, with a wing added here, a wing there, but all coming together with a sense of style and grace. It seemed perfectly suited to its surroundings. As though it had taken root and had been nurtured by the very land itself.

She drove around to the front entrance and stepped out of the car, careful to smooth down the skirt of her navy suit. As she climbed the steps she took note of the covered porch, where a single, hardy rose vine had twisted its way up a post and across the roof, apparently having shriveled and died over the winter.

She rang the bell and waited. When no one came, she rang the bell a second time, then a third. After long minutes she walked around to the back of the house. From here she had a much better view of the barns and outbuildings. And in the distance, on all the surrounding hillsides, she could see the cattle. The land seemed almost black with them.

She was just about to knock when a truck rolled up and

a woman stepped out. A woman as wide as she was tall. Two long, gray braids bounced against her ample bosom as she walked. In her hands were several trays and what looked like a Crock-Pot.

"Hello." Erin smiled. "I'm here to see Hazard Wilde."

"Huh." It was more of a grunt than a greeting. "He's out in the barn. You mind getting the door?"

Erin held the door while the woman waddled past her and clumped into the kitchen, setting things down in the sink. When she turned, Erin was still standing in the doorway.

"The barn's out there." The woman pointed.

Erin glanced over her shoulder but made no move to leave the kitchen. "Is there some way to let him know I'm here?"

"Yeah." Though the woman's face was as wrinkled as ancient parchment, her eyes were as sharp as a blackbird's, studying Erin as though she were addled. "You can walk out there and tell him."

"Yes. Of course. Thank…thank you." Flustered, Erin turned away and let herself out. She was careful to pick her way through the melting snow and pockets of mud, wishing she'd worn boots. But when she'd left for the Double W, the sun had been shining, the highway dry. Not that it mattered. She had another pair of shoes in the suitcase in her trunk. "Always prepare for the unexpected," her mother had told her. And so, whenever she left for a lecture, she always carried spare shoes, spare pantyhose, a second blouse, in case of an emergency.

She would have time to change before getting back on the road. She figured she'd get a blood sample, perform one or two simple tests, and, if her luck held, she'd be on her way in a couple of hours.

If not, she'd have to accept whatever hospitality was offered her and hope for the best. She didn't require much. A bed. A meal. That had her hoping that the woman she'd seen up at the house wasn't the one who prepared the meals around this place. The thought had a disquieting effect on her already-jangling nerves.

She stepped into the dim interior of the barn. Hearing voices nearby, she made her way toward them.

"That's why I brought her in. She's half-crazy with the pain, Hazard. You're going to have to give her a hand with that calf."

Erin paused, watching as a white-haired cowboy leaned on the rail of a stall, talking to someone just beyond her line of vision.

"You could have taken care of this out on the range." The voice was low with anger.

"Could have. But there's nothing I like better'n watching the expert do his job."

"Why you old..." The man's voice was warm with laughter, even while he uttered several rich, ripe oaths, followed by a string of insulting names.

There was another sound now. A rumble of heavy breathing that was unlike anything Erin had ever heard. Intrigued, she moved closer, until she was standing beside the cowboy. He had yet to notice her. His interest was focused on the activity inside the stall.

Erin turned her head to see what it was.

And froze.

A man with his back to her had plunged his hands inside a cow and was viciously tugging. The cow's head was raised, its eyes glazed with pain. A series of shudders seemed to pass through the animal, and a low, keening sound came from its throat.

The man swore viciously as his hands slipped and he

fell backward into dung-encrusted straw. He righted himself and plunged his hands even deeper inside the animal, pulling until the veins in his neck looked as though they might burst.

"Now you got 'er, Hazard," the cowboy shouted. "Come on, boy. Put some muscle into it."

Erin was absolutely horrified. And though the scene repulsed her, she couldn't look away. The man and animal continued in this slow, agonizing ritual that went on and on without relief. Finally, after another series of shudders, the cow seemed to tense, and suddenly a slimy blob came sliding out, landing in the straw. Seconds later there was more slime, along with what seemed to be enormous amounts of blood, drenching the man before he could step away.

While the cow began to lick at the sack of fluid, the man crossed the stall to a bucket of water, plunging his arms up to the elbows. By the time he snatched up a towel and turned toward the cow, the sack of fluid had been cleaned away and a newborn calf was already kicking its legs, struggling to right itself.

"Well, isn't she a beaut, Hazard?"

"Yeah. I just wish I could have gotten a better grip on her. I thought for a minute I'd lost her. You were right to bring her in, Cody. She'd have never made it out in the range."

"Well, well. What've we got here?" Russ Thurman spat a yellow stream of tobacco. "Looks like some city chick just got dropped here by mistake."

Hazard turned. And spotted the woman standing beside Cody at the same moment Cody did.

In her prim suit, her hair pulled back in a tidy knot and little round glasses perched on her nose, she looked as out of place in the barn as if she'd been wearing a ball gown.

Worst of all, her skin was as sickly pale as the snow outside the door.

"Excuse me, ma'am." While Russ snickered, Cody put an arm beneath her elbow. "How'd you get in here?"

"I was…" She struggled to get the words out. Her brain didn't want to cooperate. She seemed to be fading in and out. She couldn't seem to put the grizzly, bloody scene out of her mind. "I was told I would find Hazard Wilde in here."

Hazard stepped out of the stall and offered his hand, unaware of the blood that had smeared his clothes, and even splattered across his face. "I'm Hazard Wilde. And you are…?"

"Dr. Erin Ryan." She could hardly recognize her own voice. The words sounded stilted to her ears.

She was aware of dark eyes staring at her. And somewhere nearby, the sound of crude laughter.

Calling on every ounce of effort, she struggled to extend her hand.

At the same moment she felt the barn begin to tilt. Her legs turned to rubber. And then, to her complete humiliation, her world turned upside down and she could feel herself slipping into a long, dark tunnel of unconsciousness.

Chapter 2

"Please. I'm all right now." Erin was mortified to realize that Hazard had scooped her up and was carrying her out of the barn. With a single sharp word he'd silenced the man who'd been laughing at her.

His arms were unbelievably strong. As he crossed the distance from the barn to the house, he carried her as though she weighed no more than a petal on the breeze. And with such care. As if she were some fragile doll that might shatter at any moment.

"Really, Mr. Wilde." She turned her face, and to her consternation, found her lips pressed against his throat. Mortified, she turned her face away, but it was too late to undo the damage. Her heartbeat was fluttering against her chest with such force she knew he had to hear. And her breathing had become strained, as though she'd been racing up a hill. "I'm...fine now. I can walk."

In response he increased his pace, while Cody hurried along behind him, struggling to keep up.

Once inside the house he stalked toward the great room, where he gently settled her on a sofa.

She'd never seen a room quite this large. Fifty people could have gathered here without feeling crowded. The room was dominated by a raised, four-sided fireplace, with sofas drawn up on all four sides to take advantage of the warmth. There were two walls of floor-to-ceiling shelves and two walls made entirely of glass, overlooking the sweeping landscape.

"Get me some water, Cody," he shouted.

Minutes later the old cowboy was beside him, holding out a glass.

"Drink this." His tone was still gruff with worry.

Erin did as she was told, all the while aware that he was studying her with such intensity that the simple act of swallowing was painful. There was a frown line between his brows. And those deep, liquid-brown eyes were boring into her.

When the glass was empty, she handed it back. "I'm so embarrassed. I don't know what came over me. This has never happened to me before."

"How long since you last ate?" he demanded.

"This morning, I think." She tried to recall. Had she taken time to eat? It didn't matter. Food had never been a priority in her life. "It wasn't a lack of food. It was…all that blood."

"You get sick at the sight of blood?"

"No. Of course not. But…I've never seen a calf being born before. I never realized it was so…"

"Ah. I see." He nodded. "It does get a bit messy. Sorry you had to see that."

"No. It's really quite—" She stopped, bit her lip. If she wasn't careful, she was liable to start blubbering. She was still feeling a little overwhelmed. It had been the sight of the cow, licking her infant, that had been her undoing. Even in nature, it seemed, there was an instant bond between mother and child. She was sure the tender, poignant moment would be etched forever in her memory.

She still wasn't certain what had caused her blackout. Was it the pain and horror of the birth? Or the sight of the cow, its pain forgotten as it licked its newborn with such care?

She took a deep breath. "Could we start over?"

Hazard nodded, relieved that the color was returning to her cheeks. What an odd little thing she was. Not at all what he'd been expecting. In truth, when Professor Wingate had said he was sending a brilliant laboratory researcher, he'd anticipated someone like his old college professor, with a bushy beard and thick glasses, constantly forgetting to button his lab coat. Now he would have to readjust his thinking.

He offered his hand. "Dr. Ryan, I'm Hazard Wilde, owner of the Double W. And this is Cody Bridger, who can answer just about any question you might have about the operation of this place."

"Mr. Wilde. Mr. Bridger."

Hazard's eyes crinkled with a smile. "Mr. Wilde was my father. As for Cody, if you call him Mr. Bridger, I doubt he'd know who you were talking to."

She managed a shy smile. "All right. I'll remember. And my name is Erin."

Just then the door opened and Maggie and Chance came in arm in arm, their cheeks flushed, their faces crinkled with laughter.

"Do you really think you could have it done by late summer?" Maggie was so wrapped up in her husband, she hadn't yet noticed the others.

"I don't see why not. I'll get the architect started right

away.'' Chance pressed a kiss to her lips, then glanced over in surprise. ''What's this? Are we having a party in the middle of the afternoon?''

Hazard shook his head. ''Cody and I were just getting acquainted with Dr. Ryan.'' He turned. ''Erin, this is my brother Chance and his new bride, Maggie.''

They stepped closer and offered their greetings to the young woman seated primly on the sofa.

Chance turned to study his brother. ''Is this the latest ranch fashion?''

Hazard glanced down at his shirtfront and realized it was streaked with dirt and blood.

''Sorry. I was just playing midwife to a first-time mother. I'll go clean up.''

Maggie turned to their guest. ''Could I interest you in some tea, Dr. Ryan?''

''I'd love some. And I hope you'll call me Erin.''

''All right, Erin. Come on in the kitchen.'' She turned to Cody. ''How about you?''

The old cowboy shook his head with a laugh. ''I put tea drinking right up there with getting dressed in a suit and tie and going to fancy parties. It's okay for some, but it just isn't my style. If you don't mind, I'll head on out to the barn and check on our new mama.''

Erin followed Maggie into the kitchen and glanced around in admiration. ''Are all the rooms this big?''

''Yes.'' Maggie filled the kettle before setting it on the stove. ''It takes some time to get used to. Each of the brothers has his own wing. If you're not careful, you could get lost trying to find your way from one end of this house to the other.''

''I doubt I'll be here long enough for that.'' Erin took a place at the table and watched as Maggie filled a plate with biscuits and several little pots of jam.

She broke open a biscuit. "Did you make these?"

Maggie nodded. "I love to cook. It's what brought me to the Double W."

Erin tasted and gave a sigh. "Oh, this is wonderful."

"Do you cook?"

Erin merely laughed. "Not a lick. Oh, I can microwave oatmeal. And I can heat up a pretty mean pizza, if I'm hungry enough. But food has never been very important in my life."

Chance happened to stroll in at that moment and overheard her remark. "I might have said something similar just a few short months ago. But now that I've had the opportunity to eat Maggie's fine cooking, I could never go back to eating carry-out."

"See? I've spoiled you for any other woman." Maggie filled two cups with tea.

"I'm sure you planned it that way." He brushed a kiss over her cheek. "Is there any coffee?"

"I just made a fresh pot. After seeing Hazard, I figure he'll need something hot and strong."

"Good thinking." Chance poured himself a cup and lifted it to his lips for a long drink. Then he hoisted his cup in a toast. "Well, Dr. Ryan, welcome to the Double W."

Hazard stripped off his clothes and stepped into the shower. As he washed away the blood and dirt, he couldn't stop thinking about Dr. Ryan. She was so small. When he'd carried her from the barn to the house, she felt as if she weighed no more than a feather. But it wasn't just her size that was surprising. There was a fragile quality about her. He would have expected an educated woman like that to be aware of the messy side of birthing. Still, Professor Wingate had said she was a brilliant laboratory researcher. Maybe such people never actually went into the field. Maybe all their work was done under the sterile conditions of a lab. He supposed it was possible, after a few years in such an environment, to become completely detached from reality.

As he snatched a towel and began to dry, he thought about her pale, porcelain skin. He'd never seen anything quite like it. He'd wanted to reach out and touch her cheek, to see if she was real.

He tossed aside the towel and began rummaging through the closet for a clean shirt. As he began buttoning it, he paused. Yeah, she was real. At least, if that press of her lips against his throat was any indication. He'd experienced the most amazing response. In the space of one instant he'd felt a flare of heat that had his blood pulsing and at the same moment a tingle of ice along his spine that nearly stopped him in his tracks. Fire and ice. And all from one pale little female who was practically out on her feet.

What's more, in the great room, he had actually been able to see the color return to her cheeks by degree, until her skin had once again taken on a healthy glow. Funny. It was only then that his heart had returned to its normal rhythm and he'd had time to notice that her eyes behind those round glasses were the most incredible shade of blue. And the hair pinned back in that neat knot was light brown.

He slipped into clean denims, then tugged on his boots. The thought of her prim, navy suit and matching pumps had him grinning. Talk about your fish out of water. Still, as long as she could solve his problem, what did he care? He'd give her some vials of blood serum, turn her loose in his lab, and let her do the job she'd come here to do.

Running his hands through his damp hair, he pulled

open the door and headed toward the kitchen. As he drew close, he could hear Chance and Maggie laughing about something.

"It must be fun planning a new home." Erin sat back, sipping her tea, grateful for this pleasant break in routine.

"Well, we just started today. Uh, Hazard. I made coffee." Maggie started to get up but Hazard stopped her.

"I'll get it. Tell me about the house plans."

"There aren't any yet." Maggie and Chance exchanged smiles. "But we've talked about what we want, and now we'll just wait and see what the architect comes up with."

"Which reminds me." Chance caught Maggie's hand. "Come on. We have to phone the architect and get him started."

Maggie paused beside Erin. "It was nice meeting you. I hope I'll see you before you leave."

"Thanks, Maggie. And thanks for the tea. I'm feeling human again."

When they were gone, Erin watched as Hazard poured himself a cup of coffee. The plaid shirt couldn't hide the muscles of his arms and shoulders. Just thinking about the ease with which he'd carried her gave a funny tingle along her spine.

He turned. The droplets of water from the shower glistened in his shaggy dark hair. He was in need of a haircut, and it spilled over his forehead as he walked to the table.

"Are you feeling up to a little lab work?"

She nodded. "It's why I'm here."

"Okay. Follow me. And bring your tea."

He led the way through the great room, where a fire still blazed on the open hearth. Then they walked along a hallway until he threw open a door and led the way inside.

Erin didn't know what she'd been expecting. But certainly not this. She stared around in openmouthed surprise. There were three walls of floor-to-ceiling shelves. A fourth wall was all glass, allowing natural light to flood the room. More light poured from the skylights above. An island counter in the center of the room had two large sinks, several stools and a computer. Everything was white. The ceramic tile floors, the granite countertops, the cabinets and shelves. Even the walls. White and spotless.

"This is…almost as big as our laboratory at the university."

"Is it?" He shrugged and crossed to the island counter. Within minutes he'd set aside his coffee and was removing several vials of blood serum from a refrigerator.

"I took these from the dead calves." He set the vials to one side, then removed several more. "These are from their mothers. Each is labeled. I've already done the usual tests for bacteria, virus. As you'll read in my notes, so far I've come up empty."

Erin set aside her tea and took the notebook from his hand. As their fingers brushed, she almost dropped the notebook, but managed to retain her grasp on it long enough to set it down on the counter.

She hadn't imagined it. At the mere touch of their fingertips she'd felt a sizzle of heat all the way up her arm.

"Well?"

She realized he was waiting for her to study his notes. As she bent to the notebook, her admiration for him went up another notch. Not only did he have a fine lab, he kept meticulous notes.

"Why don't I run a few simple tests of my own, just to see if we come up with the same results?"

He nodded. "Good idea. While you're doing that, I hope you won't mind if I run out to the barn and check on the new calf.'' He shot her a grin. ''After all, I was the midwife.''

She watched as he turned away and let himself out. When he was gone, she took a deep breath, relieved that she was finally alone. She didn't know quite how it had happened, but ever since she'd arrived here, she seemed to have lost her bearings. For a while, there, she'd felt like Alice falling down the hole. She'd dropped into another world. One that bore no resemblance to the pristine world she'd always occupied.

But now she was back. Completely in her element. She might be a misfit in a barn, but here in the lab she was right at home.

Hazard returned to the house wearing a puzzled frown. It seemed these days at the ranch every bit of good news was countered by bad.

In the good news department, the cow and her newborn were thriving. But just to be safe, he'd taken a vial of blood from each. Tomorrow, Russ Thurman would return them to the herd.

The bad news was that Russ had confirmed that there were more than a dozen carcasses discovered overnight. All newborns. All apparently healthy.

He hoped Dr. Erin Ryan could provide him with the answer.

He paused in the doorway of the lab. She was seated at the island counter, peering through a microscope. Satisfied, she turned to write in a notebook, before returning her attention to the serum sample.

He leaned against the door, unaware of the smile of pure appreciation that touched his lips. He'd been wrong about her hair. It wasn't light brown. With the sunlight pouring down from the skylight, it proved to be a rich, honey-blond. One little strand had slipped from the neat knot and kissed her cheek in a most beguiling fashion.

She'd removed the prim jacket to reveal an equally prim, white blouse, buttoned clear to the throat. She had crossed one leg over the other while she worked, and her foot was moving to some inner music. He took a moment to admire the length of thigh visible beneath the skirt, before she tugged on the fabric, blocking his view.

She glanced up and caught sight of him in the doorway. For a moment her heart did an odd little flip-flop, before settling back to its natural rhythm.

"So." He walked closer and bent toward her notes. "Have you solved my problem?"

"Hmm? Oh. I'm afraid not. In fact, I can't find anything here at all out of the ordinary." She frowned. "Are you absolutely certain these calves weren't just killed by predators?"

"If I believed that, I wouldn't have sent out a call for help."

"I realize that. I didn't mean..." She paused, and indicated the serum sample. "Look here."

He bent his head beside hers and peered through the scope. When he did, his hair tickled her hand and she pulled it away as though burned.

"It looks perfectly normal to me."

"Yes." She reminded herself to breathe. The specimen was normal. What wasn't normal was her reaction to this man. "That's what I meant. Nothing at all out of the ordinary here. If you were dealing with infection, whether bacterial or viral, there would be changes in the blood serum. But these animals show no sign of disease."

Hazard couldn't hide his disappointment. "Sorry." He turned away and paced toward the windows, then back. "I guess I've been hoping for a quick, easy answer. But now that your conclusions are the same as mine, I realize I'm just going to have to dig deeper."

"I'm just as disappointed as you." At the arch of his brow she flushed. "For quite different reasons, of course. You have a personal stake in this. But as a researcher, I relish the opportunity to solve medical mysteries. I had even allowed myself to think I might stumble upon some new strain of bacteria that would offer a challenge to me and my colleagues."

"Yeah. Well…" He leaned a hip against the counter. "I just spoke with one of my wranglers. There are more than a dozen new calves dead since last night."

"We had snow. Maybe this is the normal attrition rate during a hard spring. I did detect some hypoglycemia in the blood samples."

He nodded. "Typical of hypothermia. But it's to be expected with all this snow. The stock is hardy enough to survive it." He shook his head. "Something else is killing off my calves. And I intend to find out what it is." He gave a sigh of resignation. "Thank you, Erin. I appreciate the fact that you came out of your way as a favor to Professor Wingate."

"Actually, I did it as much for myself as for the good professor. Though I must admit, his description of you was intriguing."

His head came up. "Really? What did he have to say?"

"He called you the most gifted, determined rancher he'd ever met."

Hazard's smile was quick and disarming. "He was equally effusive about you."

She couldn't help returning the smile. "He's a dear. We've worked together on a couple of projects. It's really his influence that brought me here. I wrote a paper that caught his eye, and he and I began corresponding. When there was an opening at the university for a fellowship, he recommended me for the position. And even though it's only for a year, I thought it would add to my store of knowledge. So here I am.'' She realized she'd been babbling. It was completely out of character. It had to be this situation.

She paused a moment, then came to a decision. ''I was on my way back to Laramie, but I think this may be far more important than anything waiting for me in the lab. Besides, it isn't often that I get the chance to do actual fieldwork. Would you mind if I stayed to do a little blood work on the calves that died last night?''

''Would I mind?'' His smile grew. ''Dr. Ryan, I'd be delighted.''

He walked to the door and beckoned her to follow. ''I'll show you the guest quarters and let Maggie know you'll be staying for dinner.''

''You don't think she'll mind the extra work?''

''Maggie?'' He laughed. ''My sister-in-law is amazing. In the time it would take most of us to open a couple of cans, she can whip up a gourmet meal that would put the experts to shame.''

He opened a door and stood aside. Just beyond the lab was a suite of rooms as impressive as all the other rooms Erin had seen at the Double W. There was a bedroom, with a king-size bed constructed of hand-hewn logs. A chaise lounge was situated in front of a double fireplace that heated both the bedroom and the adjoining bathroom. Another wall contained floor-to-ceiling bookshelves, and beside them stood a cozy writing desk and chair.

''Oh.'' Her usual reticence nearly dissolved as she looked around. ''This is…quite wonderful.''

''If you have a suitcase in the car, I'll be happy to have someone bring it to you.''

"Thank you." She dug in her pocket and produced the keys. "It's in the trunk."

As she handed him the keys she felt again the quick rush of heat, the tiny flutter around her heart. It wasn't the man, she thought. It was the situation. After years in a laboratory, she would actually spend a night at a working ranch. It was the opportunity of a lifetime.

When Hazard was gone she began to prowl the room, touching a hand to the massive stones that made up the fireplace, sitting on the edge of the mattress to test its softness.

She didn't know why she was feeling this quiet hum of excitement. As though she was about to venture into completely uncharted territory.

But she did know this: by this time tomorrow the mystery surrounding the deaths would probably be solved to everyone's satisfaction, and she would be on her way back to her tiny apartment on the campus in Laramie. But she would have the satisfaction of knowing that she'd actually spent a night at the biggest ranch in Wyoming. And, in her own small way, had had a hand in making the operation run more smoothly.

Now if only she could do something about her odd reaction to Hazard Wilde.

If Professor Wingate were here, he'd probably remind her that it had something to do with digestion. She'd be fine after a hot meal.

Chapter 3

Erin changed into her clean shoes, then repaired most of the damage to her other pair in the bathroom, scrubbing and polishing them to a high shine. Then she set about slicking back her hair, seeing to it that every errant strand was carefully tucked in place.

As she studied her reflection in the bathroom mirror, she wondered about the protocol of going to dinner without her suit jacket. This was, after all, a ranch. Still, as her mother had always cautioned, she had an image to uphold. People expected certain things of a professional woman. In the end she decided that, ranch or no, she would wear her jacket.

She left her room and started down the hall that led to the great room. Beyond that she'd spotted a formal dining room. But when she got there, she was surprised to find it empty.

She turned and followed the sound of voices to the kitchen.

Chance and Hazard were leaning against a counter, laughing, talking and drinking beer. Maggie was busy at the stove, stirring something that smelled heavenly. They all looked up as she entered.

"Come on in." Hazard took a step toward her. "Would you like something to drink?"

She started to shake her head. "I don't think…"

Maggie held up a glass of white wine. "It doesn't have to be beer. If you'd like, you can join me. I'm having a little Chardonnay."

Erin smiled. "I'd like that."

Hazard poured, then handed her a stem glass.

"Thanks." She sipped, ordering herself to relax.

"I was just telling…" Hazard stopped as the door burst open and Ace breezed in, followed by Cody. "You're back from Colorado already?"

"Yep." Ace reached into his pocket and held up a fistful of money. "With four thousand of McCormick's dollars, thanks to his lack of skill at eight ball."

"You idiot." Chance exploded, shoving Ace back against a wall. "Why in hell did you have to hustle him in a pool game?"

"Because he's such easy pickins, that's why." Ace shoved back, then managed to land a punch in Chance's forearm before stepping out of reach. "Every time we get together, the poor fool just begs me to beat him."

Now it was Hazard's turn to throw a punch. "But you were hoping for a half interest in his mine. Now you've spoiled any chance of that."

"Have I?" Ace managed two quick fists to the chest, sending Hazard hurtling backward before he straightened and slammed his younger brother against the counter.

As both brothers came at him, Ace held up a document

to stave off further attack. "Wait a minute. Do you see this?"

Chance and Hazard paused. "What is it?"

"Just a half interest in McCormick's mining operation."

"You got it?" Hazard looked thunderstruck.

"I told you I would. And when I set my mind to something, I take no prisoners."

"So first you beat him at eight ball, then you somehow persuaded him to throw in a half interest in his mine, as well?"

"Something like that. Actually, he was determined that I take half."

Hazard frowned. "If he was that insistent, it could mean we've just acquired 50 percent of bad debt."

"Hey. Do I look that stupid?" Ace held up his hand. "Don't answer that. I looked over the books. They're showing a profit."

"If that's the case, why would McCormick need WildeMining as a partner?"

"Because he needs the refining and distribution our company can offer. So I told him, if the legal department agrees, he'll have himself a partner. If legal finds any reason to nix the deal, it's off."

He glanced at Erin, who had watched this entire scene in jaw-dropping silence. The violence between these three had shocked her to the core.

Ace stuck out his hand as though he hadn't just used it to punch his brothers. "Sorry. We haven't met."

Hazard handled the introductions. "Dr. Erin Ryan, my brother Ace."

"Doctor?" Ace grinned and pressed her hand to his forehead. "I think I feel something nasty coming on. You might want to check me for a fever."

While Erin blushed clear to her toes, the others merely laughed at Ace's clowning.

"She's not that kind of doctor." Hazard twisted the tops off two bottles and handed one to Ace and one to Cody, before giving Ace a resounding punch to the shoulder. "She's a laboratory researcher. Here to find out why I'm losing so many calves."

"Oh." Ace tipped up the bottle and took a long pull, before returning the punch with one of his own. "One of those deep thinkers, who like to study things and people under microscopes. Nice to meet you, doc." He turned to Maggie. "Have I got time to change out of my let's-make-a-deal clothes before dinner?"

"I'll give you ten minutes to slip into your jeans."

"I can do it in five." He sauntered away.

Maggie turned to Cody, who was leisurely sipping his beer. "Are you staying for dinner, Cody?"

"No, ma'am. I promised to give Russ Thurman a chance to win back the five dollars I took off him last night in gin, before he heads on up to Peterson's ranch. Besides, Agnes said you were making the wranglers pot roast. I wouldn't want to miss that."

"I don't know how much will be left. Agnes took dinner to the bunkhouse about ten minutes ago."

He drained his beer and set the bottle on the counter. "If that's the case, I'll say good-night." He gave a courteous nod of his head to Erin. "And good night to you, ma'am."

"Good…good night, Cody." She was still almost speechless by the physical battering among the three brothers. How was it possible that they could nearly beat each other senseless one minute, then joke the next? Yet they truly seemed to hold no grudges.

Now she watched as the old cowboy retrieved his hat from a hook by the door and let himself out.

Minutes later Agnes waddled in and set several serving platters on the counter. "You'd have thought those wranglers were a pack of hungry wolves, the way they attacked that food." She wiped her hands on the apron that hung at a lopsided angle around her middle. "Never used to eat like that. Used to have some manners, and eat slow and easy like."

"Maybe it's the weather." Maggie was far too polite to suggest it might have been the food they'd been forced to endure for so long. She'd heard the tales of muddy chili and greasy burgers. She began filling a basket with rolls still hot from the oven. "Erin, have you met Agnes Tallfeather? Agnes, this is Dr. Ryan."

The old woman looked over at Erin. Her face creased into a sly smile. "I see you found your way to the barn."

"Yes."

"Figured you would. Hard to miss. You staying the night?"

Erin nodded.

"Well then. Guess I'll toss some clean towels in your bathroom before I go off to my room." Agnes heaped her plate with dinner. "Can't stay for dinner. Want to watch *Wheel of Fortune.*" As she waddled away she called over her shoulder, "I'll see you in the morning. 'Night."

"'Night, Agnes," the others called.

Erin turned to Maggie. "She doesn't eat dinner out here?"

Maggie shook her head. "Most nights she prefers to eat in her room in front of the television. We've been making bets among ourselves over whether or not she sleeps in her bed. I'm betting she just sleeps in the chair while the TV plays all night. In fact, I've got five dollars riding on the outcome.''

Erin's eyes widened. "Does everyone here gamble?''

Maggie looked from Erin to Chance, before bursting into gales of laughter. "You see? I told you it's contagious. Before I came here, I never thought about betting on anything. Now I'm getting as bad as the rest of you. I'm even making bets on Agnes.''

At the look on Erin's face, Hazard threw back his head and roared. "She's right. Gambling is a way of life for the Wildes. But don't worry. You can't catch it in a single night.''

"That's a relief.'' Erin was still shaking her head as she followed the others to the table.

Ace strolled in just as they were taking their places. "I told you I'd make it in five minutes.'' He settled his lanky body in the chair.

"All right,'' Chance muttered as they began to pass around platters of prime rib surrounded by fresh spring vegetables. "Let's hear about McCormick. How did you manage to relieve him of four thousand?''

"In a minute. Let me enjoy this first.'' Ace buttered a biscuit and bit into it, closing his eyes in pleasure. "Mmm. Maggie, nobody can bake biscuits like these. I've been thinking about this all the way home from Colorado.''

She merely grinned.

He opened his eyes to find his two brothers glaring at him. "Okay. The details. You know how Big John Mc-Cormick thinks he's a genius with a pool cue? Well, the first game, I let him run the table. It wasn't easy, since I had to make it look like I was really trying while managing a near miss. The guy is so bad, I thought I might have to scratch, just to give him the game. But he squeaked by and took the first one. After that our hero was so blinded by ego, he had himself convinced that I didn't have a chance. And after I beat him the second game, he went nuts and insisted we do double or nothing. From then on, he never had a shot.'' Ace shook his head and helped himself to garlic potatoes. ''I sure hope he's better at running his mining operation than he is at gambling. Because he's a lousy gambler. And a sore loser. But by the time I let him convince me to buy into his operation, he was smiling again. When I left him, Big John McCormick was one very happy man.''

Hazard chuckled. ''Just another day in the life of Ace Wilde.''

''You bet.'' Ace glanced at Erin, who was picking at her food. ''Doc, if you don't eat more than that, you'll blow away in a good wind.''

''I...'' She blushed, embarrassed by the fact that she hadn't understood a single word he'd spoken until now. That whole rambling description might as well have been given in a foreign language. Eight ball. Scratch. Run the table. These were expression that weren't even in her vocabulary. ''I've never had much of an appetite.''

''That's never been a problem in the Wilde family,'' Maggie said with a laugh. ''I've begun to think they're human garbage disposals.''

''We used to be.'' Chance closed a hand over Maggie's. ''Now we eat only the best, thanks to you.'' He lifted her hand to his lips and pressed a kiss to the palm.

Seeing the love between them, Erin felt like a voyeur. No wonder they were hoping to build their own home.

Hazard reached for the platter and helped himself to seconds. Watching, Erin wondered how these three men could eat so much and have such trim, muscled bodies. It was probably metabolism. They engaged in such hard, physical work, they needed all the fuel they could take in.

"So, Doc, you're here about all those dead calves. Have you figured out what caused them yet?"

She shook her head. "My preliminary tests matched your brother's. No bacterial or viral infection showed up in the serum samples."

"So, you think the calves were just too frail to survive?"

"I don't know what to think. But I think it's safe to say they weren't killed by bacteria or an unknown virus."

Maggie circled the table, filling cups with coffee, then passed around a tray filled with fruit tarts. "Did everyone leave room for dessert?"

Ace tasted his, then rolled his eyes. "If anyone is too full, I'll be happy to take your dessert off your hands."

He stared pointedly at Erin, until Hazard gave him a nudge. "Knock it off. Quit trying to intimidate our guest."

"Hey, you can't blame a guy for trying."

Erin ducked her head and bit back the smile that played at the corner of her lips. Though she was still feeling out of her element in this rowdy family, she realized she was enjoying herself immensely. These three brothers were unlike any she'd ever met before. Brash. Funny. Irreverent.

She thought about her own sedate childhood. Her father was a renowned physicist at Harvard. Brilliant and aloof. Her mother was an equally brilliant professor of English. A stern, serious woman who had expected, in fact demanded, that her daughter choose a profession that would do them proud.

She'd toyed briefly with the idea of studying library science, since she loved books. To the painfully shy, sweet dreamer, fiction was far more palatable than real life. But in the end, it was her natural curiosity that won out. She wanted to know the what and why and how of things. And as she delved deeper into the research, the laboratory became a safe haven. There she didn't have to deal with people. There, in the sterile environment of the lab, with its charts and graphs and data, she could be alone with her thoughts.

Alone. It seemed to her that she'd spent her entire life alone, even when she'd been with her parents. Though it was completely unintentional, they had shut her out. They had room only for their work, to the exclusion of all else.

It occurred to Erin that she had never eaten dinner in the kitchen. In fact, the only time she'd been allowed to enter was when she was home alone, and the housekeeper, Mrs. Kline, would take pity on the lonely little girl. Then Erin would be allowed to sit on a stool and sip tea with sugar, while Mrs. Kline and the cook, Hattie, would gossip about Hattie's niece, Sara, who was, according to Hattie, marrying too high above her and, therefore, doomed to a life of misery.

"So, Doc, what's your next step?"

Erin pulled herself back from her thoughts of home. "I offered to go with Hazard tomorrow and view the dead calves."

"Hey, that's nice of you."

She smiled. "Actually, it's selfish of me. As a laboratory researcher, I rarely get to work in the field. It should be quite an experience." She blushed, remembering her reaction in the barn. "I only hope I don't embarrass myself."

Hazard shook his head. "We're just going to view the carcasses and take a few samples, so that we can run more tests when we get back. I'll try to spare you as much blood and gore as possible.''

Ace glanced at Erin's clothes. ''I hope you brought something more suitable than that for your field work.''

The young woman looked embarrassed. ''I was on my way home from a symposium at the university. Except for nightclothes, these are the only things I have with me.''

Maggie eyed her. ''I can loan you some jeans and a sweater. They might be a bit big, but you'll be a lot more comfortable than you will be wearing that.''

''You don't mind?''

''Not at all.'' Maggie patted her hand before retrieving the coffeepot and topping off their cups. ''Would anybody like seconds on dessert?''

Erin watched in amazement as all three brothers helped themselves to more tarts.

Afterward, when Maggie began to clear the table, Erin stood up to give her a hand.

''Uh-uh.'' Chance took the dishes from her hands. ''You and Hazard can go in the great room and listen to more of Ace's bull—'' he caught himself in time ''—war stories, while I help my wife with the dishes.''

''But I'd like to help,'' Erin protested.

''No dice.'' He leaned close. ''The truth is, this is the only way we can ever arrange to be alone. You'd be surprised at how cozy and intimate doing dishes can be.''

Erin laughed as she followed Hazard and Ace from the room. But even before the door closed, she caught sight of Chance drawing Maggie into his arms.

She felt a little thrill and found herself wondering just how it would feel to have a man so hungry for the touch of her, the taste of her, that he could hardly control himself.

She had long ago resigned herself to the knowledge that

such things were only experienced in fiction novels. In real life, people worked. They led productive lives. And if they were lucky, they found a measure of satisfaction in their jobs and in their relationships. To ask for more was to seek the impossible.

''So, Doc.'' Ace had seen the slight flush on her cheeks, and recognized what had caused it. For some strange reason it amused him to see someone so prim, so proper, that even the sight of two people in love could be cause for embarrassment. ''How about an after-dinner drink?'' He lifted a bottle of aged brandy from a glass shelf and removed the stopper.

''All right. Just a little.''

He poured three snifters, and passed them around.

As she lifted the glass to her lips he asked, ''Where are you from originally?''

''Boston.''

''Boston. Did you go to Haavaad?'' He drew out the accent, knowing it would bring a smile to her lips.

''As a matter of fact, I did.''

''How did a Harvard grad end up in Wyoming?''

She looked down at the glass in her hands. ''It was as far as I could get from Boston.''

As she sipped her brandy Hazard stared at her with a look of astonishment. Why would a woman leave the comfort of home and family and all that was familiar, to take a job on the other side of the country? Granted, it was a very good job. And the pay would probably afford her a comfortable life-style. But she would be completely alone. No family. No friends.

He tried to imagine what his life would be like without his two rough-and-tumble brothers, who filled his days with such laughter, along with a great deal of irritation. How dull life would be if all he had to look forward to each day were rounds of endless chores. It was his family that nourished his soul and spurred him on to greater achievements. It was the sharp barb of his brother's taunts, or the pat on the back at the end of a particularly tiring day, that helped him to face another day, to leap the next hurdle.

But Dr. Erin Ryan was alone. By choice. Odd. But then, she was an odd little creature.

Not his business, he reminded himself as he set aside his brandy to add another log to the fire.

"This is a wonderful room. I can just imagine it filled to overflowing with people. Has that ever happened?"

"A few times a year. Thanksgiving. Christmas. New Year's Eve. We invite all the wranglers and their families to help us celebrate most holidays. And every year it used to be filled for our father's birthday." Hazard and Ace exchanged smiles. "Dad loved his birthday. Every year he used to throw himself one heck of a party. We'd have a barbecue, and everybody in Prosperous was invited. The women brought pot luck, and there was dancing in the barn."

"And fireworks," Ace said with a laugh. "Our old man loved fireworks. The noisier the better."

"I'll bet you didn't call him your old man to his face." Erin tasted her brandy.

"Sure we did." Hazard saw her look of surprise. "That isn't meant as a term of disrespect. Our old man was the best father in the world. He knew it. And so did we."

Erin walked to the floor-to-ceiling windows and stared out at the countryside cloaked in shadow. In the distance the mountain peaks were touched with lavender. In her mind she was picturing her father. She had never called him by any affectionate nickname. It was always the formal *father*. "Everything seems so different here."

"Different?" Hazard watched her. "How?"

She shrugged. "People are so much more casual. About their feelings. About their families."

"There's nothing wrong with casual. Whether I say I had a terrific old man, or I loved my father, the meaning is the same. No more. No less."

"If you say so." She kept her back to him, staring into the gathering darkness. "Everything's so big out here."

"That's because we aren't hemmed in by buildings." Hazard walked up to stand beside her. "You can look out and see something besides brick walls and parking lots." His voice lowered. "Do you miss Boston?"

She shook her head. "No. At least not the way I thought I would. The pace seems slower here. Maybe it's because I'm not distracted by friends or family. But it's more than that. There seems to be a connection with nature here, that's not possible in the city. But especially a city like Boston. Everyone there is so…intense."

She handed him the half-finished snifter of brandy and felt the quick little rush of heat when their fingers touched. "If you don't mind, I think I'd like to turn in now."

"Yeah. I'll bet you've put in a pretty full day. You mentioned a symposium."

"At the university. I was on a panel. I'm…not very good at public speaking, so such things tend to drain me."

As she started away she paused, turned. "What time would you like to go see the calves? I wouldn't want to hold you up."

"You can take your time in the morning. I have chores to see to before we can head on up to the herd. After morning chores, Maggie usually sends me off with a good breakfast."

"You're lucky to have her. Good night, Hazard." She

turned away. "I'll see you in the morning." She looked beyond him to call, "Good night, Ace."

"'Night, Doc."

As she walked away, she could feel Hazard's gaze burning into her back. It took all her willpower to keep from turning as she made her way to the guest room. When the door was closed, she took in a deep breath, wondering what had ever possessed her to stay here, when all her instincts had been shouting at her to leave and go back to her safe existence in the lab.

Because, she reminded herself, she would never pass this way again. It was imperative, Professor Wingate had once said, to seize the moment. This might be her only opportunity to see how a real ranch operates. Once the year ended and she returned to Boston, she would always have these memories to take out and sift through.

But there was, in fact, another, deeper reason—one she didn't want to probe too deeply. Still, as she undressed and climbed between the covers, she was forced to admit it to herself in the silence of the room.

She'd been reluctant to leave Hazard Wilde without the answers she'd come seeking. Not just because she enjoyed the challenge. But because he seemed unlike any man she'd ever known. It wasn't just the fact that he was handsome and muscled from ranch chores. Though those could have been reason enough. She was, after all, a woman. She enjoyed a good-looking hunk as much as any woman. But she sensed that there was more to Hazard Wilde than that. She'd seen a goodness, a decency, that touched a chord deep inside her.

As sleep overtook her, she was smiling. And wondering if she would feel that same thrill the next time he touched her.

*   *   *

Just a room away, Hazard was doing some heavy thinking of his own.

He'd decided to post guards around the herd, just in case there really was some predator attacking the calves. He'd ordered Peterson to have several of the wranglers patrol the perimeter of the herd until morning, with Cody heading up the first team and Russ Thurman taking the midnight-to-dawn group.

To add to the precautions, he'd ordered samples taken of the water at the creek that ran through Peterson's range, and samples of all food and water the herd came in contact with.

He just hoped Dr. Erin Ryan would find something conclusive in tomorrow's tests. His hands paused on the buttons of his shirt. Turning toward the window, he stared out into the darkness, wondering what it was about that odd little woman that tugged at him so. All his life he'd been attracted to women like himself. Women born to the soil, who were equally at home in the saddle or driving a four-wheel-drive truck. So what was it about this prim, shy, bookish woman that appealed to him?

He didn't know. And didn't want to waste time trying to figure it out. Right now what mattered most was that she was his best hope of finding an answer to this puzzle. And the fact was he needed answers quickly, before the entire herd was lost.

Chapter 4

Hazard stepped into the kitchen and, out of habit, breathed deeply. The air was perfumed with cinnamon and apple, telling him that Maggie was baking one of her wonderful coffee cakes for breakfast.

He poured himself a cup of coffee and wrapped his hands around the mug before draining it in several long swallows. Then he made his way to his room.

Just before he reached his door, he caught sight of Erin standing in the guest bedroom, looking at her reflection in the mirror.

For a moment he didn't recognize her. The hair was the same. That neat little knot at the back of her head. And the round glasses, perched on her nose. But she was wearing skinny jeans and a turtleneck. On her feet were a pair of sturdy boots.

She looked, at first glance, about sixteen.

Maggie could be seen perched on the edge of her bed,

watching her. From where he stood, Hazard could hear every word.

"I just feel so...strange wearing a pair of jeans."

"Strange?" Maggie's brow arched. "You mean you've never worn jeans before?"

"No."

"Are you saying never?"

"That's right."

"But..." Maggie studiously closed her mouth, knowing she must look as astounded as she felt. "How did you get through life without ever wearing a pair of denims? What did you wear to school, Erin?"

"Uniforms. I went to a private girls' school. We wore navy-plaid jumpers with starched white blouses. The skirts had to be long enough to cover our knees."

"You're kidding." Maggie looked at her closely. "You aren't, are you?"

"No. Why would you think such a thing?"

"No reason. Well, what about high school?"

"The same. Except that by the time I was sixteen, I was already taking college classes."

"Harvard?" Maggie knew her expression was probably one of absolute disbelief.

Erin shrugged. "It was expected, since both my parents teach there."

"I see." She was beginning to see a great deal more. This brilliant young woman was as socially inept as a twelve-year-old. "How did your high school friends feel about having a genius in their midst?"

Erin smiled almost shyly. "I've never used that term. I find if offensive."

"Prodigy then."

"Oh, no." She shook her head vigorously. "I can't

stand to be called anything that would make me feel... different.''

Maggie understood instantly. This young woman wanted desperately to fit in. And had probably spent a lifetime trying to. ''How did your classmates treat you?''

Erin shrugged, remembering the painful incidents. Her high school classmates thought she was a snob, because she was so shy. Her college classmates treated her like a joke. ''They were okay about it.''

''So what about senior year. The parties? The prom?''

Erin flushed, and Maggie realized at once she'd hit a nerve. But it was too late to call back the question.

''There weren't any parties. I was never invited to a prom. But it didn't matter. That would have just taken up too much time. My parents believed that, if you were given a gift, you had an obligation not to waste a precious moment of it.''

''And they saw parties and dances as a waste of time?''

Erin nodded.

''How old were you when you finished college, Erin?'' Maggie studied her, trying to determine her age. The slender frame and lack of makeup were deceiving. But she had a wisdom and maturity far beyond her years. Add to that a complete lack of guile, and she gave out confusing signals.

Erin smiled. ''By the time I was twenty, I was doing graduate studies. I'd earned my Ph.D. by twenty-four, and was hired as research assistant at the university that same year. And I was there four years, until this fellowship became available.''

Maggie realized that she and Erin were the same age. And yet their life experiences had made them vastly different. ''How did someone with your background decide to take a fellowship in Wyoming?''

Erin flushed. ''I realized I was almost thirty, and I'd never done anything spontaneous in my life. I knew if I talked it over with my parents, they would disapprove. So I just accepted Professor Wingate's invitation and jumped.''

''Jumped?''

Erin's shy laughter covered her embarrassment. ''Off a cliff. I thought I'd just see where I'd land.'' She crossed the room and sat beside Maggie, lacing up the borrowed walking shoes. ''I really appreciate the jeans and boots. I'll see they're properly cleaned before I return them.''

''Don't be silly, Erin. They're jeans. You can just toss them in the washer and they'll be good as new. As for the boots, they're old and worn, but sturdy enough for walking through the snow and slush out on the range. When you're through with them, just leave them in the mudroom by the back door, where we hang all the parkas.''

Maggie stood. ''I'd better get back to the kitchen. You'll be wanting a hearty breakfast before you head up to Peterson's.''

Hazard moved quickly on to his own room. As he washed away the grime of his chores, he thought about what he'd overheard. Erin Ryan had lived a life so far removed from his own, he couldn't even imagine it. And yet, he felt strangely connected to her. She'd spent her life studying, while he'd spent his working. And in the process, both had missed a lot of the high points of childhood and young adulthood that many took for granted.

He pulled on a clean shirt and ran his fingers through his damp hair. No sense brooding over what was in the past. For his part, he had no regrets. He did what he had to, in order to keep his father's dream alive. He never thought about what he'd missed; only about what he'd accomplished.

For now, he had a herd to see to. And with Erin's help, a mystery to solve.

"Good morning." Hazard walked into the kitchen and found that everyone was already at the table.

Ace and Chance were dressed for work in suits and ties, their briefcases bulging with paperwork.

Ace was gently teasing Erin about her change of wardrobe.

"I was just telling the doc. One day at the Double W, and she's starting to look like she was born to this life."

Erin blushed as Hazard took his place at the table beside her. Her blush deepened as their thighs brushed and she absorbed a little jolt.

To cover her embarrassment she blurted out, "Maggie actually made a coffee cake from scratch. I think that's just so amazing. And steak and eggs for breakfast."

Ace grinned. "Don't tell us this is a first, too."

She nodded. "In fact, we hardly ever ate red meat at home. My father is a vegetarian."

Chance arched a brow. "I hope you know you just uttered a vile obscenity. *Vegetarian* is a dirty word in this house."

"I'm sorry. I didn't mean that I am. I really like red meat. But…"

She realized that they were all laughing, including Maggie.

Hazard touched a hand to her arm and said gently. "In this family, teasing is as natural as breathing. They're having fun with you."

"Oh." She gave a sigh of relief. "Anyway, Maggie, I

want you to know that this is the most I've ever eaten in the morning. And it's all due to your good cooking.''

"I'm glad." Maggie topped off her coffee. "I couldn't see you going up to the range without something solid under your belt. It could be hours before you'll eat again."

"I'm really quite excited." Erin glanced around shyly. "I've never actually seen cattle in their natural environment. Except from a distance, of course. But to see them up close. To maybe…pet one."

"Pet one?" Ace was grinning at her. "You mean, like a dog?"

"Well, I thought…" She turned to Hazard. "Don't they allow you to pet them?"

He had to work hard to keep from laughing aloud. But she would have been mortified if she knew how funny she was. Funny and sweet. And so innocent.

"They're not exactly house pets. But I'll find one you can touch, if you'd like."

"Oh, yes." She was practically trembling with excitement. The day held such promise. As she bent to her steak and eggs she missed the looks that passed between the three brothers.

Hazard knew that Ace and Chance were thoroughly enjoying what they perceived as this little joke being played on him. The uptight little misfit who thought of ranching as some romantic storybook adventure. But, in truth, he was getting a kick out of her reaction. It was refreshing to see his life through her innocent eyes. He made a silent vow that, though he knew he couldn't completely shield her from the rough edges of life on a working ranch, he would do all in his power to act as a buffer between her imagination and stark reality.

When breakfast ended, Maggie filled an insulated con-

tainer with hot coffee and handed it to Hazard. "I think
you'll be needing this up on the range. There's a bite to
the wind today."

"Yeah. I noticed. Thanks, Maggie."

He led the way toward the mudroom off the kitchen.
"Come on, Erin. We've got to find a parka that'll fit
you."

"You mean I just take any one I want?"

He nodded, then switched on the light. "That's the rule.
We take what we need and put it back when we're
through."

She slipped a cowhide jacket from a wooden peg and
tried it on. Though it was several sizes too big, it appeared
to be the smallest one around.

"Is this okay?"

Hazard couldn't help smiling. "At least it'll keep you
warm. But try not to get lost in it."

He pulled on his own well-worn cowhide jacket and
wide-brimmed hat, then led the way outside to a truck.
He opened the door and helped her settle inside, then
walked around to the driver's side. Minutes later they had
veered from the road and were driving across an open
hillside.

For the first few minutes Erin clung to the door as the
truck lurched from side to side, passing over ruts and
boulders. But gradually she forgot about the rough ride as
she became caught up in the passing scenery.

"You know." She turned her head to stare out the window. "I love the names of places here in Wyoming. Bighorn. Yellowstone. Medicine Bow. Wind River. They
sound so…Western." She turned to Hazard. "When my
father heard that I'd accepted a fellowship here he quoted
Daniel Webster. 'All that Wyoming would bring to the

Union was savages, wild beasts, shifting sands, whirl-winds of dust, cactus and prairie dogs.'''

Hazard threw back his head and roared. ''And what did you tell your father in reply?''

''That I would tame the savages and wild beasts, and see something he might never get the opportunity to see in his lifetime.''

''And what would that be?''

''A grizzly bear, a peregrine falcon or a trumpeter swan. Or maybe all three. And in their natural environment.''

''Have you seen them yet?''

''No. But I hope to. Especially a grizzly.''

He grinned. ''Not up close, I hope.''

''Have you?''

He nodded. ''I once saw one up close and very personal. I was untangling a calf from some barbed wire. Poor thing was bawling like a baby. I was snipping away the wire with my cutters, and the next thing I knew this grizzly was coming toward me. I hadn't even heard him over the sound of the calf.''

Erin's eyes went wide. She put a hand to her throat. ''What did you do?''

''I made a mad scramble for my rifle. The only thing that saved me was that the bear reared up at the last minute. I pumped a couple of bullets into its heart. When he fell, he landed right on top of me.''

''Were you hurt?''

''Dislocated my shoulder.'' Just thinking about it had him rubbing a hand over the spot. ''I had to latch on to a tree limb and snap the shoulder back into place or I'd have gone half-mad with the pain.''

''Then did you see a doctor?''

''Doctor?'' He looked over with a grin. ''The only way

you see a doctor out here is to take a helicopter into Cheyenne and visit a hospital. And then only if you're already half-dead. I just got on with my chores. I carried the calf back to the herd and sent a couple of the wranglers out for the bear's carcass.''

Erin found herself glancing over at Hazard while he drove. What kind of man faced down a grizzly, repaired his own dislocated shoulder and then simply went about his chores as though it were all in a day's work?

She found herself hoping her father's warning didn't come back to haunt her. Maybe this ranch and this man were a lot more primitive than she'd thought.

''There's Peterson's place.'' Hazard pointed.

''Isn't this part of your ranch?''

''It is. But our land is too big, and the herds too many, to handle alone. So we hire wranglers, who help with the herds. If they're single they live in bunkhouses. If they're married, we build them a ranch house and provide for their family. Peterson's our ranch foreman. He's been with us for more than ten years now. He's a good man.''

Erin realized that this was high praise indeed from this plainspoken man.

They drove on past the ranch house and high into the range land, until they came to a gate. Hazard climbed out and opened the gate, then drove through and again stepped out to close it behind the truck.

A short time later they came to a halt. Spread out below them were hundreds of cattle. Across the field stood a cluster of men.

''There's Peterson with Cody and some of the wranglers.'' Hazard turned off the ignition. ''Let's see what they're up to.''

They met halfway across the field. As soon as Cody

recognized Erin, he whipped his hat from his head and gave her a warm smile. "Morning, Erin."

"Good morning, Cody."

Hazard greeted Peterson with a handshake, then said, "I'd like you to meet Dr. Erin Ryan. She's here to help me find out what killed so many calves."

"Dr. Ryan." Peterson touched a hand to his hat.

Behind him, Russ Thurman spat a stream of tobacco. "Careful. Our lady doctor's got a weak constitution." He turned to her with a sly smile. "We'll try not to let any calves decide to be born while you're up here. Too messy. Wouldn't want to have you passing out on us again."

Hazard shot him a killing look. "Why don't you get on back to the herd while I talk to Peterson."

Russ shrugged. "I already put in a whole night babysitting. Peterson was just taking us back to his place for a hot meal. About time, too. I told him not to be too stingy with the food now that he's been named foreman."

"We'll go up to the house in a while." Peterson frowned. "You go ahead if you'd like, Russ."

The wrangler started to amble away, then turned. "Naw. I'll hang around. But you ought to know that it didn't do any good to post guards, Boss. We lost another dozen calves last night. Tell him, Peterson. They're dropping like flies."

Hazard's eyes narrowed on his foreman. "We lost more?"

Peterson nodded. "Sorry, Hazard. I didn't want to give you the news like this. But it's the truth. Cody took the first shift. Russ took the second. We had half a dozen wranglers with the herd around the clock. But just since sunup we've found more dead calves."

"How many?"

He shrugged, avoiding Hazard's eyes. "So far we've counted fifteen."

"Fifteen. The numbers just keep increasing." Hazard's breath came out in a long, deep sigh. "I want to see them exactly as you found them."

"There's only one left that hasn't been moved."

Hazard stiffened. "Why were they moved?"

Peterson glanced at Russ, then away. "The wranglers figured they'd be sparing the rest of the herd, especially the cows that have lost their calves, by separating the carcasses from the herd."

Hazard swore. "You knew I'd want to see where they died."

"I did. But don't fault the wranglers, Hazard. They have a point. The herd is getting skittish. Too many cows, heavy with milk, wandering around in search of their calves." He put a hand on Hazard's arm. "Come on. There's one left that hasn't been disturbed yet. We just found it."

Hazard followed him across the field. His shoulders slumped as they paused beside the carcass. "I'll want to examine this one carefully, and take clot samples from all the others."

Peterson nodded.

While the others watched, Hazard rolled the calf over, his big fingers probing beneath the hide for anything that might give him a clue as to the cause of death. While he worked, Cody knelt beside him, studying both the carcass and the ground beneath it.

When the examination was complete, Hazard reached into his pocket and retrieved a surgical knife, then knelt in the snow to retrieve the sample.

Without a word he trailed Peterson to where the other carcasses had already been piled in the back of a truck.

Climbing up, he moved among them and methodically took a sample from each.

When it was done, Peterson watched him drawing on his gloves. "My wife's got plenty of food and hot coffee up at the house."

"No, thanks. You go along. Dr. Ryan and I will stay here awhile."

The ranch foreman and the wranglers took their leave. Only Cody stayed behind with Hazard and Erin.

The old cowboy put a hand on Hazard's shoulder. "I'm really sorry, son."

"Yeah." Cody turned away. "I'd like to walk for a while."

Erin and Cody watched helplessly as Hazard pushed his way through the milling cattle, stopping now and then to stare at a cow and her newborn calf.

"The boy's got a tender heart when it comes to his animals," Cody muttered.

"What do you think is killing the calves, Cody?"

He turned to her, his eyes sad. "I wish I knew. I'd give anything to spare him this pain. But I tell you, I've never seen anything like this. There's no blood, so we can rule out a predator. I don't know of any animal that can kill another without leaving traces of blood on the ground. It's got to be something in the air, or in their food or water, that's killing them. Our only hope is if you can find something in that serum when you test it in Hazard's lab."

"It has to be a virus. Or a bacteria."

He shrugged, nodded.

She turned up the collar of her parka, aware that she was freezing.

"Well, will you look at this. I guess he's found a way to soothe his hurting heart."

At Cody's words, Erin turned. Hazard was walking toward them, with a newborn calf flung over his shoulders.

"Is he...hurt?" She was almost afraid to ask.

"Nope. As healthy as can be."

"Then what...?"

He grinned. "You wanted to pet one."

"Oh, Hazard." She lifted a tentative hand to the calf's face and rubbed her fingers between two soulful eyes. "Oh, isn't he just the softest thing in the world?"

Growing a bit bolder, she pressed a kiss to the calf's warm nose. "Oh, look how beautiful you are." Caught up in the moment she forgot her self-consciousness as she traced the curve of the animal's ear, then ran her fingers down one small leg, all the while murmuring words of endearment.

For some reason Hazard couldn't quite fathom, her reaction warmed him like nothing else. She was as delighted as a child at Christmas. And he felt like a doting father. Wanting to give her everything, just to see that smile never leave her eyes.

She looked up into Hazard's smiling face. "He's... she's...it's quite wonderful. I can see why you love them so."

"Can you?" He wasn't smiling now. He was staring down into her eyes with the most intense look on his face.

"Yes. Oh, Hazard. I can't bear that this sweet little creature might die like all those others." Without thinking she pressed a hand over his. Squeezed. "We'll find the answer. I just know we will."

His eyes narrowed. For a moment he stood perfectly still, absorbing the shock waves that seemed to be exploding through him at the mere touch of her. Then he knelt down and set the calf on its feet. It stood uncertainly a moment, then hurried off to find its mother, while Hazard and Erin stood side by side watching with identical smiles of delight.

From his vantage point, Cody watched the unfolding scene with a slightly bemused expression. Old Wes Wilde used to say that love never happened when it was convenient. If Cody didn't know better, he'd guess that right now, while Wes's son was fighting the bitterest disappointment of his life, he'd just been shot with a double whammy. In the form of cupid's arrow.

Cody figured he'd just keep his thoughts to himself for a while. Because, unless he was badly mistaken, those two didn't have a clue about what was happening between them. But it would come to them, sooner or later. His guess was soon. Very soon.

Chapter 5

"**I** can't see much point in staying here." Hazard led Erin toward the truck. "We may as well get back to the house and see if these blood samples will tell us anything."

He turned to Cody. "Want a lift back, or are you staying up here?"

"I'd just as soon go back to the bunkhouse. If you want me to patrol the herd again tonight, I'll have Russ bring me back up after dinner."

Hazard nodded. "Thanks, Cody. I appreciate it." As he helped Erin into the truck, he added, "I'm thinking now that a patrol is just a waste of good manpower. Half a dozen wranglers did without sleep last night, and we lost even more calves than the previous nights."

"Don't go giving up hope, son." Cody climbed in and watched as Hazard wearily turned on the ignition and put the truck in gear. "There's an answer to this."

"You sure of that?"

"Yep. We just haven't asked the right questions yet."

"I hope you're right." As the truck swayed over the hillsides, Hazard held on to that thread of hope. He had one of the brightest researchers in the country on his side. If anyone could solve this, it was Erin.

"Hey, you two." Ace opened the door to the lab and leaned his frame against the doorway. He'd changed from suit and tie to more comfortable jeans and a shirt with the sleeves rolled to the elbows. "Maggie says to tell you dinner is ready."

"Dinner?" Hazard glanced up from the microscope and rolled his shoulders. "What time is it?"

"Almost seven. Maggie held off as long as she could. But Chance and I are starving."

Hazard glanced over at Erin, who was still peering at the serum on her slide, before scribbling notations in a notebook. Neither of them had bothered to eat since breakfast.

"Okay. Tell Maggie we're on our way." He slid off the stool and crossed to Erin. "Come on. It's time we took a break."

She shook her head. "Not yet. There must be something here I'm missing. This is the last slide. And so far they've all been the same. Completely normal. Maybe this one will tell me something new." She continued staring intently through the microscope. "Come on," she muttered in frustration. "Show me something. Anything."

Hazard waited a moment, then touched her arm. At once she looked up, then over at him.

There was no denying what she felt each time they touched. Heat. The most incredible heat. And then a trickle of ice along her spine that had her struggling not to shiver.

"Erin." He took a step back, needing some space between them. He couldn't think when he got too close to her. "It's time to admit defeat. We've been at it all afternoon. And we've found no sign of illness or disease in these samples."

"That's just it. There should be something. I mean, these calves aren't just killing themselves."

"Maybe they are." It was time he faced facts. "Maybe their immune system is too weak. Or maybe we've bred a herd with a genetic defect that will come to light someday. For now, it's time to admit that we don't have any more answers now than when we started." He turned away. "Let's wash up and head over to the kitchen for something to eat."

She gave a reluctant nod of her head. Defeat wasn't easy for her. But she'd given this her complete attention, to no avail. It was time to get back to her own work, her own lab. Her own life.

She washed her hands at the sink and followed Hazard to the kitchen.

They opened the door to the sound of raucous laughter. After the complete silence of the lab, it took a moment to adjust.

Everyone was talking at once. Ace and Chance were relating some silly story from their childhood. A story that had Maggie and Cody nearly doubled over with laughter. Even the dour Agnes was chuckling.

Between rumbles of laughter Chance was saying, "So I said to Hazard, pay up. You owe me a buck. And Hazard says, you didn't win. The bet was that I could hook Ace up with a rope and pulley and get him across the river. He only got halfway across before the rope broke. So I don't owe you a cent. You owe me."

"Yeah," Ace said with a self-deprecating grin. "And

while they're arguing about who won, I'm being swept down the river by the current. And I'm hollering like a stuck pig. And nobody cares. All they care about is collecting their bet."

Erin had paused in midstride, her mouth dropping open at the story.

Hazard casually held her chair and eased her into it, then took the seat beside her.

"And when we got home that night, Dad wailed the tar out of both of us and said if we ever tried that stunt again with our little brother, we wouldn't have any skin left."

"See?" Ace passed a basket of hot rolls. "You two really wanted to get rid of me. It's amazing that I made it through childhood with you guys around looking out for me."

"Hey, we managed to save your hide as often as we risked it," Chance said. "How about the time I hauled you out of that gravel pit, up by the old mine?"

"I always figured you only saved me because I was wearing your favorite boots and you didn't want to lose them."

"Well, there was that." Chance winked at Erin, and she began to understand that they were merely teasing. Since she'd never had a brother, she wasn't sure just how to take these three tough-talking men. And try as she might, she couldn't imagine her stern, proper father ever exchanging rollicking tales of a misspent youth at the dinner table.

"So, Doc." Ace popped a hot roll into his mouth. "How's the lab work going? Have you and Hazard solved the mystery of the dead calves?"

She shook her head. "I'm afraid not. We've exhausted all our theories. And none of them have worked out."

She glanced at Hazard, then away. "Hazard thinks we ought to admit defeat."

"What do you think, Doc?"

She stared down at her plate. "I'm not one to give up. But I'm sure the university expects me to return tomorrow. I'm already a day later than I'd anticipated. I suppose I'll do as Hazard asks and admit that this one has me stumped."

"You're going back?" Chance shot a look at his brother. "Without an answer to the deaths?"

She spread her hands. "What else can I do?"

Chance waited a beat before saying, "Did Hazard tell you why he was so concerned? Why he sent for you in the first place?"

"I would think that's obvious. A rancher hates to lose so many calves, when they're the future of his herd."

"It's a little more than that." Ace polished off another roll. "This happens to be an experimental herd, hand picked by Hazard and nurtured by our foreman, Peterson."

Erin turned to Hazard. "You never told me that. What sort of experiments are you conducting?"

Hazard shot his brother a killing look before turning his attention to Erin. Then he forced himself to say aloud what he hadn't wanted to talk about. He was such a private person. He hadn't wanted to admit just how important this was to him. "I've been concerned about the use of so many antibiotics and steroids in the food chain. I was hoping I could isolate one small herd, and raise them without any artificial additives. No enhanced food. Only range grass. No injections. Just their own immune system to keep them healthy. Then I intended to compare birth weight, body weight when they reached maturity, and a number of other factors, with those of the other herds, to see if there were any benefits.'' He shrugged, wishing it didn't mean so much to him. But it did. It hurt like hell. He'd put so much time and effort into this. Not to mention the added expense of fences and manpower, to isolate the experimental herd from the others. ''It looks like my noble experiment is dead before it gets off the ground.''

Erin was suddenly animated. ''But this is so wonderful. Scientists have been arguing for years that the antibiotics and hormones given to animals are being passed down through the food chain to the humans who consume them. This would be a chance to follow a herd through the long process, as well as follow-up tests on their offspring.''

Hazard nodded. ''It was my intention to keep one herd completely pure and isolated through several generations, so that we could determine conclusively whether or not the additives are harmful or helpful. But if the calves can't even survive the trauma of the first days of life, I think it's a clear message that I'm going in the wrong direction.'' He shrugged. ''With all these deaths among healthy calves, I'm beginning to believe that, without the use of the antibiotics and steroids they've come to depend on, they simply can't make it in this world.''

''Oh, no. Hazard, don't you see?'' Erin was so wrapped up in what he'd just told her, she completely forgot about the others around the table. ''This just makes the mystery of their deaths all the more compelling. You can't just abandon an experiment as noble as this, without knowing why it failed.''

''But you and I have spent hours—''

She put a hand on his. ''A few hours. One afternoon. That's all we've spent on this. If I've learned one thing about research, it's that it can take weeks, months, even years, before we come up with any definitive answers to life's mysteries.''

"I'm just not trained for that kind of research."

"I am." She said it simply. But her eyes were suddenly shining with excitement.

"You certainly are. But you said yourself. You don't have weeks or months. Certainly not years, to devote to this problem."

"Not years, maybe. But I do have what remains of this year."

His eyes narrowed. "What are you talking about?"

"Don't you see? I accepted a fellowship at the university. But I've been devoting all my time to following up the research of others. This could become my special project. Professor Wingate has been waiting for me to declare a field of study. Well, now I have it. Why can't I focus on just this herd and these mysterious deaths and write a paper on the results? It would certainly justify the salary I'm being paid by the university. And I'm sure the board of regents would be delighted to have my research focus on a local problem."

"Could you do the work here?"

"I don't see why not. You have a completely sophisticated laboratory. If I should find that I need more, for DNA testing, I'll return to the university and use their facilities." She looked around. Placed a hand over her mouth as she realized how bold her suggestion must sound. "I'm sorry. I've overstepped my bounds. I realize it would be an imposition to have someone staying here for an indefinite time."

"Not at all." Hazard glanced around at his brothers and then at Maggie, relieved that they were all smiling and nodding their approval. "As you said, we have the lab. And you've seen for yourself that we have plenty of room. But I think, since the bulk of the work caring for a guest will fall to Maggie and Agnes, that we need to hear from them.''

Maggie was quick to say, ''I certainly don't mind the cooking.'' She turned to Agnes. ''It will mean one more room to clean.''

''Huh.'' The old woman sniffed and barely glanced at Erin before saying, ''A couple extra towels and sheets is all. I guess I don't mind, long as she's here to solve a problem for one of my boys.''

Maggie tried not to laugh. Agnes had clearly thrown down a challenge. Erin was to remember her place. The Wilde men were Agnes's responsibility. Her boys. And Erin was to remember that she was merely a guest. Maggie had been given the same challenge when she'd first arrived at the Double W. And it had seemed like an impossible task to break through Agnes's wall of ice. But that wall had eventually thawed enough to accept Maggie as one of them.

''Well then.'' Hazard looked nearly dumbstruck at his good fortune. ''It looks like the only thing you have to do now is contact the university and see if they'll approve.''

''I'll e-mail them right after dinner. But it's a mere formality. I'm sure Professor Wingate will be delighted.'' Erin's eyes were dancing with unconcealed excitement.

Ace and Chance exchanged knowing looks. They'd seen the desolation in their brother's eyes when Hazard had thought he was losing this battle. Now they could see the growing excitement as he realized he'd won a little time.

''One more thing,'' Maggie said.

They all turned toward her.

''You're going to have to learn to eat like the rest of

us, Erin. When I knock myself out on a fancy gourmet recipe, I expect everyone to do their share of the eating.''

Erin joined in the laughter. And as the others resumed eating, she hugged the little thrill of excitement to her heart. She'd been given a reprieve. She didn't have to leave in the morning, after all. She'd bought some time. A few more days to stay at this wonderful ranch, and be a part of these fun, fascinating people.

She might tell herself she was most excited about the hope of solving the mystery. And that was true, up to a point. But, in fact, it was the thought of more time with Hazard Wilde that had her heart working overtime. And her pulse throbbing in her temples.

Chance, Hazard and Ace had closeted themselves in their father's old study, where they were going over the books. It was a monthly ritual, and one that sometimes produced cheers of victory, and at other times, quiet admissions of defeat.

Despite the fact that they had an accounting firm and a legal department, they were the first ones to see the profit-and-loss charts.

They looked up at the knock on the door.

Ace opened it, then stood back when he caught sight of Erin standing in the hallway. ''Come on in.''

''I didn't want to disturb you. Maggie told me where to find you.'' She glanced beyond Ace to where Hazard stood. ''I just got a response from Professor Wingate.''

''What did he say?''

Her eyes were glowing. ''As I'd hoped, he was delighted. And he sent his best wishes to you that we are able to quickly discover the cause and stop the deaths.''

He smiled. ''Good old Professor Wingate.''

''Well.'' She looked around to include Ace and

Chance. "If you don't mind, I'll leave you alone now and get back to my experiments."

She hurried down the hall, relieved when she reached the solitude of the lab. It wasn't that she didn't enjoy being in the company of Hazard and his brothers. But their ease with each other only served to point out how much she lacked in her own life. It wasn't just that she had no siblings in whom she could confide. But when she had left high school behind to accept the challenges of the university, she had left behind any hope of close friendship as well. The students with whom she associated at Harvard had treated her with cool acceptance in the classroom, but had never included her in their social activities. As a result, she'd never had a best friend.

A smile touched the corner of her lips as she thought about Maggie's kindness to her, and the Wilde brothers' easy acceptance of a stranger in their midst. Maybe the friendship that had always eluded her could be found right here.

Hours later, Hazard found Erin in the lab, already hard at work.

She looked up from the blood specimen she'd been examining.

He paused, wishing he had an easier time with words. "I want you to know how much this means to me."

"It means so much to me, too. If your brother hadn't told me about the fact that this herd was such a wonderful experiment, none of this would have happened. But this is exactly what my work has needed. Something worthy."

"Erin." Hazard was shaking his head. "I don't want you to think I'm some fine, noble hero. I've been wanting to do this for a long time. But it takes a great deal of extra manpower, and a whole lot of money, to see it through the long haul. My brothers and I have just spent the last couple of hours together, going over the cost of this experimental herd. It's taking a big bite out of our profits. And even if you're able to solve the mystery of the deaths, we may have to abandon this before too long.''

"But at least you'll know you tried.''

He nodded. "Yeah. But I want you to understand that all your hard work might be in vain. If I have to abandon this project, your research could prove meaningless.''

"No research is ever without merit. Even if the project is abandoned, someone else will try it. Or something like it. And they'll look at what we did here, and take what we learned here, and make it work for them.''

Smiling, he shook his head. "Tell me something, Erin. Are you always this optimistic?''

"I am when I believe. And I believe in this, Hazard.'' She looked down, afraid that he'd see the intensity that drove her. "I believe in you.''

He rolled up his sleeves. "Then what are we waiting for? Let's get to work, Doctor.''

She laughed, then returned to her microscope and blood sample.

"Do you know what time it is?'' Hazard looked up from the microscope and rubbed a hand over the back of his neck.

"No.'' Erin was peering through her scope, moving slide after slide of blood, looking for the slightest change in the pattern of cell structure.

"It's after midnight. And I've been up since dawn.''

She pushed away from the counter and rolled her shoulders. "I know. I heard you getting up.''

"Sorry. I know there's only a thin wall between our rooms. I was trying to be as quiet as possible.''

"Oh, no." She looked up, alarmed that he misunderstood. "I managed to fall back asleep. But I remember glancing at the bedside clock and wondering how someone could get started so early."

He shrugged. "I never even think about it. I've never used an alarm clock. I just have this inner clock that tells me it's time to get up and get going."

"Maybe you need an alarm clock to tell you when to go to bed. Do you realize you'll be up again in a few hours?"

"Yeah." He shot her that famous Wilde smile that always did strange things to her heart. "Come on, Doctor. Time we both got some sleep."

They carefully returned the blood samples to a refrigerator, and placed the slides in an antiseptic solution, before turning off the lights.

At the door to Erin's room, Hazard paused. "I hope I won't disturb you when I get up to start my chores. I promise I'll be as quiet as a mouse."

"Please don't feel constrained to tiptoe around because of me. This is your home, Hazard. I don't want you to feel uncomfortable because I'm here."

"But I am—" It was on the tip of his tongue to tell her that he was indeed extremely uncomfortable because she was there. But he knew this solemn, serious little woman might take it the wrong way. And so he finished lamely, "—going to try not to knock over too many pieces of furniture before I head out to the barn in the morning."

He was looking at her with such intensity she felt her heart begin to trip over itself. She had the distinct impression that he wanted to touch her. And the truth was she wanted him to. The knowledge shocked her.

He took a step back. "Good night, Erin."

"Good night, Hazard." Feeling oddly deflated, she remained in the doorway until he entered his own room and closed the door.

Then she closed her own door and leaned against it, as she waited for her heart to stop this crazy, unnatural rhythm.

What was wrong with her? Why was she allowing these strange, unsettling feelings to upset her so? This fixation on Hazard Wilde was completely out of character. And thoroughly unprofessional. In fact, she was ashamed of her behavior.

As if to test herself and her maturity, she pushed aside all thought of Hazard and forced herself through her nightly ritual. First she carefully hung up the borrowed jeans and turtleneck and set the boots on a rug by the heating vents. That done she brushed and flossed, then slathered lotion all over her body, before slipping into a pair of man-tailored pajamas. Finally she pulled the pins from her hair and bent forward to brush at least a hundred strokes. Only when everything was done did she turn off the lights and climb into bed.

She was so exhausted she expected to fall asleep instantly. But thoughts of Hazard kept sneaking into her mind, distracting her. The way he looked when he went about his ranch chores. Like a man completely at peace with himself. A man who could handle anything, no matter how painful.

She thought of the way he'd looked when told of the latest deaths of his calves. Not so much angry as wounded. She'd been deeply touched by his sadness and pain. And then she thought about the way all his features had softened when she told him she wanted to stay and solve the mystery. There had been a light in his eyes. A light that said, more than words, that she had made the right decision.

She wished she could always see that light in his eyes. She wished, more than anything in the world, that she could solve the mystery of these deaths and give him a reason to smile.

It worried her to admit that she was beginning to care much too deeply about Hazard Wilde and his problems. But, try as she might, she couldn't think of any way to turn off her feelings.

Chapter 6

In her dream Erin watched as Hazard walked slowly toward her. The snow and slush were gone, replaced by fields of flowers as far as the eye could see. She could smell the flowers. Roses. Hundred of them. Like the pale creamy roses the gardener used to plant in pots on either side of the doorway of her parents' Boston home. She smiled. She'd always thought it would be interesting to plant something and watch it grow. She'd even, over her mother's objections, persuaded their gardener to allow her to plant one single rose. But she'd never had a chance to follow through. To this day she didn't know if it had thrived because of the work she'd done or because the gardener had replaced it with one of his own.

Suddenly her dream veered from the roses to Hazard. As he drew near, Erin could make out the calf draped across his shoulders. He carried his burden as though it weighed no more than a feather. The way he'd carried her. No strain. No effort.

He stopped in front of her and bent slightly so she could reach up to pet the calf. She threw her arms around its neck and pressed her lips to the soft cheek. Then the calf disappeared as quickly as it had appeared, and Erin was holding Hazard, and pressing her lips to his. The kiss was so shocking, so unexpected, she sat bolt upright in her bed.

She pressed a hand to her heart. It was pounding like a runaway train.

She glanced at the clock. Four in the morning. She was suddenly wide awake. And far too agitated to consider trying to fall back asleep.

She lay in bed for long minutes, forcing herself to think of something, anything except the dream that had left her so shaken.

She would concentrate on the tests she'd done on the blood samples. Why hadn't they yielded anything out of the ordinary? What was she missing? Often sleep had a way of clearing the mind, so that it could look at the same old problem in fresh new ways. And since sleep was impossible now, perhaps she ought to visit the lab, on the off chance that something new would come to her.

She reached for her glasses and climbed out of bed. Because she didn't have a robe, she fumbled in the closet for her suit jacket to put on over the pajamas. Then she padded barefoot to the lab.

It was just a matter of time, she knew, until she found the answer. Until then, she had to keep plodding along, doing every test she could think of, until the code was broken.

Hazard glanced at the clock, annoyed that his mind wouldn't let him rest. Another hour and he would have to start morning chores. But he was already wide awake, a dozen different questions spinning through his brain.

It wasn't enough to have taken clot samples from the carcasses. He should have taken blood samples from healthy calves as well, so that he could do comparison testing. If he had to, he'd take a sample from every one of the herd, until he found the correlation between those that lived and those that had mysteriously died.

He slipped out of bed and pulled on a pair of jeans before crossing to the window to stare broodingly out at the land, still covered in darkness. He loved this place so much. This ranch. This land. Even the ornery cattle. Especially his experimental herd. He'd pinned such hopes on them. And now, maybe he'd exposed them to unnamed danger.

Had he been wrong to deny this herd antibiotics? Had he unknowingly exposed them to illness? What about genetic abnormalities? Was he lowering their immunity, and allowing them to reproduce, carrying a killing gene?

He rubbed the stiffness at the back of his neck and headed toward the lab. Maybe he'd run just a couple of tests before he set off on his daily chores.

At the doorway of the lab he paused. All the lights had been switched on, turning the room to dazzling white.

In the center of it all was Erin, perched on a stool. At the sight of her, his lips curved in a smile of pure appreciation. This was an Erin he hadn't seen before.

She was bent over the microscope, a study in concentration. Bare feet peeked from beneath the cuffs of man-tailored pajamas. Over her nightclothes she'd tossed her suit jacket. Whether for warmth or modesty, he couldn't be certain. But he found the look entirely too appealing. The small round glasses on her nose gave her an owlish, intelligent appearance. It was simply endearing. He studied her hair, free of pins, flowing in lovely wild tangles around her face and shoulders. Hadn't he wondered how she would look with her hair mussed? Now he could see an Erin who looked much less like a scientist and more like a woman.

She hadn't seen him yet, and he was grateful for the freedom to simply watch her as she worked. She was so fierce. So intense. Something else that he found oddly attractive. He loved the fact that she was so dedicated to her studies. So absolutely determined to find the answers.

Satisfied with what she'd observed, she turned and made some notations, then froze when she caught sight of him in the doorway.

"Working a little late, aren't you?" He started toward her.

It took her several seconds before she could find her voice. The sight of him, barefoot, shirtless, wearing only denims riding low on his hips, stole her breath. "I...guess you could say I'm just eager for the day."

"People need their sleep. Otherwise, after a while, they begin to malfunction. Are you sure you're not a robot, Dr. Ryan?"

She smiled. "I could ask the same of you." But this was no robot. This was a man. Unlike any man she'd ever seen.

The men with whom she worked were often absent-minded, with no more regard to themselves and their surroundings than the specimens they studied. Most of them wore flowing lab coats, and spent their days pouring over scientific data. The majority of them were more concerned with their minds than their bodies.

Hazard's body had her mesmerized. It was hard and sculpted from years of ranch work. His shoulders were so broad and muscled the sight of them had her throat going dry. She had to swallow twice before she could manage to ask, "Did I disturb you?"

He nearly laughed aloud at the question. She did disturb him. More than he cared to admit.

Aloud he merely said, "I couldn't sleep, and thought I'd stop by the lab before I started my chores."

"I see we both had the same idea."

"Yeah." He stepped closer. His eyes narrowed at her hair, the color of aged whisky. He had a sudden overpowering urge to plunge his hands through the tangles and kiss her until they were both breathless. To keep himself from reaching out to touch her, he clenched his hands into fists at his sides.

He seemed so fierce. So intense. She struggled to think of something, anything, to say. "You might be interested in this." She moved aside to allow him to study the specimen on the slide.

He bent his head beside hers and peered through the microscope. Though he tried to focus, all he could think of was the subtle fragrance that clung to her skin. A fragrance that had his blood pulsing.

He lifted his head and turned to her. "I don't see anything unusual."

"There's a small spot." She bent forward, sending golden tangles swirling around her cheeks. Unable to find what she was looking for, she blinked. Looked up. "It's gone. I guess it was just eye strain."

"Or maybe you just want so badly to find something, that your mind's playing tricks on you."

She touched a hand to his. "Don't say that. We'll find something. I know we will, Hazard."

He didn't seem to be listening. Ignoring the little warning, he leaned close and breathed her in. "You smell like a rose garden. What's that perfume you're wearing?"

She had to struggle to make her mind to work. It was a tremendous effort. As though some force had blocked all her thought processes. "It's not perfume. It's a body lotion. Roses and Dew. My mother sent some of hers when she heard I was coming to Wyoming. I guess she thought my delicate Boston skin wouldn't survive a year in Wyoming without help."

As she laughed she tossed her head, sending her hair drifting back to settle around her shoulders. Without thinking he reached out and caught a tangle, allowing the strands to sift through his fingers. It was as soft to the touch as it looked. As smooth and sleek as a newborn calf.

Erin's mind and body seemed to freeze. Did he know what his touch was doing?

His gaze lowered to her mouth. And though he didn't move, she could feel the heat as surely as though he had already kissed her.

Her heart slammed against her chest, leaving her dazed. To cover her feelings she did what she always did. Resorted to words.

"Actually, the air here is no more dehydrating than back home in Boston. But my mother, like so many of her ilk, allowed her preconceived notions about Wyoming to cause her to behave irrationally. And so she did the only thing she could think of to discourage me. She sent me her exotic Roses and Dew, hoping to remind me of my roots."

Hazard paused for a moment before throwing back his head and bursting into gales of laughter.

Puzzled, she could only stare at him, loving the way his eyes crinkled and the way his voice deepened as he muttered, "I love it when you talk like that, Dr. Ryan."

"Like what?"

"All those big words. My father used to call them ten-dollar words. He said that most people speak in two-bit words. But there are some who just have to use ten-dollar words. That's you, Erin. And do you know what?"

She shook her head.

"Coming from you, they sound perfectly normal. But I have to confess, it really turns me on when you talk like that."

"I don't—" Her words died as he reached out and removed her glasses. "Hazard, what are you—?"

"I've been wanting to do this for two days now." His gaze locked on hers, and he saw the startled look in her eyes.

"But I…you mustn't…. We shouldn't—" She put out a hand to stop him. But the moment her hand came in contact with his bare chest, she forgot what it was she was about to say.

In her twenty-nine years, she'd never before touched a man's naked flesh. And this was such hard, muscled flesh. Covered with dark hair that tickled her fingertips. When she realized what she was doing, she lifted her hand, but it was too late. She could see the way his eyes had narrowed on her.

"Shouldn't what? Do this?" He combed his fingers through her hair, thinking he could simply touch. But the touching wasn't enough. Not nearly enough. Almost roughly he plunged his hands into the tangles and drew her head back, all the while staring deeply into her eyes.

She was amazing to watch. Despite the brilliant mind, she was as artless as a child. Every emotion was there in her eyes to read. Shock. Fear. And then a gradual awareness that the kiss he intended was as inevitable as breathing. Not just inevitable, but welcome.

Unable to wait a moment longer, he lowered his face

to hers. Now there was only the sweetness of her mouth against his. And her breath filling his mouth. Breath as fresh, as sweet, as dawn. And her long, drawn-out sigh, as though pulled from someplace deep within her.

He absorbed a series of shock waves and struggled to hold himself together. For the space of a heartbeat he didn't move, afraid that if he did, he would crush her against him and take until he was sated. It was what he wanted…what he'd wanted from the first time he'd seen her looking so prim and proper and so vulnerable.

Erin was still seated on the stool, her back pressed against the counter. She was so swamped with feelings she wasn't even aware of the sharp edge of the counter digging into her back. Nor did she notice the whimpering sounds that escaped her lips.

She filled herself with the taste of him. So different from anything she'd known. Bold. Musky. Utterly male. His tongue met hers, teasing, tempting, causing the most amazing tingles along her spine.

"Or maybe we shouldn't do this." The words were spoken inside her mouth as his big fingers closed over the tops of her arms and he hauled her roughly against him.

Without even realizing it, she ran her fingers up his arms, thrilling to the feel of corded muscles. Then she wrapped her arms around his neck and clung to him while his mouth moved over hers in a way that stole her breath. There was no hesitation in him now. He took without asking. The more he took, the more she wanted to give.

She returned his kisses with a hunger that had them both gasping. And though he knew he was taking her too far, too fast, he couldn't seem to stop. This kiss had opened a floodgate. The need, the passion, poured between them, heating their blood, clouding their vision.

He was holding her up off the floor, against the length

of him, one hand locked around her waist so that she wouldn't fall. The other hand was cupping the back of her head, his fingers massaging her scalp as he feasted on her mouth with a hunger that rocked them both.

He hadn't known how desperately he'd wanted her. Wanted this. But now that he'd tasted her, he wanted more. He wanted all.

He lowered his head, running nibbling kisses along the smooth column of her throat. The scent of roses was stronger here, and he could imagine her rubbing the lotion across her throat, over her breasts. The blood roared in his temples.

"Hazard."

Her voice gradually penetrated the haze that clouded his mind and his judgment. He lifted his head and stared at her, loving the way she looked: her eyes heavy-lidded with desire; her lips swollen from his kisses; her skin flushed with a glow that told him, as plainly as any words, that she had been as caught up in this passion as he.

He lowered her until her feet touched the floor. Then, because the thought of letting her go was too painful, he brushed his mouth over hers one last time and absorbed another jolt to his already overcharged system.

It took all his willpower to lift his head. Then, before he could lose his resolve, he took a step back, breaking contact.

"I've...got chores to see to." He backed up another step and another, even though all his senses were screaming for him to take her in his arms and kiss her again until they were both beyond caring. "I'll see you at breakfast." He made it to the door and took a deep breath, determined to leave.

When he did, he knew he'd done the right thing. But that didn't make it easier to bear.

The taste of her was still on his lips. And the need for her was still raging through his blood.

"Good morning, Erin." Chance and Ace greeted her as they stood to one side of the kitchen, discussing the wisdom of taking the plane or helicopter, while the winds outside were increasing.

"Good morning. Something smells wonderful."

"Buttermilk biscuits," Maggie called. She was wearing thick oven mitts while she removed a pan of steaming biscuits from the oven. "There's fresh orange juice." She indicated the glasses lined up neatly on the counter.

Erin helped herself to one and stood watching as Maggie stirred an egg mixture, then turned her attention to steaks under the broiler.

"How do you do all this so efficiently? Hazard said you've even taken over catering to all the wranglers in the bunkhouses."

Maggie smiled. "Before I came to the Double W, I owned a restaurant in Chicago. It's second nature for me to think in terms of feeding huge numbers of people. It wasn't challenging enough to feed just us. I needed to do more."

"Amazing." Erin shook her head. "Often, after a long day at the lab, I've found it too challenging to open something from the freezer and put it in the microwave. Instead, I'll have a bowl of cereal and crawl into bed."

"I think that's what most people do. But food is my passion. The way laboratory research is yours." Maggie placed the egg casserole in the oven and set the timer, then looked over at Erin. "Which reminds me. How's your research coming along?"

"Not very well." Erin was aware that Ace and Chance had stopped to listen. "But we're just getting started. I have no doubt we'll find the answer.'' She pushed aside the little fear that nagged. She'd always been successful at whatever she put her mind to. Still, the fear of failure was always there, like a shadow dogging her footsteps. It was one more reason why she continued to push herself to the limit in her research.

To change the subject she asked, ''Has the Double W always had a private plane and helicopter?''

Chance nodded. ''My brothers and I are all licensed pilots. It's pretty difficult not to use a plane when you have this much land to cover. But a couple of years ago, when we realized we could afford to buy something bigger and hire a crew to maintain them, we settled on a jet and a copter. That way, we're free to go in opposite directions, or all over the world, if our business demands it.''

''I'm impressed.''

''Don't be, Doc.'' Ace laughed. ''Just think of it as slightly bigger and slightly faster than the horses our ancestors rode.''

The door opened, and Hazard and Cody stepped in on a rush of bitter air. Hazard never even bothered to acknowledge the others. The moment he caught sight of Erin across the room, his gaze locked on her.

She was wearing Maggie's jeans and turtleneck. Her hair was tied back off her face in that prim little knot. Her eyes peered from behind the round glasses. At first glance nothing about her had changed. And yet everything had. Now he could taste her sweetness. Could still smell the delicate rose fragrance that had filled his lungs. And could feel the way her lithe body fitted so perfectly against his. And right now, this minute, he wanted her. More than anything in the world.

Erin was staring at him in that same silent, watchful

manner. Reliving every touch and taste and feel of their early-morning encounter. And though the conversation swirled on around her, she was oblivious to all except Hazard.

"There's snow coming." Beside Hazard, Cody hung his hat on a peg by the door and turned to greet the others.

"I thought you said it was spring." Maggie poured coffee into a mug and handed it to him.

He grinned and wrapped his hands around the mug before taking a long drink. "That's spring in Wyoming. Sunshine one day. Buried in snow the next."

"Coffee, Hazard?" Maggie filled a second mug and turned to glance at the man who still stood by the door, staring at Erin in that quiet, thoughtful way.

"Yeah. Thanks." Forcing himself into action, he slapped his leather gloves against his thigh, then tossed them aside and crossed the room to take the mug from his sister-in-law's hand.

The phone rang, and Chance snatched it up. "Alex?" He listened to his pilot. "You're sure? Right. I'll be there in less than an hour."

He replaced the phone and turned to the others. "Alex has been in touch with the weather bureau in Cheyenne. He thinks if we're heading that way, we'd better get going soon if we want to beat the storm."

"Okay. I can take a hint." Maggie began placing platters of food on the table.

As Cody took a seat he grinned. "My old bones could have told you the same thing as the weather bureau."

The others laughed.

Hazard held a chair for Erin, then sat down beside her. While the others continued laughing and talking, he leaned close. "You okay?"

"I'm fine." She felt the heat rise to her cheeks and looked away, avoiding his eyes.

He sipped his coffee, enjoying the faint hint of roses. Would he ever again be able to smell them without thinking of her?

"Hey." Ace's voice had his head coming up sharply. "You going to hog all the eggs, Hazard? How about sharing with the rest of us?"

Hazard realized that Maggie had handed him the casserole. He'd been holding it now for nearly a full minute. With a muttered oath he filled his plate, then held it out to Erin, who avoided his eyes as she helped herself to a small amount before passing it on.

"So, Doc. What's the next step?" Ace filled his plate and buttered a biscuit.

"Step?"

"In your research. Where do you go from here?"

"Oh." She sipped her coffee, careful to avoid glancing at Hazard. If she did, she might blush, and the others would see. It occurred to her that maybe they could already see the change. Did a woman look different when she'd been kissed by a man? Kissed. That was far too simple a term. What they'd shared had been much more than a kiss. There had been all the passion and fury of a storm between them. And all in the space of a few moments.

"I have a few more tests planned for the blood samples we've already collected. Then I think we might be wise to begin taking blood samples from healthy calves as well. That way we'll have a basis for comparison."

"I was thinking that very same thing." Hazard drained his coffee and waited while Maggie refilled it. He gave her a smile of thanks. "I already phoned Peterson and told him not to dispose of the carcasses yet. If you'd like, we can drive up there after breakfast.''

''That's fine.'' Erin nodded.

From across the table Ace grinned. ''It looks like you two are on the same wavelength. I guess that means the rest of us can relax. Hazard and the doc will soon have everything under control.'' He shoved away from the table. ''Thanks, Maggie. That was a great breakfast. But since I'm taking the copter up to the mine, I'm going to get a head start on this snow.''

''I'm right behind you,'' Chance said as he walked to his wife to give her a fierce hug.

Cody finished his meal and got to his feet. ''Guess that means I'll be driving you two out to the airstrip.''

Ace and Chance picked up their briefcases and trailed the old cowboy to the door.

''When you get back, Cody, we'll head on up to Peterson's place.'' Hazard shoved away from the table and crossed to the phone. ''I'll call him now and tell him we're coming.''

Erin held her breath as he punched in some numbers. She knew that this phone call wasn't nearly as much about warning Peterson about their arrival as it was about asking the number of calves that had been lost overnight.

She watched Hazard's face as he spoke with his foreman. Her heart fell as his frown deepened. The news, she realized, wasn't good. The dying hadn't miraculously stopped. And her job, her research, was far from over.

Chapter 7

The honk of the truck's horn signaled that Cody had returned from the private airstrip. As soon as they heard it, Hazard and Erin pulled on their parkas and headed out the door.

When they climbed inside, the old cowboy put the truck in gear and they rattled off across the fields.

"Did you talk to Peterson?" Cody kept his eyes on the terrain.

"Yeah." Hazard was staring straight ahead, as well.

"What's the news?"

"Half a dozen, so far." Hazard's tone was bleak. "But the day's young."

Conversation faltered as the three of them retreated into private thoughts. Erin glanced at Hazard's tight, angry profile and wished she knew how to offer him comfort. But she knew that simple expressions of hope would sound stilted, and so she merely folded her hands in her lap and kept her silence.

When Peterson's ranch house came into view, Erin could feel the tension growing. Cody brought the truck to a shuddering stop, and Hazard flung the door wide. When Erin stepped out, she was carrying the small satchel that held her basic tools.

Peterson and several of the wranglers started toward them.

"Doctor." The ranch foreman touched a hand to the brim of his hat before turning to Hazard. "Sorry to be the bearer of bad news. But the number just rose to eight. Russ found two more after I spoke with you."

"I'll want to see where each one was found."

Peterson jammed his hands in his pockets and avoided Hazard's eyes. "The wranglers jumped the gun. Started loading the bodies into a truck before I got out here."

"By whose authority?"

Russ Thurman spat a stream of tobacco between his teeth, leaving a brown stain in the snow. "Peterson put me in charge of the crew. It was my decision."

Hazard shot him a look of surprise. "Even knowing I wanted them left at the scene of death?"

"Look, in case you haven't noticed, boss man, I've been doing double duty. And nobody's taking care of my other chores while I'm up here baby-sitting this herd."

"So you just decided to ignore the rules and do what you wanted."

"Rules? Hell, they change every day. Save the carcasses. Don't save the carcasses. Leave them where you found them. Pile them in the back of a truck and dispose of them." He chewed, spat. "We didn't know how long it would take before you got up here. As it is, the morning's half-over. So I figured I'd get the job done and get on with more important things."

"You think there's something more important than this right now?"

Russ glanced at Peterson, then looked around at the other wranglers, who were staring at their boots, at the herd, anywhere but at the owner whose famous temper was clearly growing by the minute.

"You got the biggest spread in Wyoming, Hazard. And you're spending more time and money on one dinky little herd than you are on the entire operation." He shrugged. "But, hey, it's your money."

"I'm glad you remembered that. From now on, keep it in mind. Now let's get to those carcasses." Hazard's voice lowered for emphasis. "Wherever in hell you've dumped them."

Russ showed a flash of temper before turning away.

As the procession of wranglers made their way toward a stake truck, Hazard touched a hand to Erin's arm. "Are you sure you're up to this? It isn't going to be like studying samples under a microscope. Maybe you'd rather wait in the truck while I take the samples."

She shook her head. "It would take you hours to obtain that many blood samples. I'd like to help. I—" she swallowed "—I think I'll be all right. At least I'm going to try. If it starts to get to me, I'll let you know."

He gave her a tight smile, and felt his anger begin to drain. Just looking at her helped. "That's good enough for me. All right. Let's do it."

He studied the carcasses piled in the back of the stake truck and began counting. "I only count five."

"The other three are still on the ground. We were just getting to them."

He turned to Erin. "It'll be easier for you to handle the ones in the field. I'll handle these." To Peterson he called, "Show Dr. Ryan where the others are."

She followed the ranch foreman to the first spot, where two calves lay side by side, and steeled herself against letting her feelings show.

As she knelt in the snow, she removed a vial from the satchel. Peterson worked quickly, slicing through hide to reveal the heart. Forcing herself not to think about what she was doing, Erin retrieved a clot. And all the while she reminded herself that this was necessary, for the sake of research.

One of the men hollered for the foreman. Peterson turned to Erin. "Dr. Ryan, I'll leave you here for now. When you're through with these two, I'll have one of the wranglers take you to the last carcass."

"Thank you." She didn't even look up when he walked away. Minutes later she removed the syringe and sealed the vial of blood. As she did so, she had to take several deep breaths to calm her ragged breathing. Her hands, she realized, were trembling. Through sheer willpower she managed to place the vials in plastic bags, which she labeled with a marking pen. Her usual precise penmanship was reduced to a scribble that was barely legible.

When she was through with the first carcass, she moved to the second, pushing to get through it before she lost her nerve. Though her stomach was in knots, she managed to finish. When she knelt back on her heels, fighting for composure, she looked up to see Russ Thurman standing behind her.

"Peterson wants me to take you to the where the other calf was found."

She got to her feet, gripping the satchel so tightly, her knuckles were white from the effort. She saw Thurman's glance focus on her hands, then move slowly up to her face.

"You're looking a little green, lady doctor."

"Yes." She tried to smile, but her lips felt frozen.

She followed him up a small knoll, then down the other side. She glanced around, trying to get her bearings. Though there were hundreds of cattle milling about, they were on the far side of the herd. From here Peterson's ranch house and the wranglers were out of sight.

"Here it is." Russ Thurman led the way to a snow-covered mound, where a calf lay on its side. Standing over it was a cow, heavy with milk.

After some effort, Russ managed to restrain the frantic cow. Then he returned to stand watch as Erin knelt beside the calf.

It looked for all the world as if it were sleeping. She couldn't resist checking for a heartbeat. Finding none, she removed a surgical knife from her satchel and steeled herself for the unnerving task of securing another blood sample.

As she began to slice through the hide, Russ Thurman's voice came from directly behind her. "Careful, Doctor. You're looking mighty queasy. I'd hate to have to carry you back to the boss man."

"Don't worry." She gritted her teeth. "I'm not liking this much. But I won't faint."

"Hey. It wouldn't be the first time." He spat a stream of tobacco that landed directly beside the carcass.

When she cast an annoyed glance over her shoulder, he merely grinned. "Come on, lady doctor. You're holding up my breakfast. While you were asleep in your snug little bed up at the big house, I was out here baby-sitting a herd of stupid cows. And now I've got to wait until you do your fancy research here before I get some hot food in my belly."

The talk of food had her stomach churning. The very

thought of going to breakfast after this had her nerves jumping.

Though her hands were shaking, she managed to expose the heart and retrieve a clot.

As she reached for a plastic bag, the sound of laughter stopped her.

Annoyed, she turned to Russ. "What can you possibly find amusing about this gruesome scene?"

"I was just thinking. The first time I saw you, you fainted dead away at the sight of a calf being born." He was laughing harder now, and shaking his head from side to side. "And now you're looking like you're about to pass out again. And you know what? Oh, yeah. This is a good one." He threw back his head and gave a shriek that scraped over her nerves like fingernails on a blackboard. "You're going to love this. This is that same calf. The one Hazard was delivering when you walked into the barn the other day."

Erin's face drained of all its color. She managed to get to her feet, and even managed a couple of halting steps before she dropped down in the snow and began to retch. When the sickness passed, she continued to kneel in the snow, too weak to attempt to stand.

That's where Hazard found her. Sitting back on her heels, her arms pressed to her stomach.

"Hey." He touched a hand to her shoulder and she jumped as though burned. "You all right?"

"I—" She shook her head, unable to speak.

Furious, he turned on Russ. "What's going on here? Did you say something or do something to cause this?"

"Didn't need to." Russ spat. "A woman like that can get sick and pass out all by herself, without any help from anybody. Or have you forgotten the last time, out in the barn?"

"Why you…"

"Hazard." Alarmed at the fury in his eyes, Erin caught his arm. "He's right. I'm such a coward. This isn't anyone's fault but mine. I should have known better than to think I could handle this."

"Stop being so hard on yourself. You're not a coward. This is all new to you. It isn't what you trained for." He didn't like her color. Far too pale. And her eyes. Wide with fear. "You wait here a minute. I'll just finish up and get you back to the truck." He glanced around. "Where's the satchel?"

She shrugged. "I left it…over there." She pointed.

"I'll get it." He squeezed her arm, then swung away. Kneeling beside the carcass, he retrieved the clot, then bagged and labeled it before placing it in the satchel.

When he turned, Erin had managed to get to her feet, where she stood swaying slightly.

"Think you can make it to the truck?" He took her arm.

"Yes. Of course."

He thought about scooping her up and carrying her. But he knew she'd be mortified to have the others see her weakness.

She didn't look at Russ as she turned away.

When they were gone, Russ was still chuckling as he turned toward the calf. He was surprised to see Cody standing there, staring down at the carcass.

"You here to help me drag that back to the others?" Russ called.

Cody merely looked at him.

"What's the matter with you, old man? Lost your tongue?"

"Nope." Cody stayed where he was, waiting until the

wrangler came closer. "Just wanted to let you know you'd better lay off Dr. Ryan."

"Lay off what?"

"Play that innocent act with somebody else." Cody never raised his voice. He didn't need to. He'd been around long enough that the other wranglers knew he only spoke when he had something to say. "I overheard what you told her about this calf."

"You think I was lying? Look at those markings. That's the calf Hazard delivered in the barn, the day that fancy city doctor fainted. And you know it is."

"Maybe." Cody pinned him with a cool look. "But she wouldn't have known that if you hadn't told her. And there's no denying, you enjoyed telling her."

"Maybe I did. Maybe I didn't. What business is it of yours?"

"I'm making it my business. You see you don't bother Dr. Ryan again. Or you'll answer to me, Russ."

Thurman's eyes narrowed with simmering anger. "You'd best mind your own business, old man. Or—"

"Or what?" Cody hadn't moved a muscle. But at the steely look in his eyes, Russ automatically took a step back.

"Maybe whatever's killing all these calves will decide to do the same thing to humans. If it does, you could be first in line."

Cody swung away in that loose-limbed gait of a man who had no fear. "You just remember what I told you, Russ. Dr. Ryan is off-limits."

"If you've decided to become her bodyguard, old man, she has about as much chance at safety as these calves."

Cody didn't even acknowledge him. He just kept on walking until he reached the truck.

Minutes later they had left the herd behind. And headed back to the Double W in silence.

"Erin." Hazard paused in the doorway of the lab.

Erin was peering intently at the sample under the microscope. It took her a full minute to lift her head.

Her color was back. And those intense blue eyes behind the round glasses had lost that look of panic.

She'd changed from the damp, blood-stained jeans into her navy skirt and a prim, white blouse. And after standing in the shower for a full twenty minutes, she felt as though she'd washed away the lingering stench of death. Now, after several hours in the lab, she was feeling as good as new and back in her element.

"Maggie has dinner ready. Time to take a break."

It took her a moment to realize that the light outside the wall of windows had faded to dusk. "All right. If I have to."

His grin was quick and dangerous. "Yeah. You have to. You can't spend all your time working."

"Why not? You do."

He laughed and held out his hand. "That's different. I have a ranch to run. Come on."

With a sigh she slipped off the stool and placed her hand in his. The jolt was instantaneous. It sent a rush of heat through her veins that was both shocking and pleasant. "I haven't found anything new."

"There's always tomorrow."

"You say that. But every day the mystery isn't solved, you lose more calves."

He linked his fingers with hers. "Don't remind me. Come on. Maggie's meals have a way of making us forget our troubles."

As they entered the kitchen, the sound of laughter

greeted them. Erin took her place at the table and realized how much she'd begun to look forward to the teasing humor of this family. After the grim realities of the day, being with them had a way of releasing all the tension and renewing her energy, as well as her faith that there would be a solution to the problem.

Ace was regaling Maggie with stories of their rough-and-tumble teen years. He buttered a roll and glanced at Chance. ''Do you remember the day we came home and told Hazard you'd bought an oil rig, and I'd hired a company to bore some soil samples?''

Chance nodded. ''He really came unglued.'' He touched a hand to his jaw. ''I thought for a minute he'd broken my jaw with that punch he threw.''

''You came to blows?'' Erin glanced at Hazard.

''Yeah.'' He grinned, remembering.

''Hazard thought we were going to contaminate his precious land.'' Ace passed a plate of steaming vegetables. ''We had to do some quick talking to calm him down.''

''As I recall, the talking came later.'' Chance laughed. ''After we'd pounded each other into the ground.''

''From what I've seen—'' Maggie had carved a standing rib roast and began to pass it around ''—you three have a history of fighting first and resorting to words later.''

''It just works better that way. It's a pearl of wisdom passed down from our father.'' Ace winked at Erin, who was listening to all this with her mouth open. ''First you pound the other guy into oblivion. Then he's ready to listen to reason.''

She was laughing as she shook her head in wonder. ''But what happens if the other guy refuses to be reasonable?''

''Then you pound him again. Sooner or later he comes

around.'' Ace took a bite of beef, then closed his eyes. ''You know, Maggie, it's a good thing you're already married, or I'd have to marry you, just so you could cook like this every day of my life.''

''Find your own woman,'' Chance said with a laugh.

''I think you're right. I'm going to have to keep my eye out for one. One just like Maggie. If I ever find a woman who can cook like this, I'm going to carry her off to some mountain hideaway and keep her there until she agrees to marry me.''

''That's the only way a woman would agree to be your wife.'' Hazard held the platter for Erin and frowned when she took only half a piece of beef. ''Come on. You've been working since early this morning. Your body needs fuel.''

''Thanks for your concern.'' She grinned. ''But my body will tell me when it's running on empty.''

Ace arched a brow. ''Hey, Doc. That's pretty good. If you stay here long enough, you may find yourself coming up with all sorts of smart-aleck remarks like that.''

She paused. Considered. Then her smile widened. ''It was rather smart-alecky, wasn't it?''

''Oh-oh.'' Chance threw back his head and laughed. ''I'd watch out now, if I were you, Hazard. She's starting to get the hang of how we do things around here. Next she'll be throwing a punch first and asking questions later.''

They were all laughing as they finished their meal.

''Okay,'' Ace called. ''What's for dessert, Maggie?''

''How do you know I made any?''

''Because you always do. And it's always just what we wanted.''

''You're really getting spoiled.'' She topped off their coffee, then turned away to fetch a tray of brownies. ''One of these days I'm not going to be around to fix your meals, and you're all going to have to go back to the E.Z.Diner for overdone burgers.''

Ace and Hazard groaned, while Chance merely chuckled. ''As I said. You want a good cook like Maggie? Find your own.''

Ace looked up. ''Do you cook, Doc?''

She shook her head. ''I can hardly boil water. But I'm very good at following directions. As long as it comes in a can or a box, with plenty instructions, I'll never starve.''

Ace gave an exaggerated sigh. ''I guess I'll have to look somewhere else for that wife.''

Maggie laughed. ''Believe me, Ace. When you fall for someone, it won't matter whether or not she can cook.''

''You don't think so?''

''I know it.''

''Whew. That's a relief.'' When the others merely looked at him he added, ''When I was at Clancy's the other night, I was really admiring Beryl Spence's big—''

His two brothers shot him a warning frown that had him stopping in midsentence. ''I was just going to say that she has really great—''

''We get the picture,'' Maggie said with a laugh. ''But that's one more thing that won't matter when you really fall in love.''

''It won't?''

She was laughing harder at the look on his face. ''Love just doesn't care about a person's size or shape.''

''Now I know I'm never falling in love.'' Ace shoved away from the table. ''I think I'll head on into town and see if there are any prospective victims at Clancy's.''

''While you're there, you might want to admire Beryl Spence.'' Chance kept a perfectly straight face. ''Just in case you get bit by the lovebug. After that, your looking days will be over.''

"Yeah? Well, don't ever count on that happening, Bro. The day I quit looking, I'll be dead.'' Ace snatched up his parka. Minutes later they heard the sound of his truck as he drove away.

Then, as if by some silent command, they all burst into gales of laughter.

Later, as she made her way to the lab, Erin was still smiling. She couldn't remember when she'd met a more amazing, amusing family than this.

"I can't believe you're still here.'' Hazard stood in the doorway of the lab, his arms crossed over his chest. "Chance and I have been in the library, going over the books. I was heading to bed when I saw the light in here. I thought maybe you'd just forgotten to turn it off.''

"I just wanted to check a few things.'' Erin idly rubbed the stiffness in her neck as she slid off the stool.

"Look, Erin.'' Concern was etched on Hazard's face. "I don't want you working day and night on this. It isn't worth sacrificing your sleep.''

"Don't worry about me.'' She picked up the blood sample and returned it to the refrigerator.

When she turned, he was still standing in the doorway, his arms still firmly crossed over his chest.

Disappointment washed over her. After their scene that morning, she'd been hoping they would find some time alone. But all day she'd had the distinct impression that he was deliberately keeping his distance.

Did he regret what they'd shared? She felt a sudden wrenching ache around her heart. Was that why he hadn't come near her? Because he didn't want to repeat his mistake of that morning? Was it because of what had happened up at Peterson's? Was he repulsed by the fact that she was such a coward? She didn't think she could bear it if he turned away from her because of what had happened today.

"Come on." He held the door. "I'll walk you to your room."

As she moved past him, her body brushed his and she felt him stiffen and pull back. With a wave of bitter disappointment she watched as he switched off the lights and closed the door. Then he moved to her side, keeping enough distance that they didn't touch.

When they reached her room she couldn't contain herself. Without taking time to think she blurted, "Why are you avoiding me, Hazard? Are you sorry about this morning?"

"Sorry?" He caught her roughly by the upper arms. At once he felt the jolt. Judging by the look of surprise in her eyes, he knew she'd felt it, too. He lifted his hands, then, pressed his forehead to hers and began running his fingertips up and down her arms feeling a mixture of need and frustration. It was an effort to keep his touch light. What he wanted, more than anything in the world, was to carry her through the doorway to her bed and ravish her until they were both sated.

"You're right about one thing, Erin. I have been avoiding you. But not for the reason you think."

"You don't have any regrets about this morning?"

"My only regret is that I'm so rough. I know…" He struggled with the words. They'd never been his strong suit. He'd always left the talking to Chance and Ace. "I know that you're sweet and…innocent. And I don't want to hurt you."

A sigh welled up from deep inside, and she threw her arms around his neck. "Is that all?"

"All?" He drew back so that he could see her eyes.
"Erin, I—" he swallowed "—what I want…" He shook
his head, afraid to even try to put into words all that he
was feeling. "I just want us to take it slow and easy. So
that every step along the way you can say no."

"And if I don't?"

He thought for a moment his heart was going to leap
clear out of his mouth. He swallowed, then couldn't stop
the dangerous grin that curved his lips. "If you don't tell
me no, I'm going to make those bulls out on the range
look like lapdogs."

She lifted her face to him and closed her eyes. "Then,
would you please kiss me? Right now?"

It was the sweetest invitation. But still he held back.

"First, open your eyes."

Her lids flickered, then lifted. "Why?"

"Because." He moved his hands down her back, along
her sides, until his thumbs encountered the soft swell of
her breasts. He saw the way her eyes widened. He could
feel the little jolt of fear that rippled through her. But to
her credit she didn't pull away. "I want to see you. I want
you to see me."

He lowered his head and brushed his mouth over hers.
And though she hungered for more, he took his time, tracing the outline of her lips with his tongue, before plunging
it inside to mate with hers.

"Oh, Hazard." Her hands tightened at his neck, and
she drew him closer until his body was imprinting itself
on hers.

It was such a wonderful body. All hard angles and
planes, that seemed to fit so perfectly against her softness.
And his arms, all corded with muscles, made her feel
warm and safe and…treasured.

"I've got to—" he lifted his head and took in several deep breaths to clear his head "—say good-night now."

"So soon?"

Disappointment had her eyes turning stormy. He loved her innocence. Loved the way all her feelings were there, for the whole world to see. She was, he realized, completely guileless. But he was fully aroused. And this was all too much for her. And far too soon.

"Erin, if you knew what I really wanted to do right now, you'd be running for the door. And you wouldn't stop until you were safely back in Laramie."

"But I—" She looked up and saw his eyes. They weren't warm with laughter now. Or sparkling with humor. There was something hot and fierce in them that she'd never seen before. Something dark and dangerous.

She stepped back. "All right. Good night, Hazard."

"'Night."

He left without a backward glance. When he reached his own room, he crossed to the window and stood there for long minutes, staring out into the darkness.

His father used to say that when a man cared more about what would happen to the woman than he cared about his own needs, it was a sure sign of love.

He wasn't sure about the love part. It didn't seem possible, since it had happened so fast. Without warning. It certainly wasn't something he'd wanted. Not with someone like Erin. She was all wrong for him. And this was the wrong time in his life. He had more important things to worry about right now than love. But there it was. And there was nothing to be done about it now, except hope he didn't hurt her in the process. Because a woman as fine and special as Erin Ryan could do a whole lot better than the son of a hard-drinking, hard-living Wyoming rancher.

Chapter 8

"I'm afraid I have some bad news." Chance stepped into the kitchen while the others were gathered around the table for breakfast.

Everyone looked up.

Maggie stepped out behind him. Instead of her usual jeans, she was wearing an elegant amber dress and matching coat. At her throat and ears were a gleaming topaz necklace and earrings, a gift from her husband.

"What's up?" Ace, flush from his win at Clancy's the night before, was dressed for business.

"I have to go up to New York for a couple of days." Chance turned to Cody. "Think you have time to drive to the airstrip before you head up to Peterson's?"

"Sure thing." The old cowboy tucked into his breakfast, unwilling to let it go to waste.

Chance turned to his brothers. "I've decided to combine a little business with pleasure. So I'm taking my bride along."

"Hey. No fair." Ace downed his glass of orange juice in one long swallow. "You're taking our cook."

"Huh. You think that's bad." Agnes Tallfeather made her usual grudging comment as she trudged through the kitchen carrying a bucket and rags. "I just found out I'm going to be spending a couple of days cooking for the wranglers. It won't be easy getting them to eat chili and burgers, after all that fancy food Maggie's been feeding them."

"Just remind them that you fed them for years before Maggie came along. And if they complain, tell them to drive into town and eat at the diner or try the poison at Clancy's," Chance called.

Ace grinned. "Actually, this works out really well for me. I was planning to spend a couple of days up at the mine, anyway. Looks like my timing was perfect, as always. I won't be missing a thing around here." He turned to Hazard and Erin. "You two, on the other hand, will have to make a choice. Muddle through on your own, or head on into Prosperous and take your chances at the diner."

"Now there's an idea." Hazard turned to Erin. "Did you get to see much of the town when you passed through?"

She shook her head. "I didn't even stop. I did notice a few shops and businesses along the main street, before I veered off the highway toward the Double W. But there wasn't time to investigate them."

"Then today's your lucky day." Hazard followed Cody's lead and dug into his omelette. "As soon as I finish my chores, we'll head into Prosperous, and you'll get to meet Thelma."

"Thelma?"

"She's a fixture in Prosperous. She owns the E.Z.Diner."

"Will I like her?"

Maggie nodded. "As long as you can look beyond the purple hair and green nail polish. She's quite a character. But she has a heart of gold. She was my first friend in Wyoming. And when Chance and I were married, I asked her to be my witness."

"Purple hair?" Erin's eyes widened. "She sounds as if she's really something."

Maggie saw the laughter lurking in the three brothers' eyes, and couldn't help joining in. "She is something. Something special."

"Come on, Mrs. Wilde." Chance caught her hand. "Quit gabbing. There's no time to waste. New York is waiting."

"Yes. With all those shops. And all those wonderful restaurants." She turned to Hazard. "If you get hungry, there's plenty of food in the freezer."

"I think we can manage." He kissed her cheek. "Get out of here and have a good time. You deserve it. And buy something extravagant."

She gave him a fierce hug, then hugged Ace, before allowing Chance to lead her out the door. It was clear that they were both eager to get away.

At the sound of the helicopter engines overhead, Ace picked up his briefcase. "Here's my ride. Looks like you two are on your own. Try not to spend all your time in that lab, Doc. There really is a life beyond the microscope, you know."

She smiled. "I'll try to remember that, Ace."

When the door closed behind Ace, Hazard picked up his parka. "I ought to have my chores finished by noon."

Erin nodded. "That'll give me just enough time to run a few more tests on those blood samples."

She watched as he sauntered away. Then she glanced around the huge kitchen. It seemed strange to see it so empty. But there was no time to brood about it. She was already thinking about the trip to Prosperous. And the fact that she and Hazard would be alone for the first time since her arrival.

"I'm sure that after Boston this doesn't seem like much of a town to you." Hazard drove slowly, allowing Erin to study the row of buildings that made up the main street of Prosperous.

"Every town has its own character."

"Not to mention its characters," Hazard added with a laugh.

Erin was smiling as she studied the shops. There was the E.Z.Diner, which reflected its owner's unusual taste. Painted bright pink, it sported apple-green shutters at the windows, and the shingles on the roof were lemon-yellow. A few doors down was the This N That Shop.

"What do they sell there?"

"Clothing." Hazard slowed down.

"Men's or women's?"

"Clothes for the entire family."

"And that?" She read the sign. "Wanda's Bait and Party Shoppe."

"Wanda sells gifts, party goods as well as fishing bait and tackle."

"You're kidding."

"Nope. At the end of the street is Korson's Feed and Grain. They sell everything from oats to oatmeal. And there's Clancy's Pool Hall, where my brother Ace performs almost nightly. Down there is the movie theatre, and next door is Alice's Ice Cream Shop. Alice sells hot chocolate in the winter, and cider and donuts in the autumn. Want to shop first?'' Hazard asked.

Erin nodded. ''I've been wearing Maggie's jeans and sweater since I first came here. I think it's time to buy my own.''

Hazard brought the truck to a stop outside the This N That Shop, and led the way inside, where he introduced Erin to Lucy Swan, the owner.

''Lucy, this is Dr. Erin Ryan.''

''A doctor? Somebody sick up at the Double W, Hazard?''

''No, ma'am.'' He twirled his hat in his hand just the way Cody often did. A trait Erin found endearing.

''Dr. Ryan is here to help me with some lab work.''

''Well, isn't that grand.'' The old woman was looking Erin over very closely. It was the first time she could recall seeing Hazard Wilde bring a female into her shop.

''What can I help you with?'' Lucy asked.

''I need quite a few things.'' Erin walked to a display of denims and began sorting through them.

Soon she had filled the only fitting room with so many clothes, Lucy suggested she start trying them on. ''If you need anything else, you just let me know, honey, and I'll rummage around for your size.''

As soon as Erin disappeared into the fitting room, Hazard pointed to a dress hanging in the corner. ''Lucy, do you think that would fit Erin?''

The older woman shrugged. ''Ought to. It was made for a teenager, but that little lady's so slender, she shouldn't have any trouble wearing it.'' She wrinkled her nose to show her disapproval. ''But why would you want it, Hazard?''

He just gave her one of those famous Wilde smiles,

that melted hearts from Laramie to Cheyenne. "It's a secret, Lucy. But wrap it up before she sees it. Oh, and those shoes, too."

"Are you sure?" She was studying him with a worried frown that said she thought he'd lost his mind.

"I'm sure, Lucy."

The older woman did as she was told, then handed the package to Hazard, who stashed it in the truck and made a quick stop at Wanda's Bait and Party Shoppe, adding another package to the stash before Erin walked out of the fitting room.

She proved to be a serious shopper. In slightly more than an hour she'd bought two pair of jeans, two sweaters, four simple T-shirts, hiking boots and a pair of pajamas, as well as an assortment of underthings, which she modestly tucked beneath her other purchases, much to Hazard's delight.

He carried her packages to the truck, then caught her hand. "Come on. It's time to meet Thelma."

When they stepped into the E.Z.Diner, a woman with bright-orange hair and matching lipstick looked up from the counter, which she'd been polishing to a high shine. It occurred to Erin that Maggie had described Thelma's hair as purple. Maybe, she thought, the woman changed the color as her mood dictated.

"Hazard Wilde." Thelma opened her arms wide. "Where've you been hiding?"

Without regard to the few people in the diner, he hurried forward to hug her, taking care not to wrinkle the fancy handkerchief she wore pinned to the pocket of her uniform. "Been a little busy, Thel. But I finally decided to take a day off."

"High time." She turned to study the slender, young woman who had hung back. "Who's your friend?"

"Thel, this is Dr. Erin Ryan. Erin, this is Thelma Banks."

"Hello, Thelma."

"Well. A doctor." Thelma's tobacco-roughened voice deepened an octave. "You sick, Hazard?"

He laughed. "That's the same thing Lucy asked. Erin's not a medical doctor. She's a laboratory researcher."

"Fancy title." Thelma indicated the stools at the counter. "Park it and I'll get you some coffee." She started away, then turned back. "You do drink coffee, I hope."

Erin nodded.

Thelma returned with two steaming cups. "Black for you, Hazard." She peered at Erin. "How do you take yours?"

"A little cream."

Thelma placed the pitcher in front of her, then pulled a pencil from behind her ear and leaned her hip against the counter. "Now, what'll you two have?"

"I'm not hungry," Hazard remarked. "I just wanted to see you."

"Ah." She leaned over to place a hand on his cheek and turned to Erin. "See why I love this boy?"

Erin laughed. If she didn't know better, she'd swear Hazard was blushing just a little.

"Now," Thelma said in a more serious tone. "Tell me why you're not hungry. In all the years I've known you, you've never said that before."

He shrugged. "Maybe it's Maggie's good cooking."

"Uh-huh." The old woman studied him.

Then she turned to Erin, taking note of the serious, blue eyes behind the owlish glasses and the prim, perfect knot of hair. "So, Doctor, how long have you been at the Double W?"

"Just a few days."

"What do you think of it?"

"It's unlike anything I've ever seen before. It's a little overwhelming. Everything's so big. The house. The land. The herds."

"Yeah. Not to mention the overwhelming Wilde brothers." Thelma noticed the way Erin and Hazard were holding themselves so stiffly, not allowing any part of their bodies to touch. Not an easy task on these small stools.

Her eyes crinkled into a smile. "How long do you think you'll be staying out at the ranch?"

Erin shrugged. "I'm not sure. It depends."

"On what?"

Erin glanced at Hazard, then away.

He cleared his throat. "I'm having a little problem with some cattle. Erin's giving me a hand with the research. I guess we'll just have to see how we work it out."

"I see." Thelma could see a whole lot more. And she was enjoying it immensely. Her smile grew. "When are you two heading back to the ranch?"

"Right away, I guess. We just spent some time over at Lucy's. Don't want to be away too long, since Ace and Chance are both gone."

"So, you two are alone tonight?"

"Yeah." Hazard flushed.

"Well, why don't I have Slocum make you up some food? He could fix you a pizza."

"A pizza? You mean a real one? Not like that cardboard stuff they serve at Clancy's?" He turned to Erin, who was smiling and nodding. "Yeah. That'd be great, Thel."

"I'll tell Slocum to undercook it, so all you'll have to do is stick it in the oven for a few minutes, and it'll be done."

"Sounds easy enough." Hazard laughed. "And it had better be easy. Erin and I aren't ever going to be famous for our cooking."

Thelma saw the way the two of them shared a knowing smile. "Well, there's a whole lot more important things in life than cooking. I can tell you from my own experience." She walked away and shouted their order to her cook, then returned, tucking the pencil behind her ear.

"How're Maggie and Chance?"

"Still madly in love. They're off to New York for a couple of days. They're going to build a new house up on Tower Ridge."

"A new house?" Thelma studied Chance. "How are you and Ace feeling about that?"

Hazard shrugged. "I can't fault them. They deserve some privacy. I guess if I had a new wife, I'd want to have her all to myself, without my brothers always being around. With a place on Tower Ridge, they'll have their own life, but they'll still be close enough that we can see them often." He gave her one of his famous grins. "And Maggie's already promised to have us to dinner often."

Thelma laughed. "Not to mention breakfast and lunch, if I know Maggie."

"Yeah. She has certainly changed mornings at our place." He turned to Erin. "Before Maggie came along, my brothers and I never used to see each other in the morning. We would each go to our own office in the house and drink gallons of Agnes's muddy coffee. And that was it, until we'd come together in the evening, when we'd make do with chili or burgers."

Thelma topped off their coffees. "Yep. I've got to hand it to Maggie. Inside of weeks, she took on that big, old rambling ranch house and turned it into a home. And she didn't just win over Chance. She won the hearts of his two brothers, as well. And Cody and Agnes. No small task. Especially Agnes Tallfeather." She looked from Hazard to Erin. "The right person has a way of doing that. All of a sudden things you've been doing for a lifetime take on a whole new meaning when that certain someone's around. And people and places you've known forever look different when you see them through the other person's eyes."

"Yeah. Well." Hazard drained his cup and got to his feet. "If Slocum has our pizza ready, we'd better get back."

Thelma reached up to the pass-through and accepted a cardboard box from her cook.

Hazard dug some money out of his jeans and placed it on the counter, then accepted the box from Thelma.

Balancing the box in one hand he wrapped an arm around the old woman and gave her a warm hug. "See you soon, Thel."

"You better. Or I'll come out to the Double W looking for you." She turned to Erin. "Nice meeting you, Dr. Ryan. Good luck with that research problem. And any other…problems you find out at the ranch."

Erin saw the gleam in the older woman's eyes and wondered about it. But she shrugged it aside and merely nodded. "Thanks, Thelma. It was really nice meeting you."

Hazard held the door, then trailed Erin across the street to where the truck was parked. Thelma Banks stood at the counter of the E.Z.Diner, watching the young couple through the window.

"He's done it," she said to no one in particular. "He may not know it yet, but Hazard Wilde has fallen hide over tin cups for a female. And not just any female. A lade-da lady with a fancy title. But fancy title or no, she's as crazy about him as he is about her." She was grinning as she went back to polishing the counters. She wondered how soon before Hazard and his lady love would come face-to-face with the truth.

Hazard drove the truck around to the back door of the ranch house and turned off the ignition.

As he held the door for Erin she paused, looking up into his eyes in that way that always had him catching his breath. "I suppose you'll have to make up for all the chores you missed while we were in town."

He shook his head. "I told Cody I'd be gone. He and the wranglers covered for me." He led the way up the steps, balancing the pizza box in one hand. "I'll put this in the refrigerator. Let me know when you're hungry, and we'll heat it up."

"Okay." She started toward the hallway. "I'll put my packages in my room before I get started in the lab."

As soon as she was gone, Hazard returned to the truck and removed his own packages.

At a knock on her bedroom door Erin looked up. Hazard was standing in the doorway, holding a large bag.

She gave him a smile. "I didn't know you shopped, too."

"Just something I picked up while you were trying on clothes in the fitting room." He cleared his throat. "I'd like you to put this on."

"It's for me?"

He nodded.

"You bought me a gift?" She hadn't moved. She didn't seem to know quite what to do.

"Yeah. I'd…like you to wear it tonight. I thought we'd just forget about working in the lab." He thrust it into her hands and turned on his heel.

* * *

Erin stood in front of the mirror, studying her reflection. The dress was just not her style. The fabric was some sort of silky chiffon in a pale sky-blue. It had a halter neckline that fastened at the back of the neck, leaving the arms completely bare. There was no way she could wear a bra beneath it. She felt…practically naked. And then there was the waist. It was tightly nipped. From there the fabric flowed in drifts to her ankles.

The strappy little sandals matched the dress. And were just as useless. She'd felt a bit silly just putting them on. Now, as she twirled in front of the mirror, she couldn't suppress the laughter. What in the world had Hazard been thinking? Was this what he wanted in a woman? Some silly little nymph who was all fluff and no substance?

Her first thought was to take it all off and stuff it back in the bag. But she remembered the way he'd looked, so solemn and secretive as he'd handed it to her. All right, she thought, turning away. She would model it for him. And then she would change into something more suitable.

She made her way down the hall and paused outside the kitchen door, fighting back a sudden wave of annoyance. Was this some sort of hint? Was he saying he didn't like her the way she was? That he wished she wasn't so…conservative?

Determined to get this over with, she lifted her head and stepped inside.

The first thing she noticed was crepe paper streamers strung across the ceiling and a large ornamental ball of gold and silver fastened at the center. In the background, the radio was playing oldies music. Billy Joel was singing about an uptown girl.

Hazard was standing across the room watching her. He'd showered. Beads of water still glistened in his dark hair. He was wearing fresh jeans and a starched white shirt. As he walked toward her, she noticed something in his hand. When he was close enough, she could see that it was a wrist corsage of white gardenias and deep-red roses.

"Hazard." She couldn't seem to get her bearings. "I don't understand any of this."

"I overheard you telling Maggie that you'd never gone to your prom. You were too busy studying. The truth is, I never did, either. I was too busy working the ranch. So I thought—" he held out the corsage "—I thought we'd have our prom tonight."

She couldn't speak. As he slipped the flowers on her wrist, she felt her eyes fill with tears.

"There wasn't time to rent a tux. But I thought you wouldn't mind."

Mind? She was feeling all blubbery and teary-eyed. "If I..." She swallowed and tried again. "If I'd known, I would have taken more time. My hair..." She reached up to the knot, but his hands were there first.

"Let me, Erin."

He pulled the pins from her hair and watched as it cascaded down around her shoulders in a mass of silken waves. The sight of it robbed him of breath.

Then he reached up and removed her glasses. "Can you see without these?"

"Some. Things that are too far away are a blur."

"Then it's no problem. I intend to stay close. Very close."

He set the glasses on the counter, just as a voice on the radio announced, "We had a phone-in request. So here it is, folks. From Hazard to Erin. Kenny Rogers, singing "Lady.""

Hazard opened his arms. "May I have this dance?"

"Oh, Hazard." It was all she could manage to whisper

as she stepped into the circle of his arms and began to move with him to the music. Overcome with emotion, she rested her head on his shoulder and allowed him to lead her through the steps of the dance.

When she could finally trust herself to speak she said, "No one's ever done anything like this for me. It's just so special."

"I'm glad. I was really afraid you'd think it was corny."

"Oh, no." She touched a hand to his cheek. "It's just the sweetest thing ever. I'll never forget this, Hazard."

On the radio REO Speedwagon warned not to fight this feeling. Erin and Hazard instinctively responded to the words. Their movements slowed, until they were just swaying, their bodies brushing, their gazes locked.

"You know what?" He touched a hand to her face.

"What?"

"I'm glad now that I never went to my high school prom."

"Why?" Her voice was little more than a dreamy sigh.

He smiled. "Because I won't ever have any other memories crowding this one."

"Oh, Hazard." She stood very still, no longer able to stop the tears that welled up and spilled over.

"Hey. I didn't want to make you cry." Alarmed, he reached for his handkerchief.

"It's all right." She accepted it from his hand and mopped at the moisture. "These are happy tears."

"They are?" He tipped up her chin and stared into her eyes.

"Yes. This just…" She sniffed. "This just means so much to me, Hazard. I'll never forget this night. And I'll never forget you."

"I'm glad." With his thumbs he gently wiped away the last of the tears from her cheeks.

And then, very slowly, very deliberately, he lowered his head and covered her mouth with his.

Erin felt the slow simmer begin deep inside as his lips moved over hers, tasting, teasing. And then the delicious curl of desire that inched along her spine.

She couldn't stop the sigh that escaped her lips. Couldn't prevent her arms from encircling his neck or stop the little thrill that shot through her when the dark hair at his nape brushed the backs of her hands.

Heat suddenly blazed between them, catching them both by surprise. He crushed her against him and took the kiss deeper, until they were both gasping. And still he couldn't stop. He ran wet kisses down her throat, while his hands moved down her back, then slowly up her sides, until his thumbs encountered her breasts.

At her gasp of surprise Hazard abruptly lifted his head and took a step back.

Erin's eyes widened in alarm. "What is it? What's wrong?"

"I just need a minute." He kept his hands firmly on her shoulders, holding her away a little. "Otherwise, I'm afraid I'll cross over a line here."

"Oh." She was silent for a moment, before saying softly, "I don't mind."

He stared at her in surprise. "You don't know what you're saying."

"Is that what you think?" She touched a hand to his cheek. "Why are you treating me like a child, Hazard?"

"Because—" he took a deep breath, choosing his words carefully "—I know, by the way you kiss, by the way you act, that you're an innocent."

"That's true. But I'm a woman. Just because I haven't

had any experience in love, don't think I don't know how I feel.''

He was staring at her as if he couldn't quite believe what he was hearing. ''And just how do you feel?''

She took a deep breath, then said in a rush, ''Like a woman in love.''

Her words nearly shattered his control. Still, he knew that one of them had to be sensible. And since he'd been the one to spring this on her, he felt responsible. ''I know this whole thing caught you by surprise, Erin. And I'll admit that I fantasized about this. About holding you, dancing with you, stealing a few kisses. But that doesn't mean I intended to take advantage of the situation. I didn't intend for it to get out of hand.''

She smiled. He was trying to be strong for both of them. It was one more reason why she loved him so.

In the background, Whitney Houston was singing about the greatest love of all. Erin felt her heart soar. Maybe it was the music or the fact that this night was magic. Whatever the reason, she felt a rare burst of courage.

''I know, Hazard. Neither of us intended it to happen. But it did. And I really, really want you to kiss me again.'' In fact, she thought she'd die if he didn't.

He shook his head. ''If I do, I won't be able to stop.''

Her smile changed slightly. It became, in that instant, the smile of a woman. A woman who knew exactly what effect she was having on him.

''That would be just fine with me, Hazard. In fact, I don't want you to stop. Ever.''

Chapter 9

His first instinct was to devour her. To simply kiss her until her head was spinning so wildly she couldn't think and then take her right there, before she could change her mind. But still he held back, wanting, needing, to give her every opportunity to think this through.

"I hope you understand, Erin. Tomorrow it'll be too late for regrets."

Instead of arguing, she stood on tiptoe to brush her lips over his. "Kiss me back, Hazard," she whispered against his mouth. "I need you to kiss me."

He'd wanted to take the high ground. But he was only a man. A man too close to the edge.

His arms went around her, pinning her against him, as his mouth covered hers in a kiss so hot, so hungry, it threatened to melt her bones.

"Is this what you wanted?" His hands moved along her back, igniting fires with every touch.

"Yes. Oh, yes." She returned his kisses with a fervor that matched his.

"There's still time, Erin." He brought his mouth to her temple. His hands were in her hair, though he couldn't recall how they got there. He whispered the words against her flesh, loving the taste of it. "Time to change your mind."

He tensed, afraid she might do just that. He couldn't bear it if she denied him now. For him the line had already been crossed.

"I won't. I want…" She moved in his arms, loving the way his lips burned a trail of fire down her cheek to her ear. When his tongue plunged inside, she gave a gasp. "Oh, Hazard. I want you."

A man could only take so much.

He scooped her up and started down the hallway, hoping he could make it to a bedroom. Hers or his, it didn't matter. He just wanted her. Now. The blood was roaring in his temples. His vision was nearly blinded by passion.

She wrapped her arms around his neck and nibbled his ear, sending a series of tremors along his spine. The need for her had him on the verge of exploding.

At the doorway to her room he paused to set her on her feet. His mouth covered hers in a kiss so passionate they were both trembling.

He drew her tightly against him; he could feel every delicious curve imprinting itself on his body. The press of her breasts. The lovely flare of her hips. He was practically crawling inside her skin. But still it wasn't enough. He wanted it all.

"Your dress." He reached up behind her neck, fumbling for the snap. When at last he found it, he watched as the bodice of the dress slid down, revealing pale, creamy skin.

"Oh, Erin. You're so beautiful." He trailed kisses down her throat, then lower, to the swell of her breast.

"I'm small." She felt suddenly shy. "I've always been too small."

"You're perfect." His mouth closed around a nipple, and she gasped as little darts of fire shot straight through to her core. "The most perfect woman I've ever known."

He feasted on one breast, then the other, until he lifted his head and forced himself to take a breath. He had to keep reminding himself to go slow. To touch. To savor. To draw out the moment.

His fingers found the zipper at her waist, and her dress fluttered down, pooling at her feet. He slipped his fingertips under the elastic of her modest cotton panties. It took all his willpower not to tear them from her. But he didn't want to shock her, so he gently slid them down until they joined the dress.

Erin had always thought she would feel embarrassed to stand naked before a man. But instead of shame, she felt suddenly, gloriously free. She could tell, by the blaze of heat in his eyes, that he found her desirable. And that only fueled her own desire.

"I need to touch you, Hazard." She reached her hands to the buttons of the starched white shirt and managed to slide it from his shoulders.

The touch of his hair-roughened chest caused another rush of heat, and she surprised herself by trailing her lips over him. She felt the thundering of his heart and thrilled to the fact that her touch was causing it. Growing even bolder, she reached for the fastener at his waist, fumbling in her haste. After several frustrated oaths muttered under his breath he managed to kick off his boots and jeans, leaving them in a heap beside her clothes on the floor.

"Hazard." She ran her hands up his chest, across his shoulders. "You're so beautiful."

"Beautiful?" He tried to laugh, but it sounded choked. Then he gave a long, drawn-out sigh. He'd dreamed of having her touch him like this. And now that she was, he was burning with need. Consumed with it.

"Yes. Beautiful. So strong. All these muscles." Her fingertips were igniting fires wherever they touched him.

"And you're so soft. So sweet." His big hands framed her face, and he brushed light, feathery kisses over her eyelids, down her nose, across her lips. "I'm afraid I'll hurt you."

"You won't, Hazard. You couldn't possibly hurt me." A lie, she knew. She was about to give him the power to hurt her. To break her heart. But she wouldn't think about such a thing now.

He feasted on her mouth, nearly drowning in the sweetness. He couldn't get enough of the taste of her. Her lips parted for him, and her tongue tangled with his until, on a sigh, she gave herself up completely to the pleasure.

With his mouth on hers he lowered her gently to the floor, cushioned by their scattered clothing.

Outside, the wind had picked up, sending a spray of rain laced with snow against the window. Neither of them noticed. Their world had been reduced to this room. This passion. This moment.

From the kitchen radio drifted the muted sounds of a haunting love song. Moonlight spilled through the window, casting them in a golden glow. They could hear nothing except the pounding of their own hearts. And the sound of their shallow breaths mingling.

Hazard felt the need rising and struggled to hold it at bay. It wasn't enough to take. He wanted to give. He wanted, more than anything, to make this as pleasurable as possible for Erin.

His kisses gentled, became almost reverent, as, with lips and tongue and fingertips, he explored her face, her neck, her throat. And with each touch, each taste, he felt her body become more tense, her breathing grow more shallow.

As her blood heated and her heartbeat pounded, Erin felt needs pulse through her veins. Nothing mattered now except this man. This moment. This pleasure.

Hazard saw the fear that leaped into her eyes whenever she thought about what they were going to do. And so he patiently led her, with soft, soothing touches and long, drugging kisses until the fear subsided and she slipped under the spell of passion.

With exquisite tenderness he made her feel cherished. But even while his touch calmed, it also aroused, unlocking feelings she'd never even known she possessed. Her body hummed with need. With each touch, each kiss, he uncovered another layer of need, another depth of passion.

Finally, when she could bear it no longer, she wound her arms around his neck and dragged his lips back to hers.

He sensed the change in her and thrilled to it. This was no mere surrender. This was desire so all consuming, there would be no denying its demands. He could see it in her eyes. Taste it on her lips. Hot. Hungry. Desperate.

The heat rose up between them, clogging their lungs, clouding their vision.

His touch was no longer gentle, but demanding. His kisses were no longer patient, but insistent.

With his eyes on hers he drew her head back and covered her mouth in a savage kiss. For a moment she stiffened, fearing the change in him. This was a dark side, a dangerous side of Hazard that she hadn't seen before. Then, as he took the kiss deeper, the fear was swept away by her own newly awakened passion.

She had a driving, desperate need to touch him as he was touching her. With tongue and teeth and fingertips she traced the muscles of his shoulders and chest. At his low moan of pleasure she grew even bolder, exploring all of his body as thoroughly, as erotically as he had explored hers.

He had thought he could go slowly, to allow her to set the pace. But now the need was too great. His body was alive with need. And still he struggled to hold back. He wanted this, her first time, to be a cherished memory she could carry with her for a lifetime.

With great care he brought his mouth to her breast, suckling until the nipple hardened. Then he moved to the other, feasting until she moaned and writhed beneath him.

Her breathing grew more ragged. Her hands fisted in the gown that was crushed beneath her. And still he held back, drawing out every pleasure until she cried out for release.

Erin hadn't believed it possible to feel so deeply. She was incapable of thought. Now there was only Hazard. The taste of him—dark, passionate. The look of him— fierce, powerful. His gaze—riveted on her with such intensity that he made her feel beautiful and loved. And the feel of his rough, work-worn fingers on her flesh—more heavenly than silk, making her feel desired above all else.

She moved under him and strained for release as he brought his body down hers, touching her as no one ever had. He felt her stiffen as she reached the first crest. But he gave her no time to recover as he traced his lips upward until they found hers.

He saw her eyes widen as he entered her. He wanted

desperately to be gentle. To spare her any pain. But he was beyond control now. There was a beast inside him fighting to be set free. A madness that had taken him over, body, mind and soul.

Erin had anticipated some pain. Instead, all she felt was an even deeper arousal. Driven by a desperate need for more, she surprised him by wrapping herself around him and holding him as tightly as he was holding her. Then she began to move with him, matching him strength for strength.

He could smell roses and gardenias. The perfume filled his lungs, even as he filled himself with her. And he knew that he would never again be able to smell those flowers without being reminded of her. Of this.

"Erin. Erin." He whispered her name like a litany as he began to climb with her, higher and higher.

Together they soared until they seemed to reach the very center of the moon. Then, rocked by a series of shudders, they shattered into tiny fragments and slowly drifted back to earth.

It was a journey unlike any they'd ever known.

"Are you all right?"

They lay, still joined. Hazard thought about rolling aside, but it seemed too much effort. His lips were pressed to her throat. Their bodies were still slick with sheen.

"I'm…fine." That fact amazed her. She hadn't died. Even though, for one brief moment, she'd thought she might. She'd actually felt herself breaking into pieces. Shattering, like fragile crystal. But here she was, whole, and even able to speak coherently.

"Am I too heavy?"

She sighed. "Maybe. I'm not sure." She gave a shaky laugh. "Give me a minute to think about it."

He leaned up on his elbows to stare down into her face. "Can this be Dr. Erin Ryan, the brilliant laboratory researcher, who suddenly can't put together a simple thought?"

"See what you've done to me?"

"This is serious." With a laugh he rolled to one side and drew her into the circle of his arms. He loved the way she seemed to fit so perfectly against him, as though made for him.

She snuggled close, loving the feel of his arms around her. As her heartbeat slowly returned to normal, she gave a long, deep sigh.

At once he glanced at her with a look of alarm. "Are you sure you're all right with this?"

She looked up. "You mean with what we just shared?"

He nodded and felt his heart stop. She was too solemn. Too serious.

She sat up and stared down into his eyes. "I was just thinking how glad I am that I waited. That you were my first."

His heart started beating overtime.

"But I hope you're not sorry, Hazard. I know I'm not very experienced about this…"

"Hey." He tugged on a lock of her hair, and drew her face down for a long, slow kiss. "I know that guys aren't supposed to share their secrets with women. But I'll tell you this much. There's no guy in the world who doesn't love being the first. It makes him feel like Adam at the dawn of creation. Or Tarzan in the jungle."

She started to laugh. "Really? Is that how you're feeling right now?"

"Yeah." He grinned, and her heart did a series of somersaults. "I feel like strutting around and shouting that Dr. Erin Ryan is my woman. And I'm her man."

Her laughter grew. "All right. Strut and shout if you want. But I don't think you'll want to do that out on the range in front of the wranglers."

She leaned down, tracing the mat of dark hair on his chest. Her hair fell forward, veiling her eyes. "It's funny."

"What is?"

She paused a moment, wondering if she ought to tell him what she was thinking. Then she decided to be completely honest. "I thought I'd be embarrassed to be…like this. Naked. But with you, it all seems so natural."

"Yeah. I'm just a natural guy. We ranchers are like that. One with nature." He grinned, then suddenly caught her wrist. "Besides, you're not completely naked. You still have your corsage."

She glanced down in astonishment. She'd completely forgotten about the flowers. Then she looked more closely. "Look at this. Half of one of the gardenias is gone."

He gave her a devilish grin and folded his arms behind his head. "I think I got carried away and ate it."

Their eyes met and she felt a little thrill that shot straight through her.

She touched a finger to his face, tracing the curve of his lips, the arch of his brow. "You were so…"

He wondered if she knew what her touch was doing to him. "So?" he prompted.

"So…sexy."

He felt his body begin to tense. It didn't seem possible that he wanted her again so soon. But he did.

His hand snaked out, his fingers imprisoning her wrist. "That's exactly how I feel right now. So be careful. You keep that up, we'll be right back where we started."

She looked startled. Then a lazy little cat smile touched

the corners of her lips. "Really?" She leaned down, allowing her hair to tickle his chest as she covered his mouth with hers.

"Yeah. Really." He pulled her down on top of him and ran his hands down her back, then up her sides, tracing the fullness of her breasts.

She made a sound in her throat that could have been a purr. Then she wriggled over him until he was fully aroused.

Suddenly he rolled her over and kissed her until they were both breathless. And then, with soft sighs and whispered promises, he took her on a slow, languorous journey. This time, there was none of the storm and thunder and desperation. It was all slow heat and long, lazy caresses. With soft touches and moist, butterfly kisses they drifted on a cloud of contentment, as though they had all the time in the world. And as the heat grew to an inferno and the need built until they were breathless, they took each other to an even higher plane, before settling slowly back to earth.

"Oh. This is great." Erin and Hazard sat in the middle of her bed, sharing wine and pizza.

Erin was wearing her new pajamas. Plain white cotton with white satin piping. She'd left her hair long and loose, but had retrieved her glasses. She looked, Hazard thought, like a completely different person from the one who had arrived, all buttoned up and quivering with nerves, only days ago.

Hazard had pulled on his jeans, but was still barefoot and shirtless. A man completely comfortable with himself and his surroundings. "Yeah. You did a great job of heating this up."

She glanced over. "Are you talking about the pizza or the evening?"

Surprised, he threw back his head and roared. "My, my, Dr. Ryan. Aren't you becoming a wicked woman of the world, all of a sudden."

"All your fault." She picked up another slice and tipped back her head, to catch the dripping cheese. "You've corrupted me. Now you'll just have to live with what you've done."

"Does this mean you're going to come sneaking into my room every night and seduce me?"

She arched a brow. "Hmm. Now that sounds promising. Actually, I thought you might want to come to my room."

"Just try keeping me away." He topped off her glass and then his. "Nice of my brothers to keep the bar stocked." He studied the label of the wine. "I think Ace brought this back from Spain."

"Do you ever travel with them?"

"Once in a while. When it's absolutely necessary. But I prefer to stay here at the ranch. Things just seem to run more smoothly when I'm looking over everybody's shoulder. Peterson and Cody have a handle on things, but they're not the owner, and the other wranglers know it."

"So the chores don't get done the same way as when you're here."

He nodded. "They're good guys, for the most part. But you know the old saying. When the cat's away…" He shrugged. "I'm hard on them at times. Especially during calving. This is a tricky time of year. We're dealing with newborns. With the weather. Snow one day, sunshine the next. With predators. Wolves know this is the best time to have themselves a tasty morsel of helpless calf. And now this new problem."

She touched a hand to his. "I want you to know I'll do everything I can to uncover the cause of these deaths."

He smiled, that wonderful smile that always touched her heart. "I never doubted it." He indicated the pizza. "One more slice."

She shook her head. "I can't."

"Me, neither." He lifted the carton and set it on the night table, then set his glass beside it and reached for hers.

She blinked. "What are you doing?"

"I wouldn't want you to spill red wine on those brand-new pajamas." He moved closer. "Have I told you how adorable you look in them?"

"Adorable?"

"Yeah." He reached for her glasses and set them aside. "You're so cute, I could eat you alive. In fact, I think I might." He reached for her buttons, undoing the first, then the second, all the while watching her eyes as they widened, then began to soften as he slid the top from her shoulders.

"You're not still wearing that corsage, are you?" He nibbled at her neck.

"No. Why?"

"Because." He brought his lips lower, to the sensitive column of her throat. "I can still smell roses. It's on your skin. Here." He nibbled, tasted. "And here."

She gasped and brought a hand to his chest. His heart-beat was thundering.

"Let's see if it's everywhere." With one quick tug he had her out of her clothes and lying beneath him.

He caught her foot in his hand and pressed kisses to her instep, her toes, her ankle. "Yep. The lady even has rosie tosies."

She started to giggle. "Hazard, stop. That tickles."

''Too late. I can't stop now.'' He ran nibbling kisses up the inside of her leg, pausing at her knee, then moving higher, to her thigh, then higher still.

Her giggles stopped, replaced by a gasp.

He lifted his head. ''Would you like me to stop now?''

Her eyes were already glazed with passion. For a moment she wasn't sure she could speak. But she finally managed to lift a hand, then weakly let it drop back to the sheets. ''If you stop now, I'll have to kill you.''

''I'll say this, Dr. Ryan. You're an amazingly quick study.''

He lowered his head. And slowly drove her to the edge of madness and beyond.

Chapter 10

"What are you doing?" Erin awoke to find Hazard staring down at her with almost fierce concentration.

"Watching you sleep."

In fact, he'd been awake for more than an hour, watching while Erin slept in his arms. It had been the most amazing thing to watch. The way her long, pale lashes cast shadows on her cheeks. The way her lips curved in a dreamy smile while some pleasant thought drifted through her mind. The way her hair fell in soft waves, dipping over one eye in a most seductive manner.

It was fascinating to realize that beneath this very soft, very feminine appearance, was a brilliant mind, which, until recently, had known only discipline and order. It had been so satisfying to watch her learn to relax and have fun.

She yawned. "What time is it?"

"I don't know. I never even bothered to look at the clock."

"Don't you have chores to see to?"

"Yeah." But he made no move to get up. "I'll see to them in a while."

She bit her lip. "I'm not sure I can just lie here and be lazy. I've never tried it before." She began to wiggle around.

He frowned. "What are you doing?"

"Looking for my pajamas. I wonder what happened to them."

"I think they went the way of your corsage."

"You mean…?"

He nodded. And shot her a wicked smile. "I think I ate them."

She couldn't help laughing. "What am I going to do with you?"

"You could try kissing me. I've been thinking about nothing else for the past hour."

She leaned over and pressed her mouth to his. At once his arms came around her, molding her to the length of him. She wasn't surprised to discover that he was fully aroused. She'd learned, throughout the night, that it took little more than a touch of the hand or a brush of their lips to start the fire blazing between them.

All night they'd loved, then dozed, then loved again. And each time it was different. At times soft and easy. As though they'd been together for a lifetime. At other times, so hot and fierce they were rocked by the intensity of the passion that flared between them.

"Do you know what I want to do?" he managed to whisper against her mouth.

"I think I have a pretty good idea."

He leaned over her, loving the spark of fire in her eyes. "Oh, Dr. Ryan. You haven't a clue." He ran wet, nibbling kisses across her cheek, along her jaw, before claiming her lips. His fingertips had already begun to weave their magic. "But I'm about to show you."

He cut off the words she was about to say with a kiss so filled with hunger, it robbed her of speech.

And then there was no need for words, as they lost themselves once more in their newly discovered love.

"Would you like to use the shower first?" Erin lay in bed, feeling pleasantly sated. She'd never before spent a morning like this. Of course, she'd never spent a night like the one they'd just shared, either. The thought had laughter bubbling in her throat.

"What's so funny?"

"Us." She shook her head. "Who would have believed this?"

"Yeah." He looked over at her and joined in the laughter. "Maybe it's a good thing we didn't go to our proms all those years ago. Who knows what might have happened?"

She shook her head and sat up, no longer shy about her nakedness. "This never would have happened to me back then."

"Why do you say that?" He reached up and idly twisted a strand of her hair around his finger, loving the silky feel of it against his work-roughened skin.

"Because I believe in fate. And I was fated to wait—" She almost said, *for you.* Instead, she finished lamely, "Until I was ready."

"I'm glad you waited." He drew her head down and kissed her with such tenderness she felt a lump rise to her throat.

To hide the sudden rush of emotions, she scrambled out of bed. "Since you didn't speak up, I'm going to shower first."

She walked away and turned on the taps, then stepped into the shower. A minute later she looked around to see the door open. Hazard stepped inside.

"I missed you." He walked closer, stepping under the spray with her. And as the water poured over them, they came together in a flood of passion that caught them both by surprise.

"I can't believe the mess we made in here." Erin moved around the kitchen, pulling down crepe paper streamers. She was dressed in her new jeans and sweater. Her hair fell in damp tendrils around her shoulders.

Hazard had pulled on a plaid shirt and jeans.

Both of them were barefoot.

The radio was still tuned to the oldies station. Robert Palmer was singing about being addicted to love. It had them both grinning like conspirators.

"We had other things on our minds last night, as I recall." Hazard reached for the glittery ball that hung in the center of the ceiling.

Just then the back door opened and Ace strode in, carrying his briefcase. Behind him was Cody. Both men stopped short and stared around with matching looks of surprise.

Erin froze. Her first thought was to duck out of the room. But she couldn't seem to make her mind and body work in sync. And so she stood perfectly still, while crepe paper streamers trailed from her hands to the ceiling, where they were still taped.

Hazard glowered at his brother. "What're you doing here?"

Ace grinned. "I live here. Remember?"

"I mean today. Weren't you supposed to be gone for a couple of days?"

"Yeah. I got done early. And I always look forward to your warm welcome." He turned to Erin, whose cheeks were bright pink. "Looks like somebody had a party."

"No. I mean, yes. Well, actually…" Her voice trailed off and she turned helplessly to Hazard.

"We had a little…prom here."

"A prom?" Ace's grin widened. "You two?"

"Hell." Hazard reached up and yanked down the glittery ball. "I don't owe you any explanation."

"Nope. That's true." Ace sauntered across the room and tossed his briefcase on the table. When he caught sight of the half-eaten pizza and the empty wine bottle, he arched a brow. "Now that's a new breakfast, even for you, Bro."

"We had it last night."

"Oh. Looks like you forgot to wrap the leftovers." Ace turned. "What'd you have this morning?"

"Nothing yet. We were just getting to it."

Ace lifted his hand and stared pointedly at his watch. "It's almost noon. And Cody tells me you never even bothered to show up for your chores this morning."

"I was a little busy." Hazard turned to the old cowboy. "Thanks for picking up my chores. You can go ahead up to Peterson's. I'll be along later."

"Sure thing, Hazard." Cody cleared his throat. "'Morning, Erin."

She gave him a nervous smile. "Cody."

The old cowboy looked from Erin to Hazard and began whistling a little tune as he walked out.

When he was gone, Ace glanced from Erin to his brother. They were studiously avoiding looking at each other. Erin looked for all the world like a kid with her hand caught in the cookie jar. And Hazard looked as though he'd like nothing better than to engage in a down-and-dirty brawl to clear the air.

"Guess I'll go change." Ace started past Erin, then paused. "I like your hair like that, Doc. You ought to wear it down more often."

"Thank…thank you."

He turned. "I'll be going into Prosperous in a while. You two need anything?"

"Nothing." Hazard's jaw was so tight, the word came out in a snarl.

"Yeah. Well, if you think of something…"

"Ace?"

He turned to his brother. "Yeah?"

"Get out of here."

"I'm going."

"I mean right now. Or I'm going to break you in half."

"Yeah. Sure. I can tell when I'm not wanted." Ace walked away, chuckling.

When they were alone, Hazard looked over at Erin. "Sorry. I never expected him back so soon."

"It's all right. I just feel so—" She looked down at the crepe paper streamers in her hand.

Wanting to comfort her, Hazard crossed the room and put his hands on her shoulders. They were shaking. Alarmed, he caught her by the chin, forcing her to look at him. Instead of the tears he'd anticipated, he saw that she was silently laughing.

Laughing?

Relief poured through him. "You're not mad?"

"Oh, Hazard." She could hardly speak over the laughter that bubbled up and exploded through her. "We looked so silly."

"Yeah. I don't know when I've felt more like a damned fool."

"Two fools," she said, laughing harder.

He threw back his head and roared. "You realize it'll be all over the ranch by tonight."

"It's nobody's fault but ours."

"Yeah."

They laughed harder, until tears actually streamed down their faces. Finally, when they managed to compose themselves, Hazard pressed his lips to her temple. "I guess I'll have to do at least a few of my chores. I can't ask Cody to carry the load alone. Can you finish up in here?"

She nodded.

"All right. I'll see you at dinnertime."

He started away, then returned and kissed her long and slow and deep. "I just needed that to tide me over until tonight."

"Thanks. I needed it, too." She returned the kiss.

He got almost to the door before he turned back and kissed her one more time.

Then he forced himself to walk away. Once outside he leaned against the door and filled his lungs with cold air. Then he started toward the barn. Knowing all the while that what he really wanted to do was go back inside and carry her off to her room. To shut out the world and make mad, passionate love to her all day long.

"Thelma sent some stuff for dinner." Ace walked into the house carrying a huge paper sack.

"What is it?" Hazard looked up from the freezer, where he'd been studying Maggie's neatly labeled meals and wondering how he and Erin would manage to prepare them. He slammed the door with a sigh of relief.

Erin had chosen to set the table, since it was something she thought she could handle without looking too clumsy.

"I don't know. Thel didn't say. Just said she told Slocum to fix us something special." Ace began to sort through the various carry-out cartons. "Hmm. This one's a corned beef on rye. And this is a container of salad. This looks like—" he dipped his finger, tasted "—spaghetti sauce. So I guess this must be—" he opened another "—umm-hmm. Spaghetti." He fished a package from the bottom of the bag. "Bread sticks. Fries. I think she's included everything we ever liked through the years."

"She must know you pretty well." Erin filled glasses with water and placed them on the table.

"Yeah. She was the closest thing to Mom's kitchen when we were growing up." Ace bit into a bread stick. "I think she misses cooking for us now that Maggie's in the family."

"How old were you when you lost your mom?" Erin looked up from her work.

"Five. And Hazard was eight and Chance ten. Seven years later we buried our dad."

Erin glanced from Ace to Chance. "So young. How did you manage to hang on to the ranch after you lost your dad?"

"By sheer hard work." Ace grinned. "I used to goof off at every opportunity. But not Chance and Hazard. They took it seriously. They were old enough to know what they stood to lose." He turned to study his brother, who was filling a coffeemaker with water. "Hazard was the one who kept us in line whenever Chance and I got carried away with our big dreams. He kept reminding us that without the ranch, nothing else would matter. And he was right."

Hazard shot him a quick grin. "Wait a minute. Am I hearing right? Are you actually paying me a compliment?"

"Yeah. And you'd better savor the moment. You may never get another one."

Erin began helping Hazard pour the contents of the various cartons into bowls and platters. When everything was laid out, she said, "Dinner, such as it is, is ready." She glanced around. "What about Cody?"

Just then the old cowboy walked in. "Did I hear my name?"

"You're just in time. Come and eat."

He hung his hat on a peg at the door, then crossed to the big table and took a seat. "What's all this?"

"Carry-out. From the E.Z.Diner." Ace grinned. "Thelma took pity on us because she knew Maggie's away."

"How'd she hear that?"

"She said Hazard and the doc were in for a visit yesterday." Ace sat down and waited for Erin and Hazard to join them before passing the platters and bowls. "Thelma wanted to know how you two enjoyed your pizza on your night alone. I told her it looked like you two enjoyed everything about last night."

Erin glanced at Hazard, then away.

"I didn't tell her about the prom, though."

Hazard started to do a slow burn. "I don't know why not. You'll probably tell everybody else."

"Well, you do have to admit it's not your everyday occurrence."

Cody grinned and busied himself spooning sauce over his spaghetti. These sparring matches between the Wilde brothers were as commonplace to him as the changes in the Wyoming weather. Seeing Erin's look of alarm, he smiled and winked.

At that she sat back and decided to follow the old cowboy's lead. Ace and Hazard could tease each other or even come to blows. Either way, they'd just have to work out their problems between them.

"So, Doc." Ace turned his attention to Erin. "Is my brother a good dancer?"

"The best. He's…very smooth."

"I'll just bet." Ace was having a great time. He couldn't help jabbing just a little harder. "The guys at Clancy's were telling me they heard a request on the radio last night. Some guy named Hazard." He turned up his grin a notch. "Not too many guys named Hazard in these parts. Did you happen to request a Kenny Rogers song last night, Bro?"

Instead of answering, Hazard said, "Clancy's? Wasn't it a little early for a beer?"

"Never too early for a beer. And a chance to look over the field of pool players to see if there were any suckers. Fortunately for you, the place was half empty. Otherwise I'd still be in town. And you two would still be trying to figure out how to open a can of soup." He snatched up a handful of fries. "Now about that request. Was it yours, Hazard?"

"Yeah." Now that he'd polished off a salad and spaghetti, Hazard was feeling more expansive. Besides, he figured, in a couple more hours he could get rid of Ace and Cody and have Erin all to himself again. The mere thought of it had an amazing effect. He sat back sipping coffee and feeling positively mellow. "What's it to you?"

"Nothing." Ace's smile deepened. "Bet I can guess the song."

Hazard returned the smile. "Bet you can't."

"Ten bucks says you're wrong, Bro."

Hazard reached into his pocket and slapped a ten-dollar bill on the table. "You're on."

Ace thought a minute, then said, "'Lady.'"

Hazard's eyes narrowed. "The guys at Clancy's told you."

"Nope." Ace glanced toward Erin. "The song just suits our doc." He snatched up the bill and shoved it into his shirt pocket. "Thanks for the ten spot. I'm sure I can double it tonight at Clancy's." He scraped back his chair and got to his feet. "Think I'll head on back to town now. Maybe you two would care to join me?"

Hazard shook his head, hoping he didn't look too eager at the prospect of seeing his brother leave. "I think Erin and I will just hang out here."

"Sure." Ace managed to keep a straight face. "There's probably a dance step or two you haven't tried yet."

He ignored the look of fury on Hazard's face and turned to the old cowboy, who was struggling not to give in to the laughter that threatened. "How about you, Cody? Feel like spending a couple of hours in town?"

"Might as well." Cody untangled his long legs. "My poker partner, Russ, is off this weekend."

Hazard seemed surprised. "During calving season?"

Cody shrugged. "Russ said Peterson gave him the weekend off because he's been putting in so many hours."

"Where does Russ go when he's not working?" Ace asked casually. "Seems to me he doesn't have anyplace to sleep except the bunkhouse."

"He claims he can always spend a night or two with Beryl Spence."

"Clancy's barmaid?" Surprised, Ace turned to study the old man.

Cody nodded. "That's what he says. 'Course, he could be bragging. But I saw him take off in one of the ranch trucks right after he'd finished his chores."

"What's the matter, Bro?" Hazard taunted. "Were you figuring to add Beryl's name to your little black book?"

"I might have been." Ace shook his head in disgust. "But if she's seeing Russ, I've just lost interest."

"Looks like she lost interest first."

Ace's eyes narrowed. "That's just because she hasn't had a chance to see a real man. A man in his prime."

Hazard saw this as a chance to get back at his brother for the remarks about the prom. "Speaking of prime. If you can't even beat out Russ Thurman, maybe you need to prime that pump."

Ace's temper started to rise. "You'd know all about that, wouldn't you, Bro?"

"I know as much as you."

"Why you arrogant…"

When the first punch was thrown, Cody saw Erin's eyes go wide with fear. He leaned close and muttered, "Don't let the fighting bother you. It doesn't mean a thing. It's always been their way of working through things. When it's over, the air is cleared, and they can get back to looking out for one another."

"Looking out for—" Erin didn't believe a word of it.

She watched in silence as Ace landed a solid blow to Hazard's shoulder, sending him back against the kitchen table. Hazard, in turn, countered with a fist to Ace's jaw that had his head snapping back.

"Not bad, Bro." Ace gingerly touched a hand to his chin. Finding that it was still there, he brought up his fists, deflecting a second blow aimed at his nose.

"Now I'll tell you something." Ace charged, driving Hazard back against the wall. "If I was interested in Beryl Spence, Russ Thurman and the entire crew of wranglers wouldn't be enough to discourage me."

"Yeah, right." Despite the fist in his gut, Hazard managed a laugh before landing a blow to Ace's chest that had him momentarily breathless.

"Had enough?" Hazard stayed where he was, grateful for the break in the action.

"Only if you have." Ace pressed a hand to the back of a chair and took several deep breaths.

After a prolonged silence Hazard nodded, and Ace did the same.

With matching grins they came together, punching each other's shoulders.

"You're not really interested in Beryl, are you?" Hazard asked with a chuckle.

"Not even a little bit. She's nice enough but..." Ace glanced at Erin, then said diplomatically, "She's just not my type. But she's perfect for Russ."

The two brothers laughed as though enjoying a wildly funny joke.

Ace mussed Hazard's hair. "Listen, I've got to run. Sorry about leaving you and Erin all alone tonight."

"Yeah. I bet you are." Hazard slapped him on the back. "I hope you have a successful night at Clancy's. Maybe you'll even triple my ten bucks."

Ace paused at the back door. "You coming, Cody?"

The old cowboy shot a knowing look at Erin. "Yep. I'm right behind you, boy."

As he sauntered away, Erin couldn't suppress the laughter that bubbled up.

Hazard turned. "What's so funny?"

"Nothing." She walked toward him and wrapped her arms around his waist.

"Come on." He pressed his lips to her temple. "What are you laughing at?"

"You and Ace. You really believe fistfights are a sign of affection."

"That's crazy."

"That's what I thought. But that was before I got to know the Wilde brothers." She turned away and gave a sigh of disgust at the littered table. "Come on. Let's see if we can clean up this mess. I know we won't be as good at it as Maggie, but at least we can make this place presentable before we—" She stopped, and glanced back at Hazard.

He was grinning from ear to ear. "Before we what?"

She laughed. "Before we display our own sign of affection."

"Dr. Ryan." He wrapped his arms around her waist and drew her back against him. "I much prefer your way to my brother's way."

He began nibbling her ear. As the heat pulsed through his veins he whispered, "Let's leave this cleanup for later."

He scooped her into his arms and headed for her bedroom. With a sigh of contentment she wrapped her arms around his neck and pressed her lips to his throat. This was one offer she had no intention of refusing.

Chapter 11

"You won't believe this." Hazard paused in the doorway of the lab, where Erin had already resumed testing.

"What?" At the tone of his voice she looked up from the sample she'd been studying under the microscope.

"I just talked to Peterson. So far they've found no dead calves this morning."

"Oh, Hazard." She slid from the stool and rushed toward him. "That's wonderful news."

"Yeah." He absorbed the jolt as she wrapped her arms around his waist and pressed a soft kiss to his mouth. "The day is early. But right now I'll take any good news I can get."

"Maybe the worst is behind us."

He wondered if she realized what she'd just said. Us. It warmed him to think that she already thought of them as a team. That's what they had become. The problem had become theirs instead of his. And the solution, if they found it, would be a victory for both of them.

"Maybe," she whispered against his mouth, "whatever has been killing the newborns has just gone away."

He returned her kiss. "That's a nice fantasy. But the truth is, the deaths were real. And I'm sure we'll have to hear some bad news along with the good. After all, the day is early."

"Maybe. But keep a good thought."

"Yes, Doctor. That's very good advice." He drew away. "I'll leave you to your tests. I think I'm going to head up to Peterson's. Take a look for myself."

She nodded. "I'm just about finished with all the blood work."

He picked up a pen and jotted a number on her notebook. "Here's my cell phone number. Call me if you learn anything."

She nodded and watched as he walked away. Then she returned to her work. She wanted, more than anything in the world, to end this day with even more good news.

"Now, over here…" Peterson's voice trailed off at the sound of the ringing of Hazard's cell phone.

He tugged it out of his pocket. "Yeah?" His smile immediately softened at the sound of Erin's voice on the other end.

Peterson and the wranglers saw the change in his expression and heard the softening in his voice and exchanged knowing looks. It was impossible to keep a secret from this close-knit group. They were, after all, much more than employees. They were a family. And the rumor mill was already working overtime about Hazard Wilde and Dr. Erin Ryan.

Erin's voice came over the phone. "I've decided, before I do any more testing of these specimens, that I ought to have some tissue samples. Not only from some of the dead calves, but from some healthy ones as well, for comparison. Do you think you could bring some?''

Hazard frowned. ''It's a good idea. But I don't have the necessary equipment with me.'' He thought a moment. ''Would you mind leaving the lab for a couple of hours?''

''Of course not.''

''Good. Cody's out in the barn. I'll ring him up and ask him to drive you up here.'' He paused. ''You're sure you don't mind?''

He heard the slight hesitation in her voice before she said, ''I'm sure.''

''Good girl.'' He knew how difficult this was for her. She was at home in the lab. But here in the field, she was completely out of her element. It was a measure of her dedication that she refused to give in to her fear and discomfort.

''I'll see you in an hour or so.''

He disconnected before phoning Cody in the barn. Then he returned his attention to Peterson and the wranglers as they pointed out the newest additions to the herd, as well as those cows close to giving birth. And all the while he marveled at Erin's iron will. She might appear to others to be afraid of her own shadow. He knew better. Beneath that fragile person she showed to the world there was an underlying strength and determination that would put most of these hardened wranglers to shame. It was one more reason why he loved her so.

Love.

The sudden realization caught him by surprise. When had simple lust turned into this? This all-consuming need for her. A need to be with her. To see to her comfort. Her safety. Her peace of mind.

When had he started putting Erin's needs above even his own?

He remembered something his father had once told him, after he found Hazard grieving for his dead mother. "It's easy to say you'd die for someone you love. It's harder, much harder, to live every day for them. The hardest thing I've ever done, Son, is keep going without your mother. But I do it for her. And for you and your brothers. So you'll know that it's possible to live with a broken heart. If I've learned anything in this long, miserable life, it's this. It's not *what* you have in your life but *who* you have that counts. The only thing I want for you, besides this land, is a woman who'll stand beside you and love it as fiercely as you."

Hazard shook his head in wonder, amazed that his father's words had stayed with him all these years. Could it be that Wes Wilde's wish had been granted? Without a doubt Erin Ryan, who had seemed completely unsuited to ranch life, had, in a matter of days, turned his life upside down. Not to mention his heart.

"…think about the idea, Hazard?"

Hazard pulled himself back from his thoughts and realized that Peterson and the wranglers were staring at him.

"Sorry. My mind wandered." He turned to Peterson. "What was that?"

"I asked if you thought we ought to isolate the newborns. That way we could keep them under closer observation."

Hazard shook his head. "It was never my intention to raise a hybrid that needed coddling. We'll let the calves be integrated with the rest of the herd. They either make it, or I'll have to face the fact that they simply aren't worth the effort, and I'll disband the entire project."

He looked up at the sight of Russ Thurman standing with the other men. "I heard you had the weekend off."

"Just an overnighter," Russ said with a grin. "A guy

can only take so much of these ugly critters. Then he's got to get back to civilization and see a pretty face. A female face, if you get my drift.''

Hazard turned to Peterson. ''I'm surprised you could spare a hand during calving season.''

''Russ reminded me that he hadn't had a night off in over a month. In fact, we had a few words about it, before I gave in.''

''The wranglers up on the Tower Ridge haven't had a break in more than three months, and I haven't heard them complain.''

''Maybe that's because you haven't been up there to listen to them.'' Russ spat. ''We can't all live in that big ranch house and have our fill of pretty little doctors whenever we have the urge.''

Hazard's hand was at his throat before he had time to blink. He twisted the wrangler's shirt collar, dragging him close until their faces were inches apart.

Peterson started to step between them. But one glance at the steely look in Hazard's eyes had him stepping back.

''I...didn't mean anything, Boss.'' Russ lifted his arms in a signal of surrender. ''I don't want to fight you. Sometimes my mouth just gets ahead of my brain.''

''The next time it happens, you won't have to worry. You just mention Dr. Ryan's name, I'll bust your jaw so hard, you won't be able to open that mouth ever again. You hear me?''

''Yeah.''

Hazard continued staring down into his eyes for a minute more, before slowly releasing his hold on him. When he stepped back, every man in the group took a deep breath of relief. The Wilde temper was something they'd all witnessed at one time or another. It was a fearsome thing to see. And though Russ Thurman had made more than his share of enemies among the men he worked with, none of them would choose to be in his shoes if he had to fight Hazard Wilde.

"Okay." Through sheer effort, Hazard managed to turn away. He clamped his fists at his sides. "Let's take a look at the new calves. And try to figure out why they survived while so many others didn't."

"Hi, Cody."

Erin came rushing into the kitchen, carrying a satchel filled with necessary supplies. The old cowboy stood in the kitchen, drinking a cup of coffee left over from a pot that Agnes had made that morning. It was thick as mud and nearly as tasty.

Seeing Erin, he dumped the rest down the drain.

"Dr. Ryan." In a courtly gesture he took the satchel from her hands and reached for his hat, hanging on a hook by the back door. "Hazard said I'm to drive you up to Peterson's."

"Yes. I hope this isn't taking you away from too much work."

"I'd never complain about the opportunity to drive a pretty lady somewhere."

He trailed her out the door, then pulled it firmly closed behind him. Outside, the truck was idling.

He helped her into the passenger side, then handed up the satchel before walking around to the driver's side. Moments later they rattled off across the hills.

Erin glanced at his worn, weathered profile. "Have you always lived in Wyoming, Cody?"

"No, ma'am. In my youth I drifted a bit. Worked ranches in Montana, and up into Canada. Alberta, Saskatchewan. But I always had a hankering to come back to Wyoming. There was just something about Wes Wilde and his boys that drew me, I guess.''

''Tell me about them. What was it like when they were just starting out.''

''Wes Wilde lived up to his name. He was a wild one. Hard drinking, hard gambling, hard living. But he was a good man. And he loved those boys of his. And this land. He spent the last years of his life trying to do his best to hold it all together, for their sake. It's probably what ended his life too soon. He was always just one step ahead of his creditors.'' He smiled, and she could tell he was warming to the subject. ''His boys are just like him. They're tough. They live hard. Work hard. Play hard. And they've earned every one of their successes. Nobody handed them anything. They had to go out every day and do things most folks wouldn't or couldn't face up to.''

''Like what?''

He shook his head, remembering. ''I recall one spring. It was calving season. Hazard couldn't have been more'n eighteen or so. He couldn't afford to hire any help. There was just him and Chance and Ace. And whenever we could manage it, Agnes Tallfeather's husband, Louis, and me. We'd work other ranches for pay, then come out here and help for free. We were out on the range about twenty hours, delivering calves. Finally we all fell into our beds. About two hours later Hazard woke up and heard the wind howling. When he looked outside, he realized there was a spring blizzard blowing in. He got dressed and headed back out to the range, herding the cattle toward the south ridge, where there was shelter. He drove back to the barns for hay, then went back out there, spreading the hay in the snow so the cattle wouldn't starve. By the time we got up there the next day to lend a hand, he'd been up around the clock, delivering more calves, keeping the herd together.'' The old cowboy shook his head from side to side. "He looked like—" Realizing he was about to speak a profanity in front of a lady he paused, started over. "He was bleary-eyed and ready to keel over from exhaustion. But he had a grin on his face from one ear to the other. That was probably the worst spring storm in fifty years. And Hazard didn't lose a single calf from it. He was the only rancher in Wyoming who could boast of that. And it was all because of his own hard work and determination.''

"Not to mention good friends like you and Louis Tall-feather.''

He shook his head. "We did what we could. But it was Hazard who kept this ranch going. Nobody else.'' Cody turned to Erin. "Didn't mean to brag on him so much. But he's turned into one fine man. And so have his brothers. I've always figured the measure of a man, when his life is over, is to ask if he'd have made his daddy proud. When it comes to the Wilde brothers, that one's easy. I know old Wes Wilde must be watching and smiling.''

It occurred to Erin that there was another man who shared that pride. And if Cody wasn't their father, he was the next best thing.

She looked up to see Peterson's ranch house coming into view. "Thanks, Cody. For sharing some of their past.''

"You're welcome, Erin. I think it helps to know a man better by seeing how far he's come.''

"Your memories certainly made this a pleasant drive.''

He smiled. "It helped pass the time for me, too. I can't remember when the ride up here was ever this short.''

He brought the truck to a stop and leaned over her to open the door. "I'll be waiting here when you're ready to get back to the house.''

She clutched the satchel and stepped down. "I shouldn't be long."

Erin picked her way among the cattle. Up ahead she could see a cluster of wranglers. Before she was even halfway there, Hazard had separated himself from the others and was striding toward her.

"Sorry you had to come all this way," he muttered as he gathered her against him for a moment.

"I don't mind. And Cody's such a dear."

"Don't let him hear you say that."

"For Heaven's sake, why not?"

He grinned. "It goes against the cowboy code. They want to be thought of as rugged individuals. Cody Bridger would be offended if he learned that you thought of him as dear. So keep such sentiments to yourself."

She laughed. "I'll remember."

He nibbled her temple. "You smell wonderful."

"And you smell like—" she wrinkled her nose "—something unmentionable."

He threw back his head and roared. "I've been up to my knees in cow dung. I promise I'll shower before I come near you again."

As he started to turn away, she caught him by the front of his parka. "Not on your life, cowboy. I don't care how you smell. I just want you to stay close."

He gave her a long, heart-stopping look. "Lady, you just made my day. Now come on. Let's get those tissue samples." As he led the way toward the herd he said, "I hope you remembered the tranquilizers."

She nodded.

He paused beside a couple of calves that had been culled from the herd. "These two seemed like good candidates as donors. I've examined them, and they seem in fine health."

He opened the satchel and withdrew a syringe containing a tranquilizer. In one smooth movement he injected the calf, then watched as it walked a few steps before beginning to stagger. As soon as it crumpled to the ground, Hazard reached into the satchel and took out a surgical knife. Within a matter of minutes, he had secured a tissue sample, which he slipped into a plastic bag. While Erin neatly labeled the contents, he swabbed the area with disinfectant and started on the second calf.

"Hazard." A shout went up from one of the wranglers, and Hazard turned away to hold a whispered conversation with his men. He looked back with an apologetic shrug. "Sorry, Erin. We've got a complication with one of the births." He thrust the satchel into her hands. "Think you can handle this one yourself?"

"Yes. Of course."

As he started away he shouted, "Somebody give Dr. Ryan a hand with that calf."

Russ Thurman stepped away from the others. "I'll give our lady doctor all the help she needs."

Hazard never even heard him. He was already shoving his way through the milling cows.

"Now." Russ shot a stream of tobacco between his front teeth. "You want to administer that tranc? Or would you like me to do it?"

Erin swallowed back her dislike of the man, vowing not to let him get to her again. "I think I can do it."

He shrugged. "Suit yourself. Just what is it you're looking for?"

"Healthy tissue. To compare with that of the calves that died."

"What for?"

"For two reasons. First, to see if I can detect any specific changes in the tissue of the healthy animals, as opposed to those that died."

His eyes narrowed. "And the other reason?"

"It could be that one of the herd is a carrier."

"A carrier?"

"It's just a theory. I want to see if one of the herd harbors a specific pathogen that carries a disease, but shows no sign of that disease."

"You mean, in plain language, like a kid who gives everybody else chicken pox, but never comes down with it himself?"

"Something like that."

"Why didn't you say so?"

She looked at him. "I just did."

"Yeah. I know. All those big, fancy words." He was watching her carefully. Deliberately invading her space. Crowding close enough to smell her. "I guess Hazard likes hearing his fancy lady doctor using all those fancy words. Do you talk to him that way when you're alone? Does that turn him on?"

She gave him a startled look, which very quickly turned to pure ice. "If you don't mind, we'll stick to discussing the herd, or we won't speak at all."

He shrugged. Spat. "Whatever suits your fancy. You're the doctor."

As she filled the syringe and moved toward the calf, he grinned. "Careful. These stupid dogies sometimes like to kick. You might want to avoid her hind feet."

"Thank you."

It occurred to Erin that in all the years she'd been working in a laboratory, she'd never before had to administer a tranquilizer to a living creature. When she pressed the syringe against the animal's hide, it didn't even penetrate.

Instead, it slipped from her hand and fell to the ground. As she started to bend over to pick it up, she saw the calf lift one hoof. With a cry of alarm, she ducked back and lost her footing, landing on her backside in the mud. In that same instant she realized the animal had done no more than sidestep away from her. But Russ's warning had already had the desired effect, planting the seed of fear in her mind.

He squatted down to peer at her. "You gonna pass out on me, lady doctor?"

"No, I'm—" With as much dignity as she could muster she picked up the syringe and got to her feet. "I'm going to tranquilize this animal." She reached into the satchel and began wiping the syringe with a disinfectant.

"Now what're you doing?" Russ demanded.

"Hazard said the animal was healthy. I'd like her to remain that way."

"She's just a dumb critter. Give me that." He snatched the syringe from her hand, but before he could plunge it into the animal's rump Erin caught his wrist.

He looked up in surprise. Then a slow smile spread across his face. He peeled back his lips in an imitation of a smile, revealing teeth stained yellow. "You trying to hold my hand, lady doctor? Hey, no need to go to all that trouble. All you had to do was say so."

"Step back, please." She had to struggle to keep the note of panic from her voice. "I intend to handle this myself."

He gave an exaggerated bow. "By all means. Be my guest. Doctor." He emphasized the word with extreme sarcasm.

It took her three attempts before she managed to plunge the syringe into the animal's rump. Each time, she could feel Russ watching her, thoroughly enjoying her discomfort.

Within minutes the calf began to stagger before dropping to the ground.

Erin steeled herself for what was to come. With her jaw clenched and her palms sweating, she knelt in the muddy snow, ignoring the fact that her jeans were nearly frozen to her skin.

She sliced away a strip of hide. When she'd secured the small tissue samples needed, she placed them in a plastic bag. Once again her hands were trembling so badly, she could hardly write.

Seeing it, Russ grinned and spat another stream of tobacco, watching with smug satisfaction as it landed beside her in the snow.

She looked up at him and could read the amusement in his eyes. After swabbing the cut with disinfectant, she got to her feet, clutching the satchel to her chest for courage.

Just then Hazard came hurrying up. Seeing the look on her face he turned to Russ. "What're you doing here?"

"You wanted somebody to give the doctor a hand with this calf."

"And you naturally volunteered?"

Russ shrugged. Spat. "I didn't see anybody else stepping up."

Hazard didn't bother to keep the anger from his voice. "Go give Peterson a hand. Tell him I'll be along in a minute."

"Sure thing." With a sly look at Erin, he sauntered away.

Hazard touched a hand to her arm. "You okay?"

"I'm fine." She was shivering so violently she could hardly speak over the sound of her chattering teeth.

"You're freezing." He placed an arm around her shoul-

ders and started leading her toward the waiting truck.
"Let's get you out of this cold right away."

She knew it wasn't the weather that had caused this
reaction. It was bad enough to inflict pain on a helpless
animal, in the name of science. Just the simple act of
tranquilizing and then taking tissue had left her trembling.
But the added trauma of dealing with Russ Thurman was
more than she could cope with. It shamed her to admit to
herself that she was such a coward. But whenever she was
around Russ, all she wanted to do was run and hide. And
now, with Hazard's arm around her, she felt safe again.

When they reached the truck, Hazard yanked open the
door and helped her inside, then handed up the satchel.

He looked beyond her to where Cody sat watching in
silence. "Crank up the heat, Cody. And get Erin home
fast."

He turned cool, steady eyes to her. "Forget about the
testing when you get back to the ranch. First thing I want
you to do is get a long, hot bath."

She managed a weak smile. "Yes, sir."

That brought an answering smile to his lips. "I like a
woman who can take orders." He closed the door before
she could reply, then strode quickly away to join the
wranglers.

When he was gone, Erin leaned her head back and gave
a long, deep sigh. For the space of several seconds Cody
watched her. Then he shoved the truck in reverse and
started back to the ranch house.

Chapter 12

"Maggie...Chance." Erin hurried out of the lab at the sound of their voices. "How long have you been back?"

"We got in about an hour ago." Maggie moved aside as Chance and Cody hauled bags and boxes toward their suite of rooms. "Didn't you hear our plane?"

"I guess I was too absorbed in my work." Erin smiled. "I don't hear much of anything when I'm working."

"It must be wonderful to be that much in love with your work."

Finished with his chore, Chance paused beside his wife and gave her a quick kiss. "You obviously haven't seen yourself when you're trying a new recipe. You have that same sort of concentration."

"Do I?" She returned the kiss.

"Speaking of cooking—" Erin laughed "—Ace and Hazard will be as thrilled as I am to hear you're back, Maggie. We've had to make do with carry-outs from the E.Z.Diner while you were gone."

Maggie clutched a hand to her throat in mock distress. "It's a wonder you're all still alive."

"I doubt we'd have survived much longer. Not with the sludge Agnes calls coffee." Erin clapped a hand over her mouth. "I can't believe I just said that. I've been listening to Ace and Hazard too long."

That had Maggie and Chance roaring with laughter.

"It's hard to believe," Chance said between chuckles, "that my brothers and I survived on that stuff all these years."

As they talked they made their way to the kitchen. Once inside, Maggie stared around lovingly. "I think, in honor of our return home, I'll make something special for dinner."

Chance turned away. "That's my cue to excuse myself and call my secretary."

"Coward," Maggie muttered to his retreating back.

When they were alone, Erin settled herself on a kitchen chair. "So, how did you enjoy the trip?"

"It was wonderful." Maggie hauled a large roasting pan from the cupboard. "We ate in so many fine restaurants. I was introduced to several new recipes that I hadn't thought of before. That's always fun. I can't wait to try them out and add my own variations. And we shopped. All over Manhattan. I bought a new saute pan. And a beautiful set of antique cups and saucers we found in a little shop. And an oversize stock pot that I couldn't resist. And a lovely pewter chafing dish. And a set of French cookware that's being shipped. And—'' She stopped when she saw the grin on Erin's face. "What?"

"Is that all you think of? Things to use in the kitchen?"

Maggie broke into peals of laughter. "That's just what Chance asked. But I get really excited when I look at pots and pans. Mmm." She rubbed her hands with glee, then glanced up. "Wouldn't you feel the same way if you were looking at new laboratory equipment?"

Erin nodded. "I'm sure I would. If they stocked such things in department stores. But I thought you'd be more interested in buying jewelry or clothing. Something for yourself, that you can't buy when you're here in Wyoming."

Maggie gave a quick shake of her head. "That's the wonderful thing about living here. I need so little. A warm parka. Some comfortable jeans. Speaking of shopping—" Maggie glanced pointedly at the slim-fitting jeans, the snug little sweater that Erin was wearing "—looks as if you made a trip into Prosperous while I was gone."

"Oh. Yes." Erin glanced down at herself. "I thought I'd been borrowing your things long enough. It was time for some of my own."

"You look different." Maggie studied her with a critical eye.

"You're just used to seeing me in that suit I wore when I first came here."

"Maybe. Or maybe it's the hair."

"Well." Erin could feel the heat staining her cheeks as she scraped back her chair and headed for the door. Was it possible for others to know, just by looking at her, that she was somehow different from the woman she'd been just days ago? "I guess I'd better get back to my work. I'll see you at dinner."

"Yeah. I'll see you." Maggie continued to watch her as she walked away.

There was definitely something different about Erin. But, she thought as she opened the freezer, it was more than the hair or the new clothes.

She was too busy to give it any more thought just now. But when she had more time, she'd figure it out.

* * *

"Maggie, girl, I sure am glad you're back." Cody hung his hat by the back door, then made his way to the table, where the others were just taking their places.

With the return of Maggie and Chance, the ranch house had taken on a festive air. The room was perfumed with the wonderful aroma of herbs and meat roasting. The sinful fragrance of chocolate and hazelnut drifted in heavenly clouds from Maggie's special torte.

"I agree. You don't realize how great Maggie's cooking is until you've had to rely on Thelma's carry-outs." Hazard held a platter so that Erin could help herself to a portion of rib roast.

As an afterthought he spooned garlic and thyme sauce over it. "Wait till you taste this," he whispered.

The first taste had Erin sighing. The second had her closing her eyes in sheer bliss.

"See." Hazard leaned close, until he was almost nuzzling her ear. "It's one of my favorites."

"I see what you mean."

He looked up. Their gazes met. They smiled and continued staring at each other for several long moments. The way they were looking at each other made them oblivious to everyone else in the room.

As Maggie and Chance watched in silence, they turned to each other with matching looks of disbelief and then gradual understanding.

"So." Cody broke the silence. "How was the flight home?"

"You should have seen us loading all those boxes and bags aboard the plane." Chance was shaking his head, while the others around the table merely chuckled. "Our pilot and crew warned Maggie they weren't certain they could get the plane up with all the extra weight."

"I can't believe you were able to buy so much in such a short time." Erin buttered a roll, still hot from the oven.

"That's just the tip of the iceberg." Chance smiled at his wife. "The rest is being shipped."

"The rest?" Ace paused with the fork halfway to his mouth. "What else did you buy, Maggie?"

"Some furniture. A new bedroom set. And a wonderful old antique dining room table and eight chairs." When the others merely stared at her she said sweetly, "We're building a new house, remember?" She calmly looked from Ace to Hazard. "Chance and I thought it would be fun to start with everything new."

"Yeah. Sure." Ace winked at Hazard. "That's what every guy living on a ranch in the middle of Wyoming dreams of at night. New furniture." He shook his head. "Next, Bro, you'll be picking out china patterns and silver service and—"

He saw the look on Chance's face and stopped. Grinned. "No way. You didn't."

Chance shrugged. "There was this great shop on Fifth. We both stopped to look at the window display. And the next thing we knew, we were inside picking out patterns."

"See what happens?" Ace lifted both his hands, palms outward, as if to hold back an advancing army. "Love's like a giant snowball. Once it starts rolling, there's no stopping it. One day the only decision you have to make is whether to stop at Clancy's for a beer or the E.Z.Diner for burgers. Then you find yourself married and thinking about building a house. The next thing you know you're worried about filling it. Not only with furniture, but pretty soon, with kids."

He saw the way Chance and Maggie were looking at each other, and his eyes widened. "You're not..." He tried again. "You wouldn't be having a baby or anything, would you?"

Chance merely grinned while Maggie said, "We've been talking about it."

"Talking." He wiped a hand over his brow. "Well, okay. As long as you're still talking, there's time to reconsider. You might want to think about starting out on a smaller scale. Like maybe a puppy first. Just to see if you're equipped for all that responsibility."

Chance couldn't help laughing at the look on his brother's face. "I know you can't understand this, since you haven't found the woman of your dreams yet. But someday it'll happen, Ace. And when it does, you'll wonder what took you so long. Then you'll find yourself racing ahead, trying to make up for lost time."

"Listen." Ace reached for the platter and helped himself to seconds. "I think it's great for somebody else. It's just not in the cards for me. I am worried, though. I certainly hope whatever's going around this ranch isn't contagious."

"What's that supposed to mean?" Chance watched him over the rim of his cup.

"First you and Maggie. Now Hazard and the doc." He bent to his meal, missing the furious look that came into Hazard's eyes and the color that stained Erin's cheeks. "If you could make a vaccine against love, Doc, I'd be the first one in line for it."

Seeing the way Chance and Maggie were studying her, Erin ducked her head and busied herself stirring cream into her coffee, refusing to meet their eyes.

Cody took pity on her. Clearing his throat he remarked, "Speaking of vaccines, Erin, have you come up with anything in the lab yet?"

"Nothing yet." She swallowed and prayed her voice

wouldn't reveal her utter embarrassment. "But I have some tissue samples now, and I'm hoping to do some cross studies, comparing the healthy tissue to those taken from the dead calves. Something is bound to show up. It's just a matter of carrying out the right tests."

"I don't get it." Maggie frowned. "Why can't you just look into your microscope and pinpoint the problem?"

Erin relaxed, grateful for the distraction. This was a subject she could discuss with ease. Unlike the talk of new homes and new babies.

"If it were just a matter of looking through a scope and detecting illness, medical science would have eliminated all diseases by now.

"Unless you know what you're looking for, and run specific tests designed just for that organism, you're simply operating in a maze."

Chance dropped his fork with a clatter. "You mean, after all the tests you've run, you still don't know any more than when you started?"

"Oh, I've learned a great deal. I know, for instance, that the calves haven't died from any known bacteria or virus. None showed up in their blood. And, so far, their tissue samples have revealed no known organisms that would prove fatal."

"So," Ace said with a grin, "you've eliminated the usual suspects."

"Exactly." She nodded at him. "Now I have to round up some new ones and put them through a lineup."

Ace grinned. "I can see that some of our Wyoming plain speech has finally rubbed off on you, Doc."

"Thank you." She inclined her head. "I'll take that as a compliment."

"You should." Ace winked at Cody. "When you first

came here, I didn't know what you were saying half the time. Now we're almost speaking the same language.''

"Careful," Chance said with a laugh. "This could be dangerous, Erin. If Ace can understand you, you must be losing your touch."

"That's all right. When I first got here, I couldn't understand a thing you said either, Ace." She grinned. "I believe you were talking about eight ball and scratch and running the table. I'm afraid even now I haven't a clue."

Everyone laughed. Even Hazard joined in, hoping that Ace's slip of the tongue had been forgotten. But minutes later he saw the speculative glances from both Maggie and Chance and realized that what he'd been given had been nothing more than a brief reprieve.

He knew that when his older brother got him alone, he'd be grilled mercilessly.

"All right." Chance paused in the doorway of the lab. He'd deliberately waited until Maggie and Erin were occupied with clearing away the dishes before following his brother to his usual hangout. "What's going on here?"

"I don't know what you mean." Hazard busied himself returning a blood sample to the refrigerator.

"I mean about you and the doctor. I leave you alone here for a couple of days and come back to find you acting really weird. Staring into those baby blues. Whispering in her ear. And practically feeding her."

"I wasn't feeding her."

"Only because you knew we were watching. If you'd have been alone with her, I think you'd have devoured her along with your meal."

Hazard's eyes narrowed. "I don't understand what you're hoping to gain from this inquisition. What business is it of yours what I do?"

"In case you've forgotten, Dr. Ryan is a guest in this house. And you were the one who issued the invitation."

Hazard could feel his temper rising. "I haven't forgotten."

"Well then, maybe you've forgotten that in this day and age there are laws against sexual harassment."

"Sexual…" Hazard's anger erupted. He started forward, his hands already balled into fists. "Listen, pal." He grabbed Chance by the throat and forced him against the wall.

Instinctively Chance's hand curled into Hazard's shirt-front, holding him stiffly at bay.

"You think I'm forcing myself on Erin? Is that what you think?" Hazard's eyes were hot with fury.

"I didn't mean…"

"I know exactly what you meant." Hazard tightened his grip on his brother's throat. "You don't think a woman like that could care about a guy like me?"

By bringing up both arms and pushing with all his strength, Chance was able to break his brother's grip. He took a step back and lifted an arm in defense. "Wait a minute. Are you saying…?" He managed to deflect the first blow, as the light began to dawn. "You and the doctor are both…?" The second blow caught him on the jaw, snapping his head back.

He shook his head to clear it, then managed to duck so that the next punch missed him altogether and Hazard's fist pounded into the wall beside him.

With a muttered oath Hazard flexed his fingers as pain shot through his entire arm.

"Maybe I just got lucky and you broke that hand," Chance muttered under his breath. Then, seeing Hazard's reaction, he sidestepped before another punch could be thrown. "Now wait a minute. I didn't realize it was like that between you two. You should have just told me right from the start you were in love.''

''I'm not…we're not…I didn't say—'' Hazard's eyes darkened with a frown.

''You didn't have to. Your punches said it all. You haven't lost your temper that fast since Keith Smedley stole a kiss from that little girl you had a crush on in fourth grade. What was her name? Mary Alice something.''

''Mary Alice Carter.'' Hazard huffed out a breath.

''Yeah. And now it's Dr. Erin Ryan. Who'd have thought? My brother and the little genius.''

Hazard's strong fingers closed around his brother's throat, as he slammed him hard against the wall. ''Don't call her that.''

Chance sucked in a quick breath. ''I didn't mean it as an insult.''

''I don't care. She's not just a brain. She's a person.'' Hazard's fingers tightened for just a moment, before he slowly loosened his grip. Then, aware of just how rough he'd been, he released his hold on Chance and allowed his hands to drop to his sides. ''A wonderful, kind, sensitive person.'' He shook his head in wonder. ''She's the finest woman I've ever known.''

Chance put a hand on his brother's shoulder. ''And you're in love with her.''

''I'm…Yeah.'' Hazard shook his head from side to side, still unable to believe it. Then he lifted his head to meet his brother's eyes. ''I don't know how it happened. But it did. The timing's all wrong—it's calving season, and I've got a crisis on my hands with the herd. But there it is. It can't be helped.''

Chance grinned. ''Love's like that. Just sneaks up and

sucker punches you when you least expect it. But quit looking so miserable. You're supposed to be having fun.''

''I just wish I could spend more time with her.''

''I know the feeling.'' Chance watched as Hazard crossed his arms over his chest and leaned morosely against the wall. ''But calving season won't last forever. And neither will this crisis. Between the two of you, you'll figure it all out.''

''You think so, huh?'' Hazard looked up.

''Yeah.'' Chance brightened. ''Know what you need?''

''What?''

''A night at Clancy's.''

''You mean with you and Ace?''

''Yeah. And Cody. We'll have a few beers. A few laughs. And tomorrow we'll be ready to deal with reality. What do you say?''

Hazard thought a moment, then shook his head. ''I'd rather stay here. Give Erin a hand in the lab.''

''Uh-huh.'' The corners of Chance's mouth curved into a smile. ''Now I realize just how serious this is. When you'd rather spend a night studying drops of blood and bits of tissue under a microscope than tipping a few at Clancy's, I've got to worry. It looks like there's no hope for you now. Come on. You can pry your little doctor away from kitchen duties and steal her away to the privacy of your lab. I'll finish up the dishes with my bride.''

''And you think I'm crazy. How about you? Ever since Maggie came into your life, you've been getting your kicks doing dishes.''

''Yeah.'' Chance's smile grew. ''But it's what we do after the dishes are put away that really makes me happy.''

Chuckling, the two brothers draped their arms around each other's shoulders and headed toward the kitchen, where the sound of feminine laughter lifted their spirits even higher.

"Do you miss Chicago?" Erin began to carry the dirty dishes from the table to the sink.

"So far I haven't." Maggie loaded them into the dishwasher, then turned on the taps and poured liquid detergent before settling the first of the pots and pans in the hot water. "I thought I would. But it just hasn't happened. Maybe because there's so much that's new and exciting here in Wyoming. And maybe because I didn't leave any family behind. Chance and his brothers have become my whole world." She turned to Erin. "How about you? Are you missing your family in Boston?"

Erin shook her head and reached for a towel. "Not at all. It's strange. The minute my plane left Logan Airport, I felt—" she shook her head, wondering how to explain the almost heady sense of exhilaration "—like a caged bird that had been suddenly set free."

"Really?" Maggie turned to her. "Still, it had to be a little frightening."

Erin nodded. "I wasn't certain I was heading in the right direction. I wasn't even certain my wings would work. But I knew I had to strike out blindly and see if I could really fly."

"Good for you." Maggie rinsed the first pot and handed it to Erin.

"Could I..." Erin paused, then decided to take the plunge. "Could I ask you something, Maggie?"

"Sure." Maggie washed a second pot, rinsed it, then set it on the counter.

"Did you know, the minute you met Chance, that he was the man you'd like to spend the rest of your life with?"

Maggie laughed. "Erin, the first time Chance and I met, I mistook him for an intruder. He was bearded, carrying a rifle and looked like some kind of wild mountain man. I attacked him with a butcher knife."

Erin pressed a hand to her mouth. "What did he do?"

"He managed to disarm me without breaking my neck, though I think he would have liked to. I must say, we didn't make a favorable impression on each other."

"How long did it take before you warmed to each other?"

Maggie's hands stilled. A slow smile crept into her eyes. "I couldn't pinpoint the exact moment. I think it took us awhile before extreme dislike turned to acceptance, and acceptance turned to trust, and trust finally turned to love."

"How did you know—" This one was harder to ask. But Erin forced herself to speak quickly, before she lost her nerve. "How did you know it was love, and not merely lust?"

Maggie turned. Erin's attention was fixed on the pot in her hand, which she continued to dry over and over.

"When Chance became more important to me than my own life." Maggie's voice lowered with feeling. "I would have gladly taken a bullet for him, rather than see him hurt."

Erin looked up. "You're so brave, Maggie. I wish—"

Maggie touched a hand to her shoulder. "What do you wish?"

Erin shook her head and looked away. "I wish I could be half as brave as you. When you mistook Chance for an intruder, you attacked him. If it had been me, I'd have probably fainted."

Maggie placed a hand under Erin's chin and forced her head up. "Now, why do you say that?"

"Because it's true. That's what I did the first time I met Hazard. Fainted dead away. And every time I think about it I get so embarrassed."

"Then don't think about it." Maggie closed her wet hands over Erin's. Squeezed. "We all do things that come back to embarrass us. That's part of living. When that happens, we just have to develop a sense of humor about it."

"Do you mean you and Chance can laugh about your first meeting?"

"Absolutely. He still loves teasing me about it. And I do have to admit, it makes me giggle every time he reminds me. So, Erin, stop fretting about what happened in the past. Instead, just enjoy the moment."

"Enjoy the moment." Erin met Maggie's smile with one of her own. "I like that." Then, without thinking, she threw her arms around Maggie's neck. "Thanks, Maggie. I never had a sister. And I can't imagine talking to my mother like this."

"Hey. Anytime." Maggie patted her shoulder. "And anytime you want a laugh, just ask Chance about the morning he met his new cook."

The two young women were still laughing when the door opened and Chance and Hazard came in.

Chance crossed the room and took the towel from Erin's hands.

"What are you doing?" She reached for it. "I'm not finished yet."

"Oh, yes you are, Doctor. My brother needs your help in the lab. Besides, I haven't been alone with my wife for a couple of hours now. So go on. Both of you."

Erin walked to the doorway, where Hazard was waiting. As she followed him out of the room, she caught a glimpse of Maggie and Chance, locked in an embrace.

Seeing it, Hazard leaned close to whisper, "Let's leave the lab work for morning. You've already put in too many hours."

"But what about tonight?"

He shot her a wicked smile. "I just came up with a better idea."

Chapter 13

"**A**h." Ace breathed deeply as he walked into the kitchen. "I smell real coffee. And is that—?" he leaned over Maggie's shoulder "—real food?"

Maggie shot him a glance. "As opposed to what?"

"The sewer water Agnes passes off as coffee." He touched a hand to his heart in mock distress. "And the leftovers from the E.Z.Diner's carry-outs we affectionately refer to as breakfast."

"I'd like to know what you and Hazard are going to do when I move into my own home." Maggie flipped a stack of light-as-air pancakes onto a platter.

"Be careful, Maggie," Erin said with a laugh. "Given Ace's and Hazard's appetites, you and Chance might find yourselves with a couple of unwanted boarders."

Ace grinned. "Or we could just kidnap her and force her to cook us a lifetime supply of meals before we release her."

"I think your big brother might have something to say

about that.'' Cody ambled in from the barn and hung his hat by the door before making his way to the table.

''I don't think he's big enough to take on both of us.'' Ace downed his glass of juice in one long swallow.

''Don't start feeling too frisky.'' Chance brushed a kiss over his wife's cheek, then helped himself to a cup of coffee. ''There are some things a man's willing to fight for.''

''Such as?'' Ace prompted.

''For one thing, good loving. And for another, good cooking. With Maggie, I caught the prize. So watch it. Try to kidnap my woman, I'd have to fight you both.''

They were still laughing when the phone rang. Hazard picked it up and listened in silence.

From her place at the table, Erin saw the frown line between his brows suddenly deepen. His mouth tightened into a tight line.

''Thanks, Peterson. Yeah. I'll be up there right away.'' He slammed down the receiver and turned away.

There was no need to ask. Everyone could see that the news had been grim. It could only mean more dead calves.

''How many this time?'' Ace watched as Hazard picked up his coffee cup and drained it.

''They've counted seven so far.'' He touched a hand to Erin's shoulder, and she closed a hand over his, wishing she could offer more than a touch.

''There could be more.'' Hazard turned to Cody. ''I'd like to get up to Peterson's right away.''

''Sure thing, Hazard.'' The old cowboy stuffed a last bite of pancake and sausage into his mouth, then walked to the door, where he retrieved his hat.

Hazard squeezed Erin's shoulder before turning away. He took a ring of keys from a peg beside the door and was still slipping into his parka as he made his way to the truck.

In the silence that followed, Erin pushed away from the table. "Excuse me."

As she started to leave the kitchen, Maggie glanced at her plate. "Erin, you didn't eat a thing."

"I'm not hungry. I just want to get to the lab."

"But you—" Before Maggie could issue a further protest, Chance closed his hand over hers.

He looked at Erin and could see the anguish in her eyes. "We understand. Go ahead."

She nodded.

"Erin," Maggie called. "If it won't interrupt your work, I'd like to drop by later with a snack."

"Thanks." She tried to smile, but her lips merely trembled. "I'd appreciate that."

Then she was gone. Racing along the hallway until she made her way to the one place where she could be of some use.

Erin pored over her notes all morning and into the afternoon. There had to be something she was missing. Some tiny clue that would link these deaths. She thought back to some of the tough cases she'd dealt with. There had been a parasite that had nearly decimated an entire herd before she'd identified it, and it was found breeding in the pond that was used as the herd's water supply. And then there was the new strain of virus that had been passed from a herd of deer to a nearby rancher's cattle. That had taken hours of lab work to identify. But none had challenged her like this one. She ran a hand through her hair in frustration. What good was this brain she'd been given if she couldn't use it to help the man she loved?

She took a deep breath. Maybe that was part of the

problem. She'd become so intimately involved in this, she was allowing her emotions to get in the way. She needed to take a step back. To think clearly. Like a researcher and not like a lover.

She stood, rolling her shoulders. She caught sight of the lunch Maggie had so generously brought to her. The soup was now cold. The salad wilted. She'd forgotten to take even one sip from the pot of tea.

As she moved around the room she pressed her fingers to her temples, willing herself to think. Something was killing those calves. Not a predator, Hazard said. They'd died a bloodless death. And that put the mystery squarely in her hands. This was her area of expertise. What she'd been trained for. The work she'd always carried out with such pride. Except that, in this case, she couldn't find any logical reason for these deaths. The serum samples looked normal. As did the preliminary testing on the tissue samples.

She stopped. Turned around. Paced the other way.

Think, she commanded. Something was missing. What was it? What was she overlooking?

Sometimes the path was clear from the beginning, and all it took was a confirmation of facts. At other times a researcher merely stumbled on the answer by accident. And then there were those times when every road seemed to lead to a dead end. When every question merely presented another and another. Then a researcher had to be reminded of the necessary components that led to a logical conclusion. The pathway was always the same. Through patience and persistence.

She went back to the microscope. Peered again at the tiny sample of tissue. And began jotting in her notebook.

"Okay, Doctor. Time to call it a day."

Erin looked up in surprise. The light outside the windows had faded to dusk. Hazard stood in the doorway of the lab, wearing clean denims and a plaid shirt. Drops of water from the shower still glistened in his dark hair.

"I can't stop yet. I have one more test to run on this sample."

"No more tests." He crossed the room and turned her stool around until she was facing him. Then he slipped off her glasses and lowered his mouth to hers, lingering over the sweet, clean taste of her. He was still pleasantly surprised each time he felt that little jolt to his system. "Mmm. Thanks." He took the kiss deeper. "I needed that."

"So did I." She looked up as he straightened. "Bad day?"

He nodded.

"What was the final tally?"

"Nine calves dead. All in a cluster. They looked like dominoes that had fallen, one after the other." He glanced beyond her to where the forgotten lunch had now become a congealed blob. "I'll bet you haven't eaten a thing today."

She shrugged. "I forgot."

"Yeah. I know how that is."

She touched a hand to his cheek. His eyes, she noted, looked weary. "Didn't you eat anything, either?"

"No time. But I will now. Come on. It's dinnertime."

"Tell Maggie I'll be a little late."

"Maggie isn't making dinner tonight."

Erin arched a brow. "Is she sick?"

"Nope." He gave a dry laugh. "My brothers and I have decided we all need a change of scenery. So we're taking you and Maggie into town."

"Maggie's going to eat at the E.Z.Diner?"

"Even worse." He collected the samples and placed them in their containers, then set them in the refrigerator. Then he returned to help her off the stool, linking his fingers with hers.

As they headed toward the door he said, "We're going to entertain you with the local color at Clancy's."

She paused. "Should I clean up first?"

He laughed. "If anything, you should probably try to look a bit more rumpled. In those brand-new jeans you'll be the best-dressed woman in the place."

Ace held the door. "Brace yourselves, ladies. This is the last breath of fresh air you'll breathe until you leave Clancy's."

Erin and Maggie stepped inside and glanced around, trying to see through the pall of smoke. It was a big square room with a long, narrow bar that ran the length of one wall. Scattered around the room were scarred wooden tables and chairs, some small and intimate enough for a couple, others shoved together for a party of ten or more. In the middle of the room were the pool tables. Eight of them, with a hanging lamp over each. Country music blasted from a jukebox. Waylon was wailing about lost love in a small town.

"Are there any other women in here?" Maggie studied the row of men at the bar sipping their drinks and talking among themselves. "Or are we the only ones crazy enough to be dragged inside?"

"It's pretty much a guy place." Ace sauntered inside, as comfortable as if he were in his own home.

"Which usually guarantees that there will be women here before the night is over," Chance muttered. "That is, if they want to see their men." He looked toward the bar and paused. "Hey, Hazard, isn't that Russ Thurman?"

Hazard frowned. Without a word he strode forward while the others remained by the door. He stopped behind the row of bar stools.

"Russ."

The man turned. His lips curved into a sly grin. "Hey, Boss. Didn't expect to see you here."

"I bet you didn't. I thought I spotted one of the ranch trucks parked out front. What're you doing in town?"

"Just taking a little break."

Hazard's eyes narrowed. "How little?"

"An hour or two. A quick supper and a chance to look at something prettier than all those damned cows."

"Who's handling your chores?"

The man shrugged and took a long pull on his beer. "Cody and the others will cover for me. I do the same for them sometimes."

"What time are you planning on heading back?"

"Soon as I wash the taste of manure out of my system." Russ set his empty beer bottle down on the counter and shot Hazard a challenging look. "You got a problem with that?"

"Just see that you carry your share of the load."

Thurman's voice deepened with anger. "I don't need you to tell me how to work."

"Somebody better. Did you clear this absence with Peterson?"

"Don't worry about Peterson. He knows enough to give me some room." He glanced toward the door. "I see you brought the fancy doctor. Looks like you two are getting pretty cozy."

When Hazard didn't respond he grinned. "Wouldn't have thought she'd care much for the nightlife of Prosperous. Looks more like the opera and ballet type to me.

That's probably where she'll be dragging you soon enough.''

Without a word Hazard turned his back and walked to where the others were waiting.

"Come on." He put a hand beneath Erin's elbow and steered her toward a table at the far end of the room, putting as much distance as possible between them and the men at the bar.

"I don't know why you keep Russ on," Chance muttered under his breath. "He's the laziest son of a—" He glanced at Maggie and Erin and finished, "He'll find any excuse to avoid working."

"I know. But it's calving season. I need every hand I can get. Even one as lazy as Thurman."

Erin squeezed his hand, and he forced himself to put his anger aside.

Ace trailed slowly behind the others, carefully looking over the pool players as he passed each table. They called out greetings, which he cheerfully returned.

As he took his seat Chance grinned. "Looking over potential suckers?"

"Yeah. And I think I've already found one." Ace nodded toward the lanky cowboy sporting a straggly red beard. "Cole Benson fancies himself a pool hustler. I'll let him believe that for a while longer, before I relieve him of his money."

The minute they were seated, a young woman in tight, faded jeans and a midriff-baring T-shirt hurried over to take their orders. She'd tried to tame her curly blond hair by tying it back into a wild ponytail. It looked as though it had just come through a wind tunnel.

"Hi, Chance. Hazard." She smiled at each of them in turn, but saved her biggest smile for Ace. "I didn't expect to see you in here tonight, Ace."

"It was a surprise to me, too. Beryl Spence, this is my sister-in-law, Maggie, and a friend of ours, Dr. Erin Ryan."

"Ladies." Beryl gave them each a friendly nod. "What can I bring you?"

Ace turned to Maggie and Erin. "I recommend something that comes in a bottle. Beer, preferably. Or soda."

They settled on five long-necks, and by the time Beryl returned with a tray of drinks, they had been persuaded by Ace that the only thing on the menu that was edible was the daily special.

"At least," he warned them, "you'll know it was made fresh today. There's no telling how old the rest of this stuff is."

Maggie wrinkled her nose.

Erin kept her thoughts to herself.

"So, Beryl." Ace looked up as she set their drinks in front of them. "What's today's special?"

"Chili."

"Have you tasted it?" Chance asked.

"Yep." She nodded. "Had some just before I started work."

"Is it hot?" Maggie asked dubiously.

"Hot enough that it almost blew the top of my head off. In fact, look what it did to my hair." The young waitress laughed goodnaturedly at her little joke, and the others joined in.

"Okay," Ace said. "That's good enough for me. I'll have a big bowl."

"Make it two," Chance said.

Hazard nodded. "Three." He turned. "How about you, Erin?"

She nodded. "I could use a little curl in my hair."

They laughed as they looked toward Maggie, who had

taken the time to read every item on the menu. Twice. She looked up. Sighed in resignation. "Yeah. Why not? Chili."

Beryl walked away, calling out their order to the cook who was frying burgers on a grill behind the bar.

"So this is the famous Clancy's." Maggie leaned back and took a long look around. "I just don't understand the attraction, Ace."

He shrugged, his gaze still fastened on the cowboy who was chalking his cue stick. "I guess it doesn't make any sense to anyone else. But it's been my second home since I was old enough to drink and gamble."

"You mean before you were 'legally' old enough," Chance said with a laugh. "I remember getting a call from Clancy when you were only in ninth grade. He'd tossed you out on your rear after you'd hustled a couple of cowboys out of their paychecks. He ordered you to stay out until you were old enough to drink."

Ace chuckled, remembering. "It was easier to hustle when I was younger. Everybody was eager to relieve me of my money. They couldn't believe a kid could beat them."

"And the hell of it is, you always won." Chance grinned at his brother over the edge of his bottle. "Even when you were too young to shave, you were already a whiz on a pool table."

"I come by it naturally." Ace assumed an air of false modesty. "I learned at my daddy's knee."

"Do you remember the first time you beat Dad?" Hazard sat forward in his chair. "I think you were about ten."

"Nine." Ace laughed. "We had that beat-up old three-legged pool table that Clancy had thrown away. Dad brought it home and stuck it in the middle of the great room.''

"Yeah." Chance smiled, remembering. "He put a stack of books under it until it was level. And then after supper he'd challenge us to play him for quarters.''

"That's how he managed to get us to work the ranch without ever having to pay us," Hazard said. "We always owed him a bundle by payday.''

Chance and Ace nodded.

"The first time you beat him," Hazard mused aloud, "Dad thought it was a great joke. But when you started beating him regularly, I could see that he didn't know whether to be proud of your skill or mad that he'd lost his touch.''

"The first time I won more on a pool hustle than I could earn doing ranch chores, Dad realized he'd created a monster. After that there was no stopping me." Ace kept one eye on the pool tables, watching all the different games in progress. Even when Beryl sidled up to their table with their dinner on a tray and leaned over him to pass around the food, he saw only the winners and losers of the various games.

"Here it is, folks." Beryl passed around big bowls of steaming chili, topped with cheese and onions. In the middle of the table she placed a basket of crackers and a heaping platter of chili-covered fries.

"You might want to bring us a pitcher of ice water and some glasses," Hazard suggested. "In case this chili is as hot as you described.''

"Sure thing." She walked away and returned minutes later with ice water.

Erin took her first taste and felt her eyes glaze over.

"How is it?" Hazard asked.

"It's—" she grabbed the glass and took several long gulps before managing to whisper "—very spicy."

Across the table Maggie was determined to choke down the food if it killed her, which, she feared, it might very well do. She was pleasantly surprised when she had her first taste.

"Well?" Chance demanded.

She smiled. "It's really good."

"See?" Ace's bowl was already half-empty. "And you guys thought I only came here to hustle pool."

The others burst into laughter.

"Ace," Hazard said matter-of-factly, "try that con on somebody else. We know you too well, remember? The truth is, if Clancy hired Agnes to cook, you'd still come here. You can't stay away."

"Maybe." He polished off the last of his chili and signaled Beryl for another. "At least I'd still be here challenging the pool players. But I think I'd draw the line on eating here if Agnes was doing the cooking."

"Ah, well," Hazard said with a smile, "there's always Thelma's brand of poison down the street at the E.Z.Diner."

"That reminds me." Maggie turned to Chance. "I have to stop by and have a visit with Thel before we go back to the ranch. It would be unforgivable to be this close and not take the time to see how she's doing."

He nodded. "Okay. As soon as we're finished eating, we'll have coffee and pie with Thelma." He looked over at Hazard and Erin. "Want to join us?"

Hazard shrugged. "Let's just see how the evening goes." He could see Erin staring around with a look of pure fascination. It occurred to him that she had probably never been in a bar before. At least not one as rough as Clancy's.

"So?" He pulled his chair closer and dropped an arm around her shoulders. "What do you think?"

"It looks pretty much the way I expected. Maybe a little darker. Certainly a lot smokier. But the music is good. And everybody seems to be having a good time."

"So you don't mind staying awhile?"

"I think I'd like to see if Ace can beat that cowboy."

"Not 'if,' doc." Ace was already digging through his second bowl of chili. "It's a foregone conclusion that I'll beat him."

Chance groaned and caught his wife's hand. "Come on, Maggie. It's getting thick in here. Let's go visit Thelma."

"You'll be sorry." Ace shoved the empty bowl aside. "Maggie, you'll miss seeing the master make his moves."

With a snort of laughter Chance turned to Hazard and Erin. "When you two get tired of watching the hotshot do his thing, come on down the street and join us at the diner."

Chance and Maggie strolled out arm in arm.

Ace watched his brother with a frown, then turned to Hazard. "Okay. I'm fortified now. I think it's time to issue a challenge."

As he sauntered toward the pool tables, Erin snuggled closer to Hazard. "He's really cute."

"Cute?" Hazard shot her a look of disgust. "When he was a kid, he was a royal pain in the—" He caught himself and said simply, "It's a good thing he was successful in the mining business. Otherwise, Chance and I are convinced he'd have become a professional pool hustler."

Her eyes widened. "You're joking."

He shook his head. "Think about it. Mining is really just gambling, but on a bigger scale. Instead of risking a couple thousand, you risk a couple million. And that suits

Ace perfectly. The higher the stakes, the more his adrenaline pumps.''

They watched as Ace spoke to the cowboy. Minutes later a new game was started. Ace and his opponent were chalking their sticks and studying the balls, while the guys at the bar gathered around to watch.

On the fringes of the group, Russ Thurman was making bets of his own.

Within minutes Ace missed a crucial shot. With a look of triumph the cowboy sank the ball, then went on to run the table. With a great show of reluctance, Ace reached into his pocket and removed a bill.

Behind him, Russ Thurman was forced to pay off his debts. His face mirrored his disgust.

Erin turned to Hazard with a look of surprise. ''Ace lost? I thought he was good at this game?''

Hazard merely smiled. ''He is. But he can't make it look too easy, or in a town this size, he'd soon run out of opponents. So he has to lose often enough that they'll come back for more.''

''You mean he lost on purpose?''

Hazard nodded. ''Now watch what happens.''

While they watched, Ace started to walk away. The cowboy called after him and pulled some money out of his pocket.

''I'll give you one more chance, Wilde. Double or nothing,'' the cowboy challenged.

Ace glanced over at Erin and winked before turning to face his opponent. ''Well, why not?'' With absolutely no expression he reached into his pocket and matched the cowboy's money.

The men behind him made bets of their own. Russ held back, trying to decide whether to risk any more of his paycheck. Finally he nodded and came out of his pocket with another bill.

Minutes later the second game ended much like the first, with Cole Benson winning.

As Ace started away, Benson was grinning with self-importance. "Sorry about that. How about another game? This time for some real money."

Ace paused. "How much?"

Cole Benson shrugged. "How much you got?"

Ace pulled a bill out of his pocket. "All I've got left is this hundred."

"Okay." Benson matched it.

The two men chalked their sticks. This time, when Benson missed a shot, he moved aside to watch in open-mouthed surprise as Ace ran the table, dropping every ball in sequence. His opponent never even had the chance to make another shot.

"Thanks, pal." Ace picked up the two hundred dollars and stuffed them in his pocket before returning to the table.

One lucky cowboy gave a hoot of laughter as he began collecting from those who had bet against Ace. Among the unhappy losers was Russ Thurman, who slapped his money down, then stormed out of the bar with a look of seething fury.

At their table Ace turned a chair around and straddled it. "So? What'd you think, Doc?"

She shook her head. "Hazard said you lost that first game on purpose."

"And the second." He chuckled. "It's all part of the con. Now you've seen the game of eight ball. And you've seen my opponent scratch, and you've watched me run the table."

"Thanks for the lesson."

"You're welcome. A hustler has to have a certain finesse." He waved a hand. "You know. Some smooth moves."

His hand swept the long-neck on the table, sending it toppling over, spilling beer down Erin's sweater and jeans.

"Oh." She scooted her chair back, but it was too late. Beer spread across her stomach and trickled down one leg.

"Hey, I'm really sorry." Ace jumped up and grabbed a paper napkin, then, with a flush of embarrassment, pressed it into her hand.

"It doesn't matter. I'll clean it up in the ladies' room."

As she walked away, Hazard slapped his brother on the shoulder. "Yeah. Now that was some finesse, Bro. Really smooth moves." To Erin he called, "We'll wait for you by the door."

She made her way past the bar, then opened the door marked Ladies. Inside she nearly bumped into Beryl Spence, who was standing in front of the sink. When she looked closer she realized Beryl was gripping the edge of the sink with such force her knuckles were white. Despite her pallor, she was sweating.

Erin paused beside her. "Are you sick?"

"No. I just—" The young woman sucked in a breath. "I need my insulin. I started feeling weak and came in here to give myself an injection. But I can't find my syringe."

"Where is it?"

Beryl shrugged. "I thought it was in that duffel bag." She pointed to the canvas bag resting on the floor by her feet. "But I just checked, and it's not here."

Erin dropped to her knees and began rummaging through the bag. "Do you carry a spare?"

The young woman nodded. "In my purse. It's locked up in the liquor room. Ask Benny. He's the guy behind the bar. He'll get it for you."

Erin made her way to the back of the bar and approached the man who was both cook and bartender. "Beryl sent me out here for her purse."

He nodded and disappeared in a back room, returning minutes later with a navy backpack. Erin carried it into the ladies' room and handed it to Beryl. By this time the young barmaid was bathed in sweat.

With trembling fingers she opened her purse and took out the syringe. With the ease of one who had been doing this for a lifetime, she measured the amount of insulin, then pressed the needle to her arm and pushed the plunger. Then she leaned against the wall and waited, knowing the weakness would soon pass.

"Are you all right?" Erin hesitated, reluctant to leave her alone.

"I'm fine. Thanks a lot. I really appreciate your help." Beryl gave a shaky laugh. "I know better than to let it go like that. But I got busy. And then I figured I'd just duck in here and give myself an injection. When I couldn't find my syringe, I got a little panicky. Sorry for the case of nerves."

Erin touched a hand to her arm. "No need to apologize. I'd be shaky, too, if I couldn't find something as vital as insulin." She paused. "Have you had this all your life?"

Beryl nodded. "I was diagnosed with diabetes when I was just a kid. But I'm one of the lucky ones. I take good care of myself. Don't drink. And don't usually eat the wrong things, like I did today." She shook her head. "But I'm really starting to get forgetful. I'd have sworn I had my insulin and syringe in this duffel. It's been happening to me a lot lately. Not very smart, when you consider how important it is to me." She drew in a deep breath and picked up the duffel bag, slinging it over her shoulder. "Got to get back to work. Thanks again."

"You're welcome. I'm glad I chose this minute to come in here." Erin glanced down at her jeans and realized she'd completely forgotten about the spill.

She shrugged. It had already begun to dry. She would just toss everything into the washer when she got back to the ranch.

As she stepped out of the ladies' room she saw Beryl hang the duffel on a hook beside the bar, before heading to the back room to lock up her purse.

Then she saw Hazard waiting for her at the door. Their gazes met and held. And as she walked toward him her mind seemed to empty. Her body warmed the moment his hand touched hers. And as they walked out into the night, she felt a ripple of pleasure at the thought of what they would share this night when they returned to the ranch.

Chapter 14

"Hey, Cody." Ace looked up from the breakfast table as the old cowboy came in from the barn. "You missed my performance at Clancy's last night."

"Who was the victim this time?" Cody hung his hat and made his way to the table.

Maggie passed him a platter of steak and eggs.

"Cole Benson. Been helping out at the Marshall place during calving season."

"Long way from home. How much did you win from him?" Cody cradled the mug of hot coffee between both his hands.

"A hundred. But I had to spend thirty before I could reel him in."

Cody shook his head. "You've got some smooth moves, son."

"Yeah." Hazard chuckled. "Ace is so smooth he spilled beer all over Erin."

"There was no damage done." She sipped her juice.

"I tossed everything in the washer and dryer when we came home last night, and they're as good as new this morning."

They looked up when the phone rang. As Hazard crossed the room, everyone fell silent.

"Yeah?" He listened, then frowned. "Cody and I will be right there."

He slammed down the receiver.

"How many?" Chance asked.

"The most yet. More than a dozen. And the count isn't complete." He strode to the door. "Come on, Cody. Let's roll."

The old cowboy gave a last glance at his half-finished breakfast, then shoved away from the table.

When they were gone, Ace tossed down his napkin and swore. "That herd means the world to Hazard. He's been busting his—" he glanced at Erin and Maggie and finished "—hide for more than a year now. He was so sure it was the way to go in the future. And now it's all falling apart."

Chance nodded and pushed aside his food. "What the hell is causing all those calves to die?"

They both glanced at Erin. She shook her head. "I came here thinking this would be a simple problem, with a simple solution. And I haven't been any help at all." She pushed away from the table. "Thanks for breakfast, Maggie. I have to get to the lab."

While the others watched, she hurried away.

"Erin?" Maggie poked her head in the lab.

Erin looked up from her notes.

"Ace took the helicopter over to WildeMining. He'll be gone for the day. Chance and I are driving up to Tower

Ridge to meet with the architect and builder. We'll be home in time for dinner.''

"Okay.'' Erin nodded idly as she returned her attention to the specimen under the scope.

She was only vaguely aware of the sound of doors opening and closing. Of the sound of Agnes's TV game show on in the background as the old woman went about cleaning the various rooms.

As she studied the patterns of blood under the scope, she found herself thinking about Beryl Spence, pressing the syringe to her arm. Of her gradual gain in color as the life-saving insulin pumped through her body.

It was amazing, she mused, that something that had once been manufactured in the bodies of pigs and cattle, could breathe life into millions of human beings.

Insulin. She had a sudden flash. It could not only restore life to those who didn't have enough of it, but, given to those who had no need of it, it could also snuff out life. Without a trace. What was it that Cody had said when she'd first seen the dead calves? There was no animal that could kill another without leaving blood. A wrong conclusion, she realized. But one she'd accepted at the time. Now she knew better. There was one animal that could kill another in a bloodless fashion—man.

With quickening pulse Erin placed a sample of blood serum from one of the dead calves under a second scope, and began running tests specifically for insulin.

By the time she'd completed a second set of tests, she dialed Hazard's cell phone number, quivering with excitement.

"Yeah?'' Hazard was kneeling in mud and dung, examining yet another dead calf, when he snatched the phone from his shirt pocket and uttered the single word greeting.

Peterson and the wranglers were standing and kneeling around him, examining the carcass in search of clues.

"Hazard?".Erin's voice sounded breathless.

"Sorry." At once his tone softened. "Didn't mean to snarl. It's just that it's worse than I figured. So far we've found sixteen. And the count could get a lot higher."

"Hazard. Listen." Erin struggled to hold her emotions in check. "I could be all wrong here, but I think I've found a connection."

"A connection?" His head came up. He realized he'd nearly shouted.

Peterson and the others stopped what they were doing to watch and listen.

"Do you remember what I told you about Beryl Spence needing insulin because she's diabetic?"

"Beryl?" His eyes narrowed. "What's this got to do with Beryl Spence?"

"I just tested the tissue samples for insulin. I did more than one, to make sure it wasn't a fluke. Every one tested positive. That's what is killing your calves, Hazard. They're being injected with insulin."

"And you think Beryl is injecting them? How would she manage it? And why?"

Erin ran a hand through her hair in frustration. "I don't know the answers to those questions. She seems like such a sweet girl. But I think it's just too much of a coincidence that she is insulin dependent, and your calves are dying from insulin injections. Think back, Hazard. Maybe she has a grudge against you for some reason. Maybe she's just deranged. At any rate, I think you should notify the sheriff and have him meet you at Beryl's house." She swallowed. "It could be a wild-goose chase. Or it could lead you to the solution to this mystery."

"You're right, of course." He nodded. "Cody and I will head into town right away. I'll phone the authorities from the truck."

"While you do that, I'll e-mail Dr. Wingate and run everything by him for verification. If there's a flaw in my theory, he's the one who will find it. Oh, Hazard—" her voice nearly quivered with excitement "—I'm hoping this is the answer."

"Yeah. Me too." He decided he didn't care who overheard him. "I love you, Dr. Ryan."

He disconnected, then motioned for Cody. "Come on. We're heading into Prosperous."

He strode away, with Peterson and the others staring after him in stunned silence.

Erin blessed the years of disciplined study that had brought her to this point in her life. Without it, she wouldn't be able to keep on working. Not when so many questions were whirling around in her mind, demanding answers.

As she tested yet another tissue sample and raised her head from the scope to make meticulous notes, the questions surfaced.

What would make a sweet young woman like Beryl Spence decide to inject calves with insulin? And why these particular calves? She would have to hate the Wilde family, and Hazard in particular, to do such a thing. But she hadn't acted like someone who hated them. Unless, of course, she was an excellent actress.

Besides motive, there was opportunity. When would she have time to do this without being seen? How would she get up to the range where the herd was kept?

So many questions. Too many. She bent once more to the microscope.

"Figured I'd find you in here."

At the sound of Russ Thurman's voice, Erin looked up. He was standing in the doorway, his hands hanging loosely at his sides. He was breathing hard, as though he'd been running.

"Hazard sent me to fetch you up to Peterson's right away."

It took her a moment to gather her thoughts. "He said he was going to town."

"Yeah. He is. But by the time he gets back, he wants you to have some more samples from this latest batch of dead calves."

"Oh. Yes. Of course. That makes sense." She carefully removed the samples she'd been testing and placed them in their containers before returning them to the refrigerator. Then she packed her satchel with the usual supplies. A sterile cloth, a surgical knife and several plastic bags, as well as labels and a marking pen.

"Come on. You're wasting time." Russ stood in the doorway, tapping his foot in frustration.

She deliberately ignored him.

When she closed the satchel she turned. "I'll just go tell Agnes I'm leaving."

"There's no need." He moved aside as she swept past him and started along the hallway. "I already told her."

When they entered the great room, Erin glanced around. "I thought you said you'd already informed Agnes. Where is she?"

"She was outside. Just heading toward the bunk-house."

"That's odd." Erin glanced around. "She left the TV

on. That's not like her. She's always so insistent on saving electricity.''

"Old biddy's getting absentminded." He closed his hand around Erin's wrist. "Let's get a move on."

Erin stopped dead in her tracks and stared at the offending hand.

At once he released his hold on her and took a step back. "I forgot. You only let Hazard Wilde touch you." Then, with an insolent grin, he bowed. "After you, lady doctor."

She paused at the back door to remove a parka from a hook. When she stepped outside, she could feel the bite in the air.

The truck, she noted, was still idling. She pulled herself up to the passenger seat. Before she could even secure the seat belt, Russ engaged the gears and took off, the wheels churning gravel.

"Did Hazard say if he'd contacted the sheriff yet?"

Russ shrugged. "He didn't say."

"Did Cody go with him?"

"Yeah. His ever-present sidekick. The old man acts like a doting father."

Erin nodded. "I think he's proud of Hazard. And he should be."

"You mean 'cause Hazard's made himself millions on his old man's ranch?"

"Not because of the money. But because he's made himself into a fine man."

Russ shot her a sideways glance. "A fine catch, don't you mean?"

She arched a brow. Her tone was pure ice. "I beg your pardon?"

"Don't play fancy lady with me. You females are all the same. Walk right over the poor slob who's got to work

for a living, and cozy up to the guy with all the money.''
His foot pressed the accelerator nearly to the floor. The
truck bounced over ruts and rocks as it raced up a hill and
flew down the other side. "Tell me. How long did it take
for Hazard to flash his money and get you into his bed?"

Erin's fingers gripped the door. "I intend to tell Hazard
about your insolence. I won't have you speaking to me in
this way."

"You won't have…?" He reached out and closed his
big hand over her arm.

Despite the protection of the parka, she cried out in
surprise and pain. Her surprise turned to fear as he
dragged her across the seat until the seat belt dug into her
ribs. His face was inches from hers. His breath hot against
her cheek.

"Let's get one thing straight, fancy lady doctor. That
old coot, Cody, isn't around to play bodyguard now."

"Cody?" She struggled to keep the fear from her voice.

"Yeah. He's always thought he was better'n me. Like
you. But out here, you're no better'n anybody else. In fact,
you're less than anybody. That brain of yours won't do
you any good at all. What counts here is muscle. And if
you think you'd like to go up against mine, be my guest."
His eyes narrowed. "As for your big protector, Hazard
Wilde, he doesn't scare me."

He released her and returned his hand to the wheel as
they careened into a wood.

Erin peered out the window. "This isn't the way to
Peterson's."

"That's real smart, Doctor."

Her eyes widened as her fear grew. "Where are you
taking me?"

"Someplace where we can be alone."

"Why?" Even as the question slipped from her mouth, her fear turned to a quick rush of panic.

"Because I've finally figured out a way to really hurt Hazard Wilde. The calves were good, as far as they went. They just didn't go far enough."

Her hand flew to her mouth. "It was you who killed all those calves?"

He flashed her a look of triumph. "Smart, wasn't I? See, you aren't the only one with brains."

"But how? Why?"

"The 'how' was easy. I just helped myself to Beryl's syringes and insulin. Whenever I had a few minutes alone with the herd, I'd poke a couple of calves. When I saw how easy it was, I started ordering bigger doses from a connection in the medical supply business. I only used Beryl's supply in an emergency. The 'why' is even easier. To destroy Hazard Wilde."

The truck emerged from the wood into an isolated area bounded by tree-shrouded hills. As Erin looked around she realized there were no herds nearby. No wranglers. She shivered. No one who could come to her rescue.

"Come on." Russ turned off the ignition and reached over, releasing her seat belt. Then he grasped her hand in a viselike grip, tugging her across the seat.

She had no choice but to stumble along beside him as he exited the truck and started past a stand of trees. They came to a clearing. It was a desolate spot. Beneath a layer of melting snow were the charred remains of what may have been a house. The only thing still standing was a stone chimney.

"Cozy, isn't it?" Russ dragged her closer. "This is where I spent my happiest years."

"Here? On the Wilde ranch?"

"My old man was foreman." His voice lowered. "It

was a good life. For a while. Then it turned into a living hell.''

"Why—'' Erin's teeth were chattering, and she had to swallow before she could manage to ask, "Why did you bring me here, Russ?''

"I told you. I've figured out the perfect way to hurt Hazard Wilde. The calves were a start. But this'll be even better.'' He turned to stare at her and she could see the madness in his eyes. "I'm going to kill everything he loves. Including you.''

Hazard drove with one hand, holding the cell phone to his ear with the other. "What do you mean, Russ isn't there? Where did he go?''

Peterson's voice sounded puzzled. "He's just following your orders.''

"My orders?''

"He told me you called and wanted him in town right away. I figured it had something to do with this Beryl Spence business.''

Hazard gave a hiss of annoyance. "I never phoned him. And he didn't come into town. I'm almost at the ranch and I haven't passed another vehicle on the road.''

"Maybe he stopped at the bunkhouse.''

"Yeah. Maybe.'' Hazard felt the first trickle of ice along his spine.

Beryl had told the sheriff that she'd been misplacing her insulin and syringes lately. Suddenly it was all beginning to make more sense. Russ Thurman had just become the prime suspect. When he found him, Hazard vowed, he'd get to the truth in all this.

"I'll check.'' He disconnected and jammed the phone into his shirt pocket.

With a twist of the wheel he veered up the driveway

and pulled around to the back of the house. There was no sign of another truck. Despite the chill, he started sweating.

He turned to Cody. "Check the bunkhouse. See if there's any sign of Russ Thurman."

While Cody started off in the direction of the bunkhouse, Hazard sprinted up the steps and let himself in through the back door.

"Agnes?" Hearing the sound of the TV, he hurried through the kitchen toward the great room. It was empty. He moved on until he came to the lab.

"Erin?" He paused in the doorway. As he'd feared, it was empty.

Very deliberately he turned away and made his way to Erin's bedroom, willing himself not to panic. When he found it empty, as well, his heart plummeted all the way to his toes.

He turned and retraced his steps through the house. When he got to the back door, he saw Cody helping Agnes Tallfeather up the steps.

"What's going on? Is she hurt?"

"More mad than hurt." Cody caught the old woman's hands and held them up. They were bloody and battered.

"Bastard locked me in the closet," she muttered. "Hauled me out of the house like a sack of potatoes and locked me up in the bunkhouse closet. Said he'd figured out the perfect revenge against the Wildes."

Hazard's heart stopped. "Russ Thurman?"

She nodded. "Crazy as a loon. Always said that about him. Him and that drunken father of his."

Cody looked around. "Where's Erin?"

"Gone." The word nearly stuck in Hazard's throat.

"With Russ Thurman?"

Hazard nodded.

"After he locked me up, he shouted that you'd know where to find him." Agnes rubbed at her bruised and bloody hands. "He called it the old homestead."

"Of course." Cody froze. "You realize he's gone off the deep end. Erin's no match for a brute like that."

Hazard's eyes were as hard as chips of steel. "Notify the sheriff." He was already racing out the door. "Tell him I intend to kill Russ Thurman. Unless he kills me first."

"It doesn't look so big now." Russ had hold of Erin's wrist as he circled the crumbling foundation, half-buried beneath overgrown roots and shrubs. "But when I was a kid, I thought it was the grandest ranch house in all of Wyoming. It was the first real home we'd ever had. Before that, my old man and I used to go from ranch to ranch, pitching a tent in the woods, or bunking in one of the range shacks while we helped with the calving. None of the jobs ever lasted beyond a few months. Then we'd be forced to move on. I hated it. Until I was twelve, I never had a home or a friend. Then we came here, and Wes Wilde hired my old man on as foreman of the ranch."

He stopped, kicked at a half-buried stone. Something caught his eye, and he bent to retrieve a silver chain. Without realizing it, he let go of Erin's wrist while he examined the dull silver.

She glanced toward the truck. The driver's door was still open. Had he left the keys in the ignition? She'd been too distracted to notice. She mentally measured the distance, wondering if she could outrun him and lock herself inside. Her heart started pounding at the thought of what she was about to do.

"Belonged to my mother." He held up the chain, and she pretended to be interested.

"That's pretty." Her mind raced. She had to keep him distracted. "Was your mother pretty?"

"Yeah." His eyes narrowed on her. "When you're twelve, you don't really notice. But looking back, I should have. She was little. No bigger'n you. Blue eyes and hair like cornsilk. She used to wait in some dingy room in some dingy town until my father would get another job and send for her. When she came here, she thought she'd died and gone to heaven. But then she started liking it too much."

"Too much?" Erin glanced toward the truck, then back to Russ.

"She was always running into her room and brushing her hair or smoothing her skirts whenever she heard the sound of someone coming."

"That's what…" Erin tried to speak, though her face felt frozen. Whether from cold or fear, she wasn't certain. But she could no longer feel her hands or feet. In fact, her whole body seemed numb, and she wondered if she would stumble and fall when she started running. "That's what most women do when they have company."

"Yeah." His eyes went flat. Flat and dead. "Especially if the company is the rich owner of the ranch."

He kicked at the ground, his eyes scanning the dirt. "Wonder what happened to the little heart that used to be on this chain."

Erin knew she would never have a better opportunity. She had to use this momentary distraction. She turned and started racing toward the truck. Before she'd even taken two steps she heard his muttered exclamation.

She dared not look back. With her lungs burning from

the effort, she ran as fast as she could. When she reached the truck she leaped inside and grabbed the door.

Instead of cold steel, her hand encountered flesh. She looked up to see Russ just one step behind her, holding the door.

"Why you little…" He swung the door wide and caught her by the shoulder, yanking her with such force she fell to the ground.

As she started to get to her knees, he caught her by her hair and pulled her head back. "You think you're smart." He slapped her so hard it snapped her head to one side.

For a moment Erin was forced to grasp the door of the truck for balance as a shower of stars swam in front of her eyes. Then, as she slowly struggled to her feet, she became aware of a sound.

A truck barreled over the hill and came to a screeching halt just inches from them. As Hazard stepped out holding a rifle, Erin felt her hopes soar. Then, just as quickly, her hopes were dashed as Russ grabbed her and held her in front of him like a shield.

After one quick glance at Erin, Hazard kept his gaze steady on Russ. He couldn't bear to see the deathly pallor that robbed her of all color, or the terror in her eyes.

He'd driven like a madman, almost blinded by the rage that drove him. In his whole life, he'd never known this kind of fear. And now that he knew Erin was still alive, nothing else mattered. He would save her. Or die trying.

"Let her go, Russ."

"Oh. Yeah. Sure." Russ laughed. A wild, high-pitched sound that scraped over raw nerves. "That's why I brought her here and lured you to follow. So I could just give up without a fight."

Almost casually he reached into his pocket and withdrew a syringe, pressing it to her throat. "Now I'll give the orders. And you'll do as I say. 'Cause I'm the one with the power now. And you're going to know what it feels like to be less than nothing.'' He motioned with the syringe. ''Toss down that rifle and kick it over this way, or I'll have to stick your woman. You know those calves that keeled over without a whimper? She'll be just like 'em.''

''Don't hurt her.'' Hazard held the rifle in one hand and started to toss it aside.

''No, Hazard.'' Erin let out a cry of despair. ''Don't you see? He's going to kill me, anyway. But if you do as he says, you'll have no way to defend yourself.''

Hazard's eyes narrowed on Russ as he tossed aside the rifle. ''If you hurt her. If you so much as harm her in any way, I'll kill you with my bare hands. That's not a threat, Russ. That's a promise.''

''That's right. Talk tough for your woman. That's what the Wildes are famous for, aren't they?''

Hazard shot him a puzzled look. ''What's that supposed to mean?''

''Don't play dumb with me. You knew. You all knew.''

''I don't know what you're talking about, Russ.'' Hazard wondered how many seconds it would take to cross the distance between them. Was there time to snatch Erin from this madman's hands before he could plunge the syringe? Or would he risk her death in the attempt? He knew one thing. He had to try.

''Never could figure out why Wes Wilde would hire my old man as foreman. Oh, sure, he'd been bouncing around ranches all his life. Knew a good bit about cattle and such. But he liked to drink. And when he drank he tended to slack off and let the other wranglers cover for him. So, I had to wonder why a man like that would be foreman. And then, all those years later, I found out why.''

''Why?'' Hazard was determined to keep him talking until he could find a chance, no matter how slim, to attack.

''When my old man died, I found a packet of letters written to my long-dead mother from Wes Wilde. My old man had read them, too. Every one of them. Telling her she had a right to leave a man who beat her. Telling her he'd give her protection if she asked for it. After he found those letters, my old man sank into a bottle and never crawled out. He drank himself to death. And one night in a drunken rage he burned down the only home I'd ever had. They found his body right next to the tin box filled with those letters.''

Erin saw the stunned look that came into Hazard's eyes and knew that he'd never known about the letters.

To his credit he managed to keep his tone even. ''And you've decided that my father hired your father because he was in love with your mother?''

''Why else?''

''When my father hired your father, he hadn't even met your mother yet. There was only you and your old man, living hand-to-mouth. Your mother didn't come into the picture until she joined the two of you much later. If there was…something between them, they kept it to themselves. My mother had long since passed away, and your parents' marriage was just as dead.''

Russ's voice went up a notch. ''Then if it wasn't to impress my mother, you tell me why Wes Wilde hired a man like my father to be his foreman.''

Hazard shook his head. ''You damned fool. Don't you see? My father had three sons of his own. And he took pity on a twelve-year-old boy who had never had a home or a friend.''

Russ stiffened. His face drained of all color. This was something he'd never even considered. And now his mind simply wouldn't accept it. He'd nursed this anger, fueling it almost lovingly through the years with every real or imagined slight, until it consumed him. There was no way he could now deny something that had become so much a part of his life. "You're lying," he screamed. "It's all a lie."

Hazard used that moment to rush forward and forcibly yank Erin free. With one quick shove he pushed Russ back against the truck hard enough to stun him. The syringe fell to the ground.

"Get inside," Hazard commanded. "Lock the doors. And no matter what happens, stay inside."

Erin turned, clawing and scrambling into the truck with a strength driven by panic. When the door slammed behind her, she couldn't even remember how she got there. She watched as Russ punched Hazard so hard he fell to the ground. Then Russ fell on top of him, pummeling him with his fists. A moment later both men had regained their footing. The two exchanged blow for blow, until their faces were bloodied. Erin had to look away, to keep from being sick. She had never seen such violence. And still they fought, each desperate to subdue the other.

Erin breathed a sigh of relief when she saw Hazard knock Russ to the ground. For a moment she closed her eyes and whispered a prayer that it was finally over. But then there was a terrible roar, so powerful it rocked the truck. She opened her eyes and saw the rifle in Russ's hands. Then she looked toward Hazard and saw him stiffen, then slide slowly to the ground.

"No!" Erin reflexively clutched the satchel to her chest. Without realizing what she was doing, she threw open the door and hurried to Hazard's side. There seemed to be blood everywhere. Staining his shirt. Spilling like a river from his body, turning the snow beneath him to crimson.

She was a doctor, yet not a doctor. She had never in her life tended a patient. Still, she had to do what she could to save him. She unzipped the satchel and grabbed up the surgical knife, cutting away his shirt to press a sterile cloth to the wound.

"Go…back." This was Hazard's worst nightmare. She had given up her safety for him. And now he was helpless to protect her. "Go back…truck."

"No, Hazard. Oh, please don't die." Tears coursed down her cheeks, blurring her vision as she fell to her knees and cradled him in her arms.

"Not…dead." He had to struggle to get the words out from between chattering teeth. He knew the bullet had been fired from such close range, it had passed completely through his shoulder. He knew, too, that at any moment he would surely lose consciousness. Still, he had to stay alert. Erin's life depended on it.

"Oh, this is too good." Russ leaned over them, a look of triumph in his eyes. In his hand was the syringe. "Hazard Wilde lying in the mud, where he belongs. Unable to do more than watch while I snuff out the life of the woman he loves." He laughed, a wild, hysterical sound that carried on the breeze like a ghostly echo. "I'll tell you what, boss. When I'm through with your fancy woman, I'll put you out of your misery so you can join her."

Erin had never been so terrified in her life. The man facing her was absolutely mad. Of that she had no doubt. It was there in his eyes. In the high-pitched sound of his laughter.

As if in a daze she watched as his hand holding the

syringe moved ever closer. Then suddenly she felt the
cold steel of the surgical knife against her fingertips. She
was trembling so violently she wasn't even certain she
could hold it in her hand. But she knew she had to try.
For Hazard's sake.

As Russ leaned down for the final thrust, she brought
the knife upward with all her strength. Felt the blade bite
effortlessly through skin and tissue until it was buried
deep in his chest.

For a moment he merely stared at her in dull surprise.
Then a vicious oath was torn from his lips. He started to
reach for her, but couldn't make his body obey his com-
mands. The syringe fell to the ground, and he brought
both hands to the source of the white hot pain that had
him staggering backward.

He sank to his knees, still staring wordlessly at Erin.
And then he seemed to fold, collapsing in on himself,
dropping face first in the snow.

"What have I done?" She stared at the still figure, who
only moments before had seemed so menacing. She went
rigid with shock as she realized the enormity of what she
had done. She, who had always been so sheltered, had
taken a life.

With a cry she fell into Hazard's arms. "Oh Hazard.
Oh, dear Heaven, what have I done?"

"Oh, baby. What have you...done?" Through a blur
of pain he gathered her close and held her while she
sobbed her heart out. Against her cheek he crooned, "You
just saved our lives."

Chapter 15

"Sorry, Chance. Ace." A sheriff's deputy stuck his hand out to hold them back. "The sheriff wants everybody to stay behind these trucks. You're not to contaminate the crime scene."

"Don't even think about trying to stop us, Brad." Chance brushed past him with Ace following.

The two brothers strode through the barricade until they located Hazard and Erin. Hazard was sitting in the snow, leaning against the trunk of a tree. His face was bloody and battered. Someone had applied a tourniquet to his shoulder to stem the flow of blood. A blanket had been wrapped loosely around him.

Erin had her arms locked firmly around his waist, her face buried against his chest. From the occasional muffled sounds, it appeared that she was weeping softly.

Russ Thurman lay nearby. The sheriff was busy writing, while his deputy was taking pictures of the scene.

And what a scene. It looked almost surreal. The snow had been churned into a sea of mud, attesting to the fierceness of the battle that had been waged between two desperate men. Blood was splattered everywhere.

Chance dropped to his knees beside Hazard. "You all right?"

"I'm alive."

"Erin?" Chance saw his brother's hands close around her shoulders.

"She's fine. Better than fine. She's—" he pressed his mouth to her hair, as much to reassure himself that she was all right, as to comfort her "—just a little shaken."

Ace stood over them. Now that he could see for himself that they were indeed alive and well, he started grinning. "I've seen you looking better, Bro."

"Yeah. I've felt better, too."

"There's a lot of blood on that ugly face. Did he break your nose?"

"He tried."

The sheriff pushed past Ace and Chance. "I need to ask a few more questions."

Hazard closed his eyes. "Can't you do that back at the house?"

"Yeah. Sure. But I don't want to haul away the body until I have all the facts. Now, as I understand it, Russ Thurman befriended Beryl Spence, then got the bright idea to use her insulin in order to kill off your calves. He ordered massive amounts from a medical supply place, then when he needed more, helped himself to some of Beryl's as well. This was in retaliation for an old grudge?"

"That's right." Hazard leaned his head back, feeling weary beyond belief. He'd never been so afraid in his life.

Afraid he would be too late to save the only woman he'd ever loved. Afraid he'd have to watch her die at the hands of that madman. And now he couldn't seem to wrap his mind around the fact that it was truly over.

The sheriff coughed discreetly. "Dr. Ryan, I need to ask you a few things, as well."

Erin lifted her head.

Chance and Ace noticed that she kept both her hands locked firmly in Hazard's. Her eyes were red and puffy, her face as pale as the snow.

"As I understand it, Russ kidnapped you and brought you here, not only so he could kill you, but also so he could force Hazard to watch?"

She nodded. Sniffed. "That's right."

"He wrestled the rifle away from you, Hazard?"

"No." Hazard passed a hand over his forehead. "He ordered me to toss it, or he'd inject Erin with the insulin."

"Then you managed to wrestle Dr. Ryan away from him, and got her safely in the truck."

His hands tightened on hers. "Yes."

"Then you and Russ struggled, and he managed to shoot you with your rifle?"

Hazard nodded.

"So, how were you able to find the strength to kill him with the knife?"

"I didn't."

The sheriff looked perplexed. As did Chance and Ace. "But then who…?"

Erin's voice was little more than a whisper. "I…I was the one who…"

"You, Dr. Ryan?" The sheriff looked from Hazard to Erin. "But I thought you were safe in the truck."

"I was."

"But why…?"

"How could I remain safe when Hazard was wounded and bleeding? I had to go to his aid."

Beside the sheriff, Ace and Chance felt their jaws go slack. Was this the same timid little woman who was afraid of her own shadow?

"So you climbed out of the truck and went to Hazard's side."

She nodded. Her lips trembled. "I was trying to stop the bleeding. But then Russ came at me with a syringe. You must believe me. I didn't want to…" She couldn't say the words aloud. "I just wanted to stop him, so that I could take care of Hazard's wounds."

Seeing how fragile she appeared, the sheriff kept his tone easy. "Now this knife you used, Dr. Ryan. Where did you get it?"

"It's a surgical knife. It was in my satchel. I was using it to cut away Hazard's shirt, so I could get at the wound." Her eyes filled. "I was afraid Hazard would die before I could stop the bleeding. And then…" She started trembling again. "I didn't care about myself. But I knew I couldn't let Hazard die. So I—" she took a deep breath and spoke the words before the fear would paralyze her again "—I killed Russ Thurman."

While she sobbed against his chest, Hazard looked up at the men. Despite the pain, a slow smile spread across his mouth, lighting all his features. "Isn't she something?"

"Yeah." Ace shook his head. "Something."

Then he shot a glance at his older brother. The two shared a knowing grin.

"I've called for a 'copter." The sheriff closed his notebook and shoved it in his pocket. "We'll have you airlifted to the hospital, Hazard."

Hazard vehemently shook his head. "I'll think about it later. Right now I want to go home."

Erin wiped her tears and lifted her head. "Do you think that's wise? You need proper medical attention."

"I'm a doctor, remember?" He smiled at her. "Well, an animal doctor. And besides, I'll be in the best hands possible."

At her questioning look he winked. "Your capable hands, Doctor." He brought both her hands to his mouth and tenderly kissed each one.

"Come on. I'll drive your truck." Ace tossed his keys to Chance. "Follow me, Bro."

With Chance on one side, and Ace on the other, they managed to get Hazard to his feet. Erin led the way to the truck and watched as the two brothers managed to ease Hazard up to the passenger seat. Ace slid behind the wheel, and Erin sat next to Hazard. With the heater going full blast, they turned away from the scene of carnage and headed toward the lights of home.

Ignoring his pain, Hazard drew Erin into the circle of his arms. She closed her eyes and snuggled against his chest, listening to the steady beat of his heart. *Safe.* The word kept playing through her mind like a litany. *Safe.* He was safe.

Hazard brushed his mouth over her hair and breathed her in. And found he still couldn't quite believe what they'd just come through together.

Together. It was the sweetest word he knew.

They rode the entire distance in silence.

"Dr. Ryan?" Agnes paused in the doorway to Erin's bedroom.

After the chaos of the previous day, the house suddenly seemed too silent.

"Yes, Agnes? Come in, please." Erin was wrapped in a robe, drying her hair with a towel.

"I just want you to know." Agnes paused just inside the bedroom. Her big, work-worn hands were worrying the edge of her apron. "I haven't gone out of my way to make you feel welcome. But I know what you did for Hazard. I just wanted to thank you for saving my boy."

My boy. Erin felt her heart twist. Those two words spoke volumes about the way this old woman felt about the Wilde brothers. Like a mother hen. She had every reason to guard them so jealously.

Since Agnes wouldn't come any closer, Erin walked to her.

"I heard how hard you fought to break free after Russ locked you up, Agnes. How are your hands?"

The old lady held them up like a victorious prizefighter. "Hardly a scratch."

Erin caught them in both of hers and examined them closely. Then she squeezed them. "I'm glad."

"Well." Agnes cleared her throat. Turned away to hide the moisture in her eyes. "Better get to my chores."

"Yes. I guess I'd better get to my packing."

"Packing?" Agnes turned. "You're leaving?"

Erin shrugged. "My work here is done."

"Yeah." Agnes spun away. "Well. Got to go." She stormed out of the house like a woman on a mission.

"How're you feeling?" Ace set his briefcase aside and studied his brother. Except for a black eye and a swollen lip, he seemed to be mending nicely.

"Fine." Hazard idly rubbed at the bulge of dressing that covered the bullet wound in his shoulder. After the excitement had died down the previous night, he'd finally given in to the sheriff's insistence that he go to the hospital. Using the family helicopter and pilot Brady Warren, he'd flown all the way to Cheyenne and back. Thanks to the doctors probing his wound, and the painkillers they'd administered, there had been no chance for him to tell Erin all the things that were on his mind.

"Okay." Chance led Maggie inside the barn. "What's so important that we have to meet in secret out here?"

Hazard turned to his sister-in-law. "Maggie, I was hoping you might make a special dinner tonight."

Chance frowned. "What's wrong with the dinners she's been making?"

"Nothing." Hazard touched a hand to Maggie's arm. "But I'd like tonight to be special."

With a woman's intuition, Maggie understood at once. Her smile bloomed. "Oh, Hazard. I just knew it. You're going to ask her, aren't you?"

"Ask who what?" Cody strolled inside and joined the others.

"Hazard is going to ask Erin…"

"Here you are." Agnes waddled up and placed herself squarely in front of Hazard, her hands on her hips. "Tell me. Didn't that fancy little doctor risk her life to save yours?"

He blinked. "You know she did."

"And haven't you been sneaking into her room at night, after the rest of us are asleep?"

Behind her back he could see the others grinning at him like idiots. He could feel his temper beginning to rise. "That's none of your business, Agnes."

"Well, I'm making it my business. What do I have to do to get you to appreciate Dr. Ryan?"

"Appreciate her?"

"That's right." She pointed a finger at his chest.
"Now, granted, she might not be what I'd have picked
out for you. Huh." She sniffed just thinking about all the
things that were wrong with Erin Ryan. "Dresses like a
lady. Never drove a truck, let alone a tractor. Can't ride
a horse. Faints at the sight of a calf being born. Wrinkles
her nose at barnyard smells." She seemed to catch herself.
"But none of those things are important when two people
love each other. And make no mistake," she said, poking
her finger hard into his chest. "She wouldn't have risked
her life if she didn't love you. And I happen to know you
feel the same way about her, even if you are too pig-
headed to admit it."

"As a matter of fact I was just…"

"Don't go denying it." She put both big hands on his
shoulders and pushed him backward. "And don't go
thinking you're too old for me to tell you what to do. You
get yourself in that house and tell that little lady exactly
how you feel before she finishes packing her suitcase."

"Packing?"

"That's what I said. She's in there packing. She told
me her job here is done."

"You know something, Agnes? I'd forgotten just how
tough you can be. I hope you're always on my side. Now
I guess I'd…better do what I'm told." He shot a quick
glance at the others, who were nearly doubled over in
silent laughter.

Then he glanced back at Agnes and did something he'd
never done before. He wrapped his arms around her and
gave her a big kiss. "Thanks, Agnes. I don't know what
I'd do without you."

"Huh. That's the truth. Don't you forget it, either."

As he hurried away, she stood perfectly still, touching a finger to her mouth. Then, seeing that the others were watching, she put her hands on her hips. "Well? What're you looking at? There's work to be done."

They stepped apart and beat a hasty retreat.

"Agnes said you were packing."

Erin looked up. The sight of Hazard's black eye and swollen lip made her heart turn over. "Professor Wingate will want a full report of the laboratory tests."

"You could e-mail them."

"Well." She looked away. "I could. But now that my work is completed, the university will be expecting me back. I have to serve out my year of fellowship."

"Back to the world of academics." He felt a momentary twinge of fear. "I suppose you miss it?"

She shrugged. "It's all I know."

"I suppose, when your year ends, you'll be eager to get back to Boston."

"I…thought I would. But I've learned to love Wyoming."

"You have?" He studied the way she looked in her jeans and sweater, her hair falling softly around her face. Such a contrast to the young woman who had arrived, all prim and buttoned up, in a proper business suit, her hair in that awful knot. "Do you think you could learn to love…the people of Wyoming, as well?"

She smiled. "I guess that would depend on the people."

"Maybe you could start with me."

Her smile deepened. "I already love you, Hazard. You know that."

He started to relax a little.

"But love is one thing. Believing in happily-ever-after is another. I was raised to believe in doing what is right."

"What's right?" The tension was back, and he could feel a throbbing in his temples.

She nodded. "I believe that my mother and father love each other. After all, they've been married for more than thirty years. But do you know that in all that time I've never seen them kiss?"

"I'm sorry for them. But what's that got to do with—"

She held up a hand. "My mother told me that after passion fades, the glue that holds a marriage together is what two people have in common. My parents are both involved in the academic life. They come from similar backgrounds."

He could feel the panic starting to grow. When she opened her mouth he said, "Wait, Erin. Before you say anything, just listen to me. I realize I can't offer you the things you were used to. Here in the middle of nowhere, I can't compete with the academic life-style you've always known. But I could add to the lab, so that you could still do the work you love. You could be in constant contact with your co-workers. I'll install as many computers as you need. Just…" He closed his eyes a moment. "Please, Erin, don't leave."

"Oh, Hazard." She let out a long deep sigh. "Don't you see? What you're offering is everything I've ever dreamed of." She took a step back. "It would be so tempting to just selfishly take it all and grab all the happiness I can."

"But then why—"

She shook her head. "All my life I've been reminded

of the importance of being sensible. And common sense tells me that I have nothing to offer you in return.''

''Nothing to offer?'' He would laugh if she weren't so damnably serious.

''I can't cook like Maggie.''

His tone lowered with feeling. ''I don't want a cook.''

''I can't help around the ranch. I could never jump in the truck and lend a hand with the calving.''

His eyes narrowed. ''I have wranglers for that.''

''I'm not even very good with people. That's why I chose laboratory research for my field of endeavor. It keeps me alone with my thoughts and away from people.''

''Erin, I wouldn't care if you locked yourself away in a laboratory forever. As long as you'd let me inside with you.''

He could see that she was wavering, and he decided it was time to press his advantage. He stepped closer and laid a hand on her arm. Felt the beginnings of warmth tingling through his fingertips. ''You say you're not good with people, but you've won the love and admiration of my whole family. Even Agnes wants you to stay.''

''Agnes?'' She couldn't think when he was touching her. Would it always be like this? ''Now I know you're joking.''

''You can ask her yourself. If anyone would tell you the truth, without sugarcoating, it's Agnes.''

''But—''

''You said you love me.'' He stepped closer. Touched a hand to her cheek. ''Was that a lie?''

She moved against his hand like a kitten. ''Of course not. I do love you.''

''And I love you. Desperately.'' He framed her face with his hands and brushed his lips over hers. Just the merest touch of mouth to mouth, but it started the fire building deep inside. "Erin, you're worried about seeing the passion die between us. I'm worried about how I'll live if you leave me. I could never love again. Would you do that to me? Doom me to a life of loneliness?"

She started to draw back. "I'm afraid."

"You?" He smiled, that heart-stopping smile that never failed to melt her resistance. "Is this the woman who stood up to a madman, with nothing more than a little knife?"

She seemed surprised. Then she returned the smile. "I'm not used to thinking of myself as brave. I guess I was. But that was different."

"How?"

"I wasn't thinking. I was feeling."

"Then do that now. Feel, Erin. Feel that sense of amazement you had when you first arrived here. Remember? You told me you wanted to tame the savages and wild beasts. And see a bear, a peregrine falcon and a trumpeter swan. If you stay, I'll show them to you. All of them. I promise."

Her eyes were shining. "I'd love that."

"So would I." He dragged her close and wrapped his arms around her. "Feel the love we have for each other."

"But what if...?"

"What if? Erin, there are a million what-ifs. What if the world were to end? Is there any place you'd rather be than here?"

"Of course not."

"Then stay. Marry me. Spend the rest of your life with me."

"Oh, Hazard." She lifted wide eyes to him. "I'm afraid."

"So am I. But as long as we believe in each other, we can make it."

She couldn't help laughing. "Why is it so easy to believe you?"

"Because—" He covered her mouth with his and kissed her until they were both breathless. The heat was gradually becoming a raging inferno. "—your heart tells you it's true." He took the kiss deeper. "Besides, you need to learn to take a few risks if you're going to live in a family of gamblers."

"Does that mean I'll learn to be one, too?"

"It's a possibility." He nuzzled her mouth. "Say the words, Erin. I need to hear them."

"I…"

Against her cheek he murmured, "I couldn't stand to lose you again."

She wrapped her arms around his neck and pressed her lips to his throat, sending heat spiraling through him. Then she lifted her mouth to his. He knew, by the way she returned his kisses, that her decision was finally, irrevocably sealed.

"Don't worry, Hazard," she whispered against his lips. "There won't be a third time. You're never going to be rid of me."

"Promise?"

"I do promise. Oh, I love you, Hazard. With all my heart."

From behind them came the sound of wild applause and cheering. They looked up to find Chance and Maggie, Ace, Agnes and Cody gathered around the doorway, their faces wreathed in smiles.

"It's about time," Ace shouted above the din. "We've

been standing here for the past five minutes, taking bets on who'd cave first.''

"Welcome to the family," Chance called. "And thanks for making me the big winner of the day."

"Wrong." Laughing, Hazard lifted Erin in his arms and spun her around. As he set her back on her feet he added, "I'm the big winner this day. Now get out of here. All of you."

As he kicked the door shut, the sounds of laughter and voices faded.

And then there was no need to speak as Erin and Hazard told each other, in the way of lovers from the beginning of time, all the things that were in their hearts.

Epilogue

"Quit your pacing." Ace leaned against the wall and watched as Hazard stalked from the desk to the window to the bed, then back again.

Hazard turned on him with a snarl. "Who invited you in here?"

"Cody did."

The old cowboy looked up from the chair he was straddling and grinned.

"Neither of you could get your big fat fingers around the little buttons of that shirt." Ace straightened his brother's jacket and tie. "If it weren't for me, you'd be walking up the aisle with your shirt hanging open and your tie flapping in the breeze."

Hazard glanced down at his tuxedo. "This is just plain stupid. I don't see why we couldn't get married in jeans. This is a ranch, not the Taj Mahal."

Chance opened the door and stepped inside in time to overhear his brother's complaint. "I remember saying pretty much the same thing." He grinned. "But don't worry. It'll all be over soon. And then things can settle down to normal."

"Whatever that is." Too nervous to stand still, Hazard started pacing again. "When's the last time we had anything close to normal around here? It seems like lately all we've dealt with are crazed loonies with guns and syringes."

Chance winked at Ace and Cody. "I think it's time to break out some cigars and whisky." He reached into the cabinet and removed a bottle of aged whisky, while Ace passed around the cigars.

Chance filled four crystal tumblers. "The last time we drank this was the day of my wedding."

"I don't think there were this many people here, were there?" Hazard expelled a stream of smoke and peered out the window, watching as more cars and trucks rolled up the drive. "I think the whole state of Wyoming is here to watch me make a fool of myself."

"At least the entire town of Prosperous. Here." Ace handed him a tumbler of whisky, then hoisted his own. "This ought to settle those nerves."

Ace and Cody followed suit.

"Here's to Dad," Chance said softly. "The guy who started it all."

They drank in respectful silence.

Hazard turned to Cody. "Do you believe what Russ Thurman said about our dad and his mother?"

The old man thought a moment. "I know this about your daddy. He always stood for the underdog. And Russ's ma seemed, to most of us, afraid of her husband, who was a drunk and a bully. Wes may have just tried to help her find her courage. Or he may have had some other, deeper feelings for her. Either way, I think it's best to let the dead rest in peace.''

The three brothers nodded, grateful, as always, for the old cowboy's wisdom.

Cody cleared his throat and lifted his glass. ''Here's to you, Hazard. I always knew you'd make this ranch work the way your daddy wanted.''

Hazard put a hand on the old man's shoulder and squeezed. Then he tossed back his drink.

''Here's to that pretty little genius who stole your heart,'' Ace said.

At Ace's words, Hazard managed to smile, for the first time in nearly an hour.

''By the way.'' Chance laughed. ''I saw her folks out in the great room. They were standing off to one side, looking like they'd just stepped onto another planet. The last I saw of them, Agnes had them pinned against the wall and was boasting that she'd practically raised you.''

Hazard moaned.

His older brother couldn't resist adding, ''And how lucky their daughter was to have a catch like you.''

While the others roared, Hazard pressed a hand to his forehead. He was sweating. And his stomach was roiling.

''Look.'' He set down his glass and stubbed his cigar in a crystal ashtray. ''I can't stay here any longer. I've got to go see Erin.''

''Maggie's with her,'' Chance said. ''And if I know Agnes, she's guarding that door like a Doberman. She'll never let you in.''

''Want to bet?''

As Hazard yanked open the door and stormed away, Ace pulled a bill from his pocket. ''Ten dollars says he sees her.''

Chance shook his head. "This'll be the easiest ten I ever made."

They both turned to Cody. The old cowboy shook his head. "My money's on Hazard."

Chance just grinned. "That makes twenty I'm going to earn today. I think I'll just tag along and see how it goes down."

"I'm going with you." Ace finished his drink and took a final puff on his cigar.

The two brothers stepped from the room and started down the hall.

"Oh, Erin." Maggie sighed as she zipped up the long, sleek column of white silk. "You're such a beautiful bride." She studied their reflections in the mirror. "And I feel so honored that you asked me to be your witness and to help you dress on this special day."

"And I'm so thrilled that you agreed to handle all the food." Erin turned and hugged her. "I never had a sister, Maggie. But if I did, I'd want her to be just like you."

Maggie blinked away the tears that threatened. "Are you sure you don't want your mother to be in here with us?"

Erin shook her head. "We had a lovely visit. And we shed a few tears together. But I don't want my father to be alone out there." She laughed. "He's already feeling completely out of place."

"They'll get used to the fact that their daughter is married to a cowboy."

"Maybe. After fifty years or so," Erin said with a laugh.

She was still laughing when the door was yanked open and Hazard stormed inside.

Maggie stepped in front of Erin, trying to block his

view. "You know the rules, Hazard. You're not supposed to see the bride before the ceremony."

"Maggie." Hazard's eyes looked as hot and fierce as they had when he'd faced Russ Thurman. "I love you. But if you don't get out of here right now, I'm going to have to throw you out."

She turned to Erin for confirmation. Erin merely nodded.

"All right." Maggie kissed Erin's cheek, then stood on tiptoe to kiss Hazard's cheek, as well. "I have to see to the hors d'oeuvres, anyway. I'll see you both in a few minutes." She patted his arm. "And don't look so serious. It's going to be just fine."

"I know." He waited until the door closed behind her. Then he turned. When Erin started to speak, he touched a finger to her lips. "Wait a minute. Let me just look at you."

He held her a little away from him and drank in the sight of her. Then he drew her close and pressed his forehead to hers. "Okay. Now I think I can get through this."

"You were having doubts?"

"Not about us. But this—" He ran his hands up her arms and across her shoulders. "Why are we putting ourselves through this?"

"So we can live happily ever after."

"We could have done it without the circus."

She touched a hand to his cheek. He caught it and pressed it to his lips and felt the slow, simmering flame that sparked and began to burn deep inside.

"It was so sweet of you to send the plane for my parents, Hazard."

He shook his head. "It was a cold, calculated act to impress them. Were they impressed?"

"Very."

"Good." He shot her that wicked grin that always made her heart hitch. "I didn't want them to think their daughter was marrying a yokel."

"They wouldn't think that."

"They wouldn't?"

When she avoided his eyes he caught her by the chin and forced her to look at him.

She smiled. "Well. Maybe they would. But only because they don't know you the way I do. Now that they've had a chance to see the way you live, they're truly happy for us. They've given us their blessing. Of course, that was only after I assured them that I wouldn't be going on cattle drives and giving birth along the trail." Her smile grew. "Speaking of birth. I did have to promise them a grandchild."

"Anytime soon?"

"We didn't set a date. But I told them I didn't intend to keep them waiting too long."

"If you'd like—" he nuzzled her lips and felt the strain of the past few hours beginning to dissolve "—we could start working on that right now."

"It's tempting." She moved in his arms, loving the little curls of pleasure that danced along her spine. Would it always be this way? she wondered. Would he always have the power to make her feel so thoroughly loved? "But we have a date with the preacher. And I wouldn't want to miss this chance to become Mrs. Hazard Wilde."

"Umm." He kissed her, long and slow and deep. "I like the sound of that."

"So do I."

They both looked up at the knock on the door.

Maggie poked her head inside. "Erin. Hazard. It's time."

Hazard kissed both her hands, then released them and

started toward the door. Before he reached it he returned to kiss her cheek. This time he made it to the door before returning for one last slow kiss. Then he walked out without a backward glance, knowing it was the only way he could leave her.

Minutes later he stood beside the preacher in front of their assembled guests in the great room. It had been transformed into a garden paradise, with baskets of roses and gardenias flanking the doorways and windows, lending their perfume to the festive occasion.

Hazard and his brothers had added another touch, in honor of their father. As soon as the sky was dark enough, they planned a fireworks display for the guests.

Hazard glanced around at their eager faces. Agnes sat proudly in her place of honor beside Erin's mother. Maggie, in a simple gown of pale-peach silk, walked in and stood between Chance and Ace, who were both witnesses to their brother's marriage. There was a murmur from the crowd as the bride entered, walking demurely beside her father. She kissed him and then turned to link fingers with the groom.

Hazard stared into those wonderful blue eyes and marveled that he had survived all these years without this woman. The crowd seemed to slip away. All he could see was Erin: that shy smile that never failed to touch him; the sweetness, the goodness that seemed to radiate from her and set her apart from anyone else he'd ever known.

And then she was speaking the words that would forever bind them. *Bind.* How had it happened, that one little female had become so important in his life, that he wanted, needed desperately to be bound to her for a lifetime? The thought of spending even one day without her was beyond imagination.

"You may kiss your bride," Reverend Young said.

"I love you, Erin." Hazard stared into her eyes as he brushed his mouth over hers.

"And I love you, Hazard."

Love. As their mouths met, she felt a joy unlike anything she'd ever known before. Her heart felt so full she feared it would burst.

How had this transformation occurred? She'd come so far. Not just in miles, from Boston to Wyoming. But also in life-style. From academic to the earthy life on a ranch. She'd undergone such changes. From shy loner to this life, rich with family. Where she had once lived a life of rules and regulations, she now felt free to take risks. Best of all, she'd been accepted by his family and friends, not for just her mind but for herself.

All because of this man, who completely owned her heart. "Be warned, my husband," she whispered against his mouth. "I intend to love you for a lifetime."

"I'll go you one better." He brushed his lips over hers. "My love will last through eternity."

As they were surrounded by friends and family who wished them well, the love they felt for each other was there in their eyes for all to see.

* * * * *

*Watch surly, sexy Ace Wilde gamble
his heart on love in talented author
Ruth Langan's upcoming*

The Wildes of Wyoming—Ace

*available June 2000 from
Silhouette Intimate Moments.*

INTIMATE MOMENTS®
Silhouette®

presents a riveting 12-book continuity series:

A YEAR OF LOVING DANGEROUSLY

When dishonor threatens a top-secret agency, twelve
of the best agents in the world are determined to
uncover a deadly traitor in their midst. These brave
men and women are prepared to risk it all as they
put their lives—and their hearts—on the line. But
will justice…and true love…prevail?

**You won't want to miss a moment of the
heart-pounding adventure when the year
of loving dangerously begins in July 2000:**

*Available only from Silhouette Intimate Moments
at your favorite retail outlet.*

Silhouette®

Where love comes alive™

Look Who's Celebrating Our 20th Anniversary:

Celebrate 20 YEARS

"Working with Silhouette has always been a privilege—I've known the nicest people, and I've been delighted by the way the books have grown and changed with time. I've had the opportunity to take chances…and I'm grateful for the books I've done with the company. Bravo! And onward, Silhouette, to the new millennium."

—*New York Times* bestselling author
Heather Graham Pozzessere

"Twenty years of laughter and love… It's not hard to imagine Silhouette Books celebrating twenty years of quality publishing, but it is hard to imagine a publishing world without it. Congratulations…"

—International bestselling author
Emilie Richards

INTIMATE MOMENTS®
Silhouette®

SILHOUETTE'S 20ᵀᴴ ANNIVERSARY CONTEST
OFFICIAL RULES
NO PURCHASE NECESSARY TO ENTER

1. To enter, follow directions published in the offer to which you are responding. Contest begins 1/1/00 and ends on 8/24/00 (the "Promotion Period"). Method of entry may vary. Mailed entries must be postmarked by 8/24/00, and received by 8/31/00.

2. During the Promotion Period, the Contest may be presented via the Internet. Entry via the Internet may be restricted to residents of certain geographic areas that are disclosed on the Web site. To enter via the Internet, if you are a resident of a geographic area in which Internet entry is permissible, follow the directions displayed on-line, including typing your essay of 100 words or fewer telling us "Where In The World Your Love Will Come Alive." On-line entries must be received by 11:59 p.m. Eastern Standard time on 8/24/00. Limit one e-mail entry per person, household and e-mail address per day, per presentation. If you are a resident of a geographic area in which entry via the Internet is permissible, you may, in lieu of submitting an entry on-line, enter by mail, by hand-printing your name, address, telephone number and contest number/name on an 8"x 11" plain piece of paper and telling us in 100 words or fewer "Where In The World Your Love Will Come Alive," and mailing via first-class mail to: Silhouette 20ᵗʰ Anniversary Contest, (in the U.S.) P.O. Box 9069, Buffalo, NY 14269-9069; (In Canada) P.O. Box 637, Fort Erie, Ontario, Canada L2A 5X3. Limit one 8"x 11" mailed entry per person, household and e-mail address per day. On-line and/or 8"x 11" mailed entries received from persons residing in geographic areas in which Internet entry is not permissible will be disqualified. No liability is assumed for lost, late, incomplete, inaccurate, nondelivered or misdirected mail, or misdirected e-mail, for technical, hardware or software failures of any kind, lost or unavailable network connection, or failed, incomplete, garbled or delayed computer transmission or any human error which may occur in the receipt or processing of the entries in the contest.

3. Essays will be judged by a panel of members of the Silhouette editorial and marketing staff based on the following criteria:

   Sincerity (believability, credibility)—50%
   Originality (freshness, creativity)—30%
   Aptness (appropriateness to contest ideas)—20%

   Purchase or acceptance of a product offer does not improve your chances of winning. In the event of a tie, duplicate prizes will be awarded.

4. All entries become the property of Harlequin Enterprises Ltd., and will not be returned. Winner will be determined no later than 10/31/00 and will be notified by mail. Grand Prize winner will be required to sign and return Affidavit of Eligibility within 15 days of receipt of notification. Noncompliance within the time period may result in disqualification and an alternative winner may be selected. All municipal, provincial, federal, state and local laws and regulations apply. Contest open only to residents of the U.S. and Canada who are 18 years of age or older, and is void wherever prohibited by law. Internet entry is restricted solely to residents of those geographical areas in which Internet entry is permissible. Employees of Torstar Corp., their affiliates, agents and members of their immediate families are not eligible. Taxes on the prizes are the sole responsibility of winners. Entry and acceptance of any prize offered constitutes permission to use winner's name, photograph or other likeness for the purposes of advertising, trade and promotion on behalf of Torstar Corp. without further compensation to the winner, unless prohibited by law. Torstar Corp and D.L. Blair, Inc., their parents, affiliates and subsidiaries, are not responsible for errors in printing or electronic presentation of contest or entries. In the event of printing or other errors which may result in unintended prize values or duplication of prizes, all affected contest materials or entries shall be null and void. If for any reason the Internet portion of the contest is not capable of running as planned, including infection by computer virus, bugs, tampering, unauthorized intervention, fraud, technical failures, or any other causes beyond the control of Torstar Corp. which corrupt or affect the administration, secrecy, fairness, integrity or proper conduct of the contest, Torstar Corp. reserves the right, at its sole discretion, to disqualify any individual who tampers with the entry process and to cancel, terminate, modify or suspend the contest or the Internet portion thereof. In the event of a dispute regarding an on-line entry, the entry will be deemed submitted by the authorized holder of the e-mail account submitted at the time of entry. Authorized account holder is defined as the natural person who is assigned to an e-mail address by an Internet access provider, on-line service provider or other organization that is responsible for arranging e-mail address for the domain associated with the submitted e-mail address.

5. Prizes: Grand Prize—a $10,000 vacation to anywhere in the world. Travelers (at least one must be 18 years of age or older) or parent or guardian if one traveler is a minor, must sign and return a Release of Liability prior to departure. Travel must be completed by December 31, 2001, and is subject to space and accommodations availability. Two hundred (200) Second Prizes—a two-book limited edition autographed collector set from one of the Silhouette Anniversary authors: Nora Roberts, Diana Palmer, Linda Howard or Annette Broadrick (value $10.00 each set). All prizes are valued in U.S. dollars.

6. For a list of winners (available after 10/31/00), send a self-addressed, stamped envelope to: Harlequin Silhouette 20ᵗʰ Anniversary Winners, P.O. Box 4200, Blair, NE 68009-4200.

Contest sponsored by Torstar Corp., P.O. Box 9042, Buffalo, NY 14269-9042.

PS20RULES

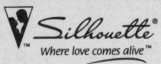